THE SUN CHILDREN (draft)

ROBERT PEATE

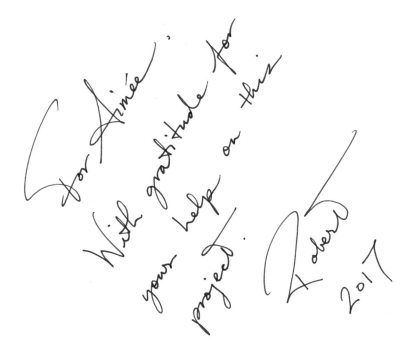

For Aimée,
With gratitude for
your help on this
project.

Robert
2017

For more information:
robertpeate.com

Printed in the United States of America

ISBN-13: 978-1492248507
ISBN-10: 1492248509

Also by Robert Peate

The Recovery
Mister Negative and Other Stories
Visits with Catholicism
Sisyphus Shrugged
Money's Men

Praise for *Sisyphus Shrugged*

"Robert, reading SS and enjoying it greatly, tho' it scares the hell out of me. Every day, politics gets closer to the reality you project, as concerns about the next election emerge."

—Bob Cone, inventor of Liquid Light

"The world that would be if capitalism, selfishness, lack of humanity, absence of social and caring attitude in society would win the upper hand is shown in great detail and with many well chosen examples, such as health care, age care, and environmental protection, to name but a few. The intellectual argumentation against Rand is sound and well presented.

"In my case Peate is preaching to the converted. I found Atlas Shrugged heartless and wrong on so many levels, let alone her overdrawn and exaggerated and one-dimensional characters. Peate has the advantage of any parody that can resort to humor and bounce off the work it reflects upon.

" . . . I enjoyed the book and think that this is an important piece of literature and a well written story."

—Christoph Fischer,
christophfischerbooks.com

"Wednesday Talk Radio on KBOO this morning had about 30 percent more callers than usual, all wanting to talk about Ayn Rand and Robert Peate's new novel taking off from her book Atlas Shrugged. Wild!"

—Lisa Loving, KBOO-FM

"Overheard in the bookstore, from a person holding *Sisyphus Shrugged*: 'Wow, this is intriguing. Daunting, but intriguing.'
"We chatted about Ayn Rand and Fiction of Ideas. Book gone."

—Néna Rawdah,
Saint Johns Booksellers

"If you have ever read *Atlas Shrugged*, whether you liked it or not, you really should read this book."

—David Scott Moyer

"I really like your quote 'I live for Humanity, and I ask Humanity to live for me (and for everyone else).' That is the way it should be."

—Paul Buchheit, DePaul University

"I showed it to wife Linda, and she screamed so loudly she hurt my ears (my left ear is particularly sensitive, and she keeps forgetting this)."

—David E. Block

"Can't wait for it to be made into a movie."

—Larry Parrish

Praise for *The Sun Children*

"WOW, Robert. Really good stuff!"

—Dan Marshall, author of *The Lightcap*

"To be honest, Cassiopeia reminds me of myself at that age. Her naiveté and blind devotion to duty—contrasted with the wisdom, doubts, and duplicity of her elders—is perfectly believable to me. I remember at 23 being oddly numb to the possibility, though theoretical, of being killed in the line of duty. I don't think I was alone in that. There is something about that age range, especially if you are single, where you don't quite understand what you will be missing if you get killed right now. You can't see or imagine the future, so I guess it is hard to mourn what you don't feel you have in the first place. And the women in their 30s have gone past that stage and lived just enough longer to 'see over the hill' that you can't see past at 23. I also identify with being the naïve person among others more cynical or wise. Cassiopeia also reminds me of Sara [in I and You]: a true believer among others who are less 'devoted'. The malicious god masquerading as a 'benevolent' father rings my bell too."

—Beverly Garside, author of *I and You*

"I am excited and intrigued to be a part of this project! It reminded me of *The Handmaid's Tale* by Margaret Atwood."

—Aimee Rose Reed

Author's Note

This entire story takes place in Latin. I have sprinkled a little throughout to give it a flavor, but I cannot write in Latin. Perhaps someone can translate it into Latin someday.

"THE BLESSED-BLUE SKY, THE TINY BABY SUNS IN EACH BADGE,
FACES UNCLOUDED BY THE FOLLY OF THOUGHT . . .
ALL THESE WERE RAYS, YOU SEE—
ALL MADE OF SOME SORT OF UNIFIED, RADIANT, SMILING MATTER."

—YEVGENY ZAMYATIN

SOLIS   FILIIS

Prologo

"Now, who can tell me when the Day began?"

"A hundred and thirty years ago."

"Close. Anyone else?"

"A hundred and forty?"

"Oh, even closer! Good, both of you. A hundred and thirty seven. And what do we call the time before?"

"The Night."

"Why do we call it the Night?"

"Because not everyone saw Havo's Light yet."

"That is right. And what else can you tell me about that time?"

"We had space ships."

"Well, we still have the ability to make space ships now, and the Church has one or two it uses to study the Moon, but it is true that we've been focusing more on Terra. Why is that?"

"So we can enjoy life here before we go out into Space?"

The teacher, Cassiopeia Ovatio, nodded. "That makes sense to me," she said. "Why explore when we enjoy paradise here? We have everything we need."

"I heard the biggest space ship ever was a space station."

"Station Michael," Cassiopeia said. "Does anyone know what happened to it?"

"It is still up there?"

"No. Anyone?"

"It got blown up?"

The teacher nodded. "Yes."

"Was anyone on it?"

"Oh, yes. Many good Havians perished."

"The apostates did it."

"Yes, during the war of Night and Day. But thankfully, even the apostates became peaceful Havians. Everyone knows Havo now. Speaking of Havo, we've got Havo's Eve coming up. Which member of Havo's family will you be going as?"

"I am going as a star!"

"I am going to be Havo Himself."

"I want to be a planet."

"All good choices," Cassiopeia Ovatio said.

Pars Unum:

Omnia sol Temperat

Walking in the forest near my home, I do not see or hear another human being. I see only the snow, the bare trees, and myself. I remember the empty space is one of the good things about the World now. It was overcrowded before. When I feel sad for our declining population, I curse my own disobedience to Havo and command myself to rejoice in His will. He sometimes works in mysterious ways and tests us. He has a plan and never asks us to bear more than we can bear.

I hear the hard snow under my booted feet, the slight breeze swaying the trees, even the gurgle of the creek on the edge of our property through the trees. I do not enjoy the cold, but my robes, coat, and hat suffice as long as I keep moving. I like the winter weather much more than the others in town do, others who complain far more than they should. They are alive, after all. They are here on this planet, unlike the dead. But there I go being ungrateful again. I should be more compassionate. They too cannot have children. I know this. But *we* are the Children of the Sun, Havo, whose presence I feel everywhere. Even in the cold I feel His warmth inside me, keeping me well and bringing me joy. His light, His love for us creates everything good in the Universe. How can anyone complain of anything? How can anyone feel anything but joy and certainty in His love for us all? Yes, it is true we have been suffering without children, but we must have done something morally wrong, and our scientists will find what is scientifically wrong. We must have faith and purify ourselves. My cheeks are numb, yet they sting. I see my own breath and smell the crisp air. I sigh in contentment and keep moving.

It will be spring soon. I can feel it in the air.

I find my way to the creek and crouch down by its edge. The water, though frozen over in some places, still runs in others. Mother liked to bathe in a deep spot in spring and summer. I come here sometimes that I may feel closer to her. I touch the icy water. I often wonder how a woman who came to this spot almost every day for many years could have drowned. I remember Father saying, "We must always beware the Evil One, Havo's son Diab." He told me when I was young how Diab was usually called Scar, "the Evil that Stays".

"If we stay true to Havo," he said, "Scar cannot reach us easily. To the extent bad things happen to good persons who stray from Havo, this is what they deserve. To the extent bad things happen to good persons who do not stray, this is Havo using Scar to test us. Scar is a servant of Havo, which sometimes we forget. Either way, when bad things happen, we must not question our lot. We deserve whatever Havo brings to us—pain or pleasure, sorrow or joy."

Did Mother deserve to die? She was always true to Havo. Is Havo testing Father and me? Was this how she served Havo, by sacrificing herself? No—it is too terrible to contemplate. Our Sun would never do that to us.

Havo, I long for her.

Havo chooses not to answer my pain directly.

Until the Day, there were disbelief and rebellion. How could anyone suffer such an error in judgement, I have long wondered? Only pain could cause that to happen—pain causing confusion. Despite my pain, I see the truth and the light of Havo's love. I look at the spot where my mother died. If I had lived then, and I had met someone doubting Havo, I would have responded with compassion and love. Only these can conquer pain and grief, and Havo would expect no less of me. *No amount of pain will ever distract me from the truth of your love*, I promise Havo. I cannot help smiling.

Everyone knows Havo now.

The Father and Mother of Us All, Havo and His Consort, Havia, take care of all human beings, their Rays, as my father takes care of me and I take care of him. Since the day of Mother's drowning, my father hates my leaving him alone for long periods, especially when I go walking by myself in the woods. I do not wish to cause him worry, so I never tarry long.

I tear myself away from Nature more easily in winter, when Havo chooses to pull away from us, to remind us of His importance, to make us appreciate Him all the more. I remind myself that Havo's perfect creation is everyplace, even in the mundane home we have made as instruments of His will. I must not begrudge the mundane. Despite my mother's loss, I return home feeling strengthened and blessed, to find my father weeping.

"What is wrong, Father?" I ask, but he cannot answer me. He makes a feeble gesture, but his arms drop, and he bursts into a fresh round of tears. I feel both alarmed and confounded. He sobs and gestures toward the floor.

I look down to see a wrinkled piece of fine vellum, an official church correspondence, and a part of me feels shock and outrage that my father could desecrate a holy document. With the love I feel my father should have shown to those who serve Havo by caring for us all most selflessly, I gently pick up the correspondence. I see the seal reading, "SACRED CONGREGATION FOR THE WORLD INSTITUTION." This is the letterhead of the entire Church, but I see this correspondence has come from our province office. I continue reading words I will never forget:

Brother Tertius:

As you know, in this time of trial known as the Inopia, we are all called upon to make sacrifices for the good of the World in perpetuity. Our lives and concerns are as nothing compared to those of the good for which we must all suffer at times, as Havo wills. Now is one of those times.

Each year, each of the ten Provinces chooses one person to send as Offerings to Our Sun Havo. To decide who the fortunate Offering will be, we pray and beseech Havo for wisdom.

As you know, we send only Offerings between the ages of three and twenty-five. We try to choose older children to lessen the pain and sorrow of losing younger ones. It truly saddens me to write this, but as your daughter is not yet twenty-four . . .

I stop reading and drop the paper. I am the daughter. I am to be sent to the Sun. A fire burns in my soul. I look up toward the Havens. I will meet Havo soon. A part of me feels overjoyed, exhilarated beyond words, though I am sad to part from my father. I look over at my father, who continues crying in his chair, and feel confused.

"No," he says through tears. "No more."

"The Church is wise," I say. I hold him. I understand his sadness. I feel the simultaneous loss and gain of my future, uncertain yet excited. I think of Octavius, a year younger than I am, chosen three years ago. He would be twenty-two now. His family bore it bravely.

My father does not answer. He turns toward me with an expression I cannot understand. He masters his pain and grief, wipes his tears away, and pulls himself up to face me.

"Cassiopeia, my darling," he says, holding my face in his hands. "My beautiful daughter." He embraces me as if his arms are hoops of steel, the strongest embrace I can remember from him. "I do not want to lose you."

"You will not lose me," I say. "I will be here." I touch his chest, to indicate his heart. He nods absently.

"No," he protests. I am surprised, having never seen him like this before. I have also never heard him disagree with the will of Havo or His Church. I take this as a sign of his grief and forgive him. Everyone knows Havo, Our Sun and Source, is loving and fair, the provider of all good things.

"Father, you do not know what you are saying," I assure him. "You think you will lose me, but you will not. I will always be with you, and we will be reunited in Haven. Think of what this means. Think of how wrong it would be to go against Havo's will."

My father does not seem to feel much better. I try again. "Father, I love you," I say, caressing his arm. "I thank you for all you have done and endured. Your strength has always made me feel secure, as it does now. I cannot feel fear, thanks to you. You bore Mother's loss. You will bear this too. I have faith in you. We will be separated, but only for a time, after which you will join us forever."

"I am sorry, Cassiopeia . . . " he says, looking directly at me for the first time. "I would take you away from here if I thought you would go. But I know you will not." He says this last sentence as if to himself.

"Do you mean to hide from Our Sun Havo?" I ask in shock more than outrage. "To evade my holy duty?" I do not mean to admonish him, but I can hardly believe he has spoken blasphemy, something I have never heard him do before. I see him shrivel before my eyes.

"I am . . . sorry, Cassie," he says.

"Father, Our Sun and His Church in their wisdom have chosen me to save our world," I say. "How could anyone wish to thwart this divine mission? I wish to save our world. I am but an instrument of Havo's will, and I serve him with the greatest of joys in my heart. To refuse would earn me eternal damnation, but, worse than that, it would be evil. Scar is acting against our world, and I will not aid him." I hope that my reminding him of these truths will help him to see reason.

"Yes. Yes, of course, Cassiopeia." He composes himself, and we speak of other matters: of my walk, of his work in town, of Mother, and of dinner.

The launch will occur on March the thirteenth, which means I have a little more than a month to bid farewell to everyone in Soul River. I must also prepare myself and our home for my father, who will learn to live without me. I make more trips to town than ever before in one month, to repair small damage to our home and fill our larder with enough stores to last him the better part of a year. Not the most appealing food, but it will save him having to make trips for a while. He begs me not to do it. He says he will go to town. I do not believe him. I know how he neglects himself, and I expect him to do so even more in my absence. He can do many things, but in some respects, he is helpless without someone to care for him.

Soul River, far from the province center, Urbis Stella, has about a thousand residents. The even after the letter arrives, I visit the market, the post office, and the hardware store. I had hoped to attend the races in Urbis Stella on the fourteenth honoring Havo's lieutenant Mars, the Fourth of Eight, but now I will not. I will honor him in a much more important way.

I am walking down Vita Way, the spectrum-trimmed silver banners hanging from the lamp-posts, when I see our Prism, Arcturus, leaving the town church for the day. The church itself, of course, has its silver and spectrum cloth banners hanging down at either side of its main triangle-shaped, prism-colored window. Beneath the window, above the main doors, a video screen shows comforting verses from the *Book of Havo* accompanied by pastoral scenes.

Havians wear silver in public, with spectrum-trimmed cuffs, collars, and triangular caps with fabric flowing down at either side (from the flat front to the pointed rear), almost reaching the ground. At home we may dress as we choose. My father wears fewer colors at home, but I always wear the silver and spectrum. I do not always wear the cap, as I know he likes to see my hair. I greet Prism Arcturus.

"Love and Light," I say.

"Love and Light," he says, then turns to see it is me. He becomes silent.

"Good even, Father," I say hopefully.

"Good even, Cassiopeia Ovatio," he says uncomfortably. I am surprised.

"Father, you have known me my entire life. You led my Harmony ceremony, bringing me into full communion with Havo and Havia. We have known each other since I was a child, and you call me by both names?"

"I am sorry, Cassiopeia," he says.

I stare into his eyes, but I do not know the expression I see in them. He seems pained.

"What troubles you, Father?"

I try to discern the matter, but he looks off over my head.

"I am to meet Havo," I say, and this brings his eyes back to me.

"Yes, you are," he says.

"Are not you proud? Are not you pleased? For me?"

He regards me penetratingly, then says, "Yes. Yes, I am."

"Then why do not you show it, Father?" I demand, my boldness surprising even me.

"I am . . . pleased for you, Cassiopeia . . . ," he says. "And yet I am also saddened that we will lose you."

"Do not feel sad! My father and you are the same. Is not it a treason against Havo to feel sorrow at His pleasure? Who are we to miss those we love, placing our loss over Haven's gain and even that of those we profess to love and miss? My mother is dead, yet I do not grieve! I rejoice that she is with Our Sun, Our Father!" I wish I could see on his face the joy I feel in my heart, but still he does not to wish to look at me.

"I . . . will not rejoice," he says. "I will pray for your soul."

"Do not pray for my soul," I say, making the most forward statement I have ever made to a Prism. "My soul is at peace, for I go to a better place to make this world a better place. I do so for you and everyone else here. Rejoice with me, Father. That is all I ask." I reach out my hands for his, and he places them in mine without a word. I squeeze his hands and recite Havo's Prayer:

Our sun, which art in the Sky,
Havo be thy name.
Thy Kingdom come, thy will be done,
on Terra as it is in Haven.
Give us this day our daily warmth,
which giveth us all things,
and forgive us all things,
as we forgive others all things.
Lead us not astray,
and deliver us from evil.
Thine is the heat, the light, and the life,
forever and ever, amen.

I finish reciting the prayer the whole World knows and loves.

"I know the prayer, Cassiopeia," the Prism says.

I study his face but learn nothing. "Father, I do not understand your reactions. You have spoken of our love and joy in Havo every Sunday."

"Cassiopeia, to me you have always embodied all that is good and pure on this world. I wish you nothing but joy and peace. I love you as I would have loved a daughter of my own. That is why I mourn the loss."

"Father, you must not forget your faith and love in Havo's will."

"I do not, which is why . . . "

I wait for him to finish, but he does not.

"Why what, Father?"

"Cassiopeia, you must forgive me. There were others they could have selected, but . . . I put your name forward to the committee."

"Then I have you to thank most!"

"No," Father says, apparently trying hard not to raise his voice. "You have me to curse." I am at a loss.

"To curse? Clearly it was Havo's will! You are an agent of Havo, and I bless you, Father!"

"I know that no one could represent this world, this church, or our need better than you," Prism Arcturus says, placing his hand on my shoulder. "I regretted the recommendation, but I knew it was the obvious one. You are our most precious jewel, Cassiopeia, the only Offering in this province *worthy* of Havo and Havia." He pauses, looks around, then takes his hand off my shoulder.

"Please do not regret your choice, Father. I do not."

"You are a credit to your family," he says. Then, in a more resigned tone: "Comfort your father."

Soul River's Prism walks away, leaving me feeling secure in the ultimate knowledge that I am going to meet my maker, and that I was chosen for this honor by the most admired man in the province.

I am filled with joy . . . but baffled by his sadness, and my father's.

Why did Father seem so distressed by my having been chosen? Why did Prism Arcturus, when he said he himself played the most important role in the choosing? How could anyone be distressed or dismayed by the choice? I decide Prism Arcturus must feel sorry for my father and me, which is of course kind but misplaced in this case. Prism Arcturus temporarily forgot the greater benefit and glory of Havo, but he will remember them. I decide he was simply surprised by seeing me, and of course there is sometimes difficulty when things change, but change is a part of Life.

The day of my departure is less than one month away, and the prospect of meeting Havo thrills me beyond expression. I can never thank the Church enough for this greatest of blessings.

I do not share my news with anyone else at first. I go through my next day at work normally. I confess a part of me will miss every moment, even the moments of displeasure that make up a typical day. When the school day ends and the children run home, barely saying goodbye as they are wont to do, I feel a stab of longing. I had hoped to have children someday. Now I never will.

I finish my work, pack up, and bid the co-workers I see a good evening. Everyone takes everything for granted, every day. I did until yesterday. Now everything is different. Better, I know, but change means change.

I go home to hear female voices inside. I open the door to find a group of women I do not know sitting around our main entertaining room. "Your father excused himself, dear," one of the ladies says. "He said you would be along soon, and here you are."

"Thank you and welcome, Sisters," I say. "Might I offer you some food or drink? We are about to sup, and you are all most welcome to join us."

"No, thank you, Sister Cassiopeia," the woman who is clearly the leader says. "We are from the province center, so you do not know us, but we know you have been chosen for the upcoming Offering."

I listen.

"We are all over twenty-five, but the Lead Prism of the Provincia suggested that, as women under thirty, we visit to offer our support at this time of trial. Some of us have made such visits in years past, to other Offerings."

"I am sorry," I say. "I do not understand."

"You are naturally confused, even dismayed, by this turn of events," the woman explains calmly.

"Sisters," I say, "I cannot thank you enough for the beauty of your care for me at this most significant of times. It is true that my father and even the Prism of Soul River are saddened, so perhaps you should tend to them. But I have been blessed by Havo, and nothing could please me more." I see surprise and doubt in their faces, which cause me more puzzlement. "I go to meet my maker with an open face, an open heart, and joy in my soul. I do this out of love for my world. If you are sad not to be among this year's Offerings, this is understandable. It is true you are too old for this honor. But you too will meet Havo in due course, when Havo decides. Havo has chosen different paths, different fates, for you."

The leader's face changes to one of soothing pleasance.

"I can see this one does not need support," she says. "She is truly blessed by Our Sun." She stands. "Let us go, Sisters. We can only hope someday to achieve this level of faith and devotion."

"Pray, stay," I urge them all.

"No, many thanks, Sister Cassiopeia Ovatio," the leader says. "We do not wish to intrude upon your joy."

"Light be unto you all," I say, bowing to their will.

"And also with you," they say in unison. They rise and depart.

At the door, the leader remembers something, turns, and says to me, "Oh, yes. Provincia Media would like to interview you before your meeting with Havo, and I was asked to arrange this."

"You do me too great an honor, Sister," I say.

"I will have the station contact you." She smiles, then purses her lips and turns to go.

"Thank you."

I seek my father and find him whittling in the back yard. I know that he often does this to work out frustration or stress, but this time, he seems surprisingly content.

"I am sorry for that," he says without looking up.

"For what?" I ask.

"For that visit by those Provincia women."

"I am sorry their faith is not as strong as my own," I say.

Father says nothing for a time, then, "My daughter, you will find that not everyone's professed faith is sincere."

I say nothing. I had of course thought this for years. I had seen small hints of lack of complete faith in many of the townspeople. But I told myself I was mistaken. I had not wanted to believe it of them. Now, thinking of these women, I tell myself their faith is sincere; they just do not understand the full blessing I am about to receive. They love their life here too much. They will see the joy of Havo when they die. Of course, if my assessment is true, that does mean their faith is incomplete. These women from the Provincia believe in a Havo who is far, not Havo who is near and everywhere at once, including inside us. That is the answer: they do not believe in themselves.

I believe in Havo and myself.

This is why we have teachers, not only to help Havians learn reading, writing, mathematics, science, and history, but to help perfect their understanding of Havo's love.

"I understand, Father," I say. "But yours is, yes? Earlier, you were distressed. I cannot bear the thought of leaving you if your trust in Havo is not absolute."

"It is," he says gravely, filling me with relief and gratitude.

"Thank you, Father. I do this for our world, for Mother, and for you." I embrace him.

"I know," he says, touching my arm.

At that moment, I know I am ready.

The next morning I wake and give morning praise as always:

O Havo, through the Immaculate Ray of Your Beloved Consort Havia, I offer you my prayers, works, joys, and sufferings of this day in union with the Holy Abundance of the Rays throughout the World. I offer them for all the intentions of your Sacred Suns: the salvation of souls, the reparation for our former sin, and the reunion of all Havians at the end of the World. I offer them for the intentions of our Prisms, and in particular for those recommended by our Lead Prisms this month.

Without my telling anyone, the whole village knows my secret. The students pepper me with questions:

"Domina Ovatio, is it true?"

"Are you going to meet Havo?"

"Are you scared?"

"Are you excited?"

"Will you come back?"

"Who's going to be our teacher for the rest of the year?"

"What about next year?"

After saying, "One question at a time!" and laughing, I calmly answer each question. In the days that follow, my life returns to normal, to the point that the students and I do not talk about it. It is possible that some of them forget. My father and I do not.

I do not notice the rest of the month. I begin to feel only a calm eagerness to join the nine other Offerings. I trust they feel the same, wherever they are.

I always feel Havo surrounding and inside me, so I almost never pray, but the night before our departure, I do.

My sun and moon, I thank you for the Universe, this galaxy, and this world. I thank you for all the blessings you have bestowed on Humanity, on my family, and on me. I am eager to meet you. Please look after my father in my absence, as it will be hard for him.

I say "absence", but I know I will never come back. I am coming to meet you, Havenly Father and Mother. I am coming home.

I should say a few words to explain my references to Havia. Havia, as the consort of Havo, has great power, though She came second and did not create the Universe. It is to Havia that Havians pray to intercede with Havo on their behalf. They do not know if She will intercede or if He will act on her intercession. But Havo rules the Universe and has bequeathed this duty, among others, to Havia. She is extremely important in this way, also in that She provides the softening of all Nature. It is her spirit that tempers anger, fosters mercy and compassion, even, some say, inspires all artistic creation.

Havia is represented by the Moon.

Why are we infertile? Our scientists determined our gametes were defective, but they could not find the cause of the defect and attributed it to Havo's will. At first there was panic, but Our Mother and Father, the leaders of our global church, counseled trust in Havo. We have prayed for over a century. As the population has aged and died, it has diminished in number. Now, in the 137th year of Day, we have a billion Havians left worldwide. We still have children, just not enough to exceed the deaths. We are still losing ground. Why would Havo do this to us? This is the World's most popular question, though rarely voiced aloud.

"We must not question beyond what we can see," we are often told. "What we see points to Havo's will. That is sufficient."

But it is clear to me that Havo has more than one reason, as more than one good thing has resulted from this population trend. Our planet is less burdened and polluted. Everything human is more special now too, due to being more rare. Is this another of Havo's gifts? Is this a lesson He wants us to learn, to appreciate the glory of Nature and each other more?

I will ask Him soon.

I conclude my lessons and bid my students, their families emotional farewells. My school and town throw me celebrations. I get through them, somehow. My father remains quiet.

Meeting Havo means going to Roma, in Provincia Exemplar, our greatest city, the Seat of Havo, and meeting the current Father and Mother of All. As a teacher, I value knowledge and wisdom, and Roma is the heart of our world's knowledge and wisdom. I am of course nervous. It is the duty of all Havians to visit Roma once in their lives, but I have not made the journey. I preferred to wait until I was older and wiser. Now I hope my current knowledge and wisdom will be sufficient, though I fear I will come across as a country fool.

Before I leave Provincia Cascadia forever, I visit the media station in Urbis Stella, the large town nearest to Soul River. A Church car drives me there and back. It is my second time riding in an automobile; I did so once when I was a girl riding in a parade. I study the houses, the businesses, the factories on the way to Urbis Stella and back, everything old and beautiful, as everything is on Terra.

In the media studio, I am tended to and lighted. Though teaching involves performing, I am not comfortable being at the center of adult attention, let alone the subject of adult inquiry. I tell myself no one will watch this interview, but I know the reverse is true—the Offering interviews are among the most popular viewed programs each year. The man interviewing me is not a church official, but we are recorded in advance, so any mistakes I make can be corrected upon broadcast. I am thankful for this and laugh about it with the staff.

"Have no fear," they all say. "You will do well."

I find myself wearing a microphone, being interviewed by a man whose name I can subtly sense I am expected to recognize when I hear it but do not. He wears a dark suit, popular in more urban areas, with hints of the spectrum on the cuffs and pant legs instead of robes, and smiles more often than is natural. Something about him displeases me, but I try to ignore it.

"Good afternoon, Cassiopeia Ovatio," he says when someone tells us we are being seen by millions of persons across the continent.

"Good afternoon," I say.

"How does it feel, going to meet Havo?"

"I can imagine no higher joy or honor. It is what we all seek and desire, is not it?"

"Indeed. But what is it like?"

"It is like nothing else. But I understand that you wish me to describe it. Everything will change. I feel humbled and hope to prove worthy."

"And you are a schoolteacher, is that right?"

"I was, yes."

"That must have been very emotional, saying good bye to your students."

"Yes, it was."

"Is there anything you'd like to say to them now?"

"I love you and will await your joining me someday."

"That is sweet. And now you are going to meet Havo. How does one prepare for meeting one's maker?"

"I have been praying, stocking my father's larder, taking walks in the woods, and praying some more. Also reading *The Book of Havo*."

"Any favorite passages? Particularly inspiring?"

"Yes. Well, I think perhaps the one most directly relevant to my situation is Prism 23:4: 'Even though I walk through the valley of the shadow of death, I will fear no evil, for you are with me; your ray and your light, they comfort me."

"Of course, you are not going into a valley of *shadow*, are you?" the man chuckles.

"No," I say. "It is a metaphor. It is saying first and foremost that even though we might be alone, Havo walks with us. It is saying second that even though we might be afraid of imminent danger, Havo protects us. I am not afraid because I feel Havo's protection. I know all will be well. I am happy. And to meet Havo will be my greatest joy."

"You are truly blessed, sister. I see here it says you will leave just your father. How did he take the news?"

"He is sad, but he understands the need. We must get our children back, for the sake of the World. We must petition Havo for mercy. I will do so, for all of you, I promise."

"That is a very charitable mission."

"Havo asks us to do what we must, and we are proud to serve our world in any way the Church sees fit."

"We thank you and honor you, Cassiopeia Ovatio. You will long be remembered as a faithful daughter of Havo."

I nod and thank him and everyone else. Though I am uncomfortable with the attention and do not feel I have done anything to deserve honors, I even pose for photographs in the studio. I am pleased to serve Havo, grateful to bring honor and glory to Him. Soon I am on my way home.

I return to our small but cozy house, its oval spectrum-banded rug under the living-room furniture, the wooden rocking chair and central table, the old and mismatched furniture throughout. I look at the artwork on the walls, painted by my artist mother. I say goodbye to this place in my heart.

"There is something I want you to have," Father says, surprising me.

"What is it?" I ask.

"Your mother's prism."

"No. You can't."

Each Havian's prism is a personal object representing the Havian's connection with Havo and his consort, Havia. It is the medium through which their love reaches the adherent and becomes a rainbow inside that adherent. It is also the medium through which the adherent prays to them in all matters, every day. My mother's prism has been in its small wooden box on its shelf in my parents' bedroom since her death. I do not wish to take what is hers. In her absence, I do not wish to take what must have brought my father comfort.

"Cassiopeia," my father says. "I want you to have it."

"Why?" I ask. I suddenly feel more emotional than I have allowed myself to feel for weeks.

"Well, first because she's not using it. Second, because I am not using it. Third, because it may bring you comfort. Fourth, because I believe Havo would want you to bring it with you to return it to her. And fifth, because it is already in your bag."

I cry and embrace him. He is right that I must bring it to her. I do not mention it again.

The night before I leave, my father drinks alcohol, though I urge him not to do so. He says, "It shouldn't have been you. They could have chosen someone else."

"Of course it should have been me," I say, surprising myself. How far I have come from my days of expecting a long life on Terra! I did not know then I was destined for a greater duty. "I am as prepared to meet Havo as anyone. Let the children live longer."

"That is how I feel about you."

I bid farewell to my beloved horse, Valens, in our small barn. I recall my father's childhood nickname for me, "Verbosia". I do not have many words now.

"Take care of Father," I say to Valens. Valens does not answer. He is old but still strong.

A church car comes for me. My father asks to ride along. The driver says that is not standard procedure, but he relents in the face of my father's apparent grief. We ride to Urbis Stella in silence.

The airport there used to fly many planes, during the Night. I am glad I did not know such stress and madness. Now the Church controls most technology, and planes only fly on official Church business, for which fact I am grateful. We do not need to rush willy-nilly all over the World in endless pursuit of distraction. We need only to focus on Havo.

At the airport, a small group of Havians meets us. "Welcome," they say. "Blessed Cassiopeia Ovatio."

"And her father, Tertius," my father says.

"Doubly honored you are, to give your daughter to Havo."

My father does not answer.

They lead us through the airport, my father holding my hand.

We reach the gate. "We will await you in the plane," the Havians say, leaving my father and me to say farewell.

"My daughter, I . . . ," he says. "I love you." He embraces me more strongly than he has in years, smells my hair, holds my head to his.

"I love you," I say. "Do not feel sorrow."

"Oh, Cassie," he says, holding the side of my face. "I am sorry." He breaks down, and I embrace him.

"Be glad for me," I say. "I go to meet Havo, and I will await you."

He pulls back, nods, and wipes his face with his arm.

I squeeze his hand, turn, and walk a short walkway to the plane. I will never see my father again. I do not look back, to preserve his dignity, and because I want him to feel proud of his daughter's strength.

The first flight of my life, to Roma, is long but uneventful. Everyone is exceptionally kind to me, and I read *The Book of Havo* for inspiration. As I have before, I ponder why Havo can not or will not defeat his son Scar's evil once and for all. I have heard it said that Scar is useful to Him, even that Scar serves Havo. Which is it, I wonder? I will ask Him, or hope to be shown, when I meet Him.

My first glimpse of the Seat of Havo comes from the window of our plane when we land. I see ancient and modern. I gasp at the sight of the dome of Saint Peter's, where the Havians have guided the World for over two thousand years, fighting for justice before the final victory of the Day. I triangle myself in gratitude.

I step into the ancient, modern city that feels like more than a place. It feels like a soup in which I am swimming. The sights, the lights, the sounds, the smells! Everything is big and tall. I follow my guide from our plane to our car to our hotel looking about in awe. This ancient city is alive.

I have heard of Roma my whole life, of course. I have seen pictures of Our Father and Mother, leading worship services, visiting other cities, but never before have I been here. The ancient buildings mix with the modern. Everyone seems happy. This afternoon we meet Our Father and Mother in person.

My escorts take me to the Havican, where five others and I are brought into a room to wait. Only two of them are children, a boy and a girl. Everything is ancient. Marble statues, tapestries, and paintings line the walls. I am gladdened by the proper reverence this shows to our lord and light-bringer. As happy as I am, I do not speak with the other Offerings. I am preparing myself to meet the Mother and Father of All. The others seem to be doing the same.

An attendant comes and brings us to the public Havican receiving room, which I have seen on video screens at my school. My father and I do not own a screen. Whereas I did not care very much about being interviewed in Urbis Stella, I am overcome by the honor of being in this room. Havo is everywhere, even in the most mundane places, but the Havican represents the fullest expression of Terra's love for Havo and Havia. The attendant leads us to stand in a line facing Terra's Lead Prisms, the Father and Mother of Us All, seated on their thrones. The Father of Us All, Lux Aduro, addresses us first, standing from his throne to speak.

"Sons and daughters of Havo, bright and multicolored Rays," Father says, "you have traveled far, from the ten Provinces of Terra. Soon you will return to Sol. My heart is full with joy for your reunion with Havo and Havia. Long have I wished to look upon the face of our beloved maker and his consort. I will follow you later of course, but you will precede me in that. You are truly blessed." He comes toward us, then descends the dais steps to the main floor. Father starts at one end of our line, looking directly at each one, asking questions and offering words of encouragement to each. He clasps one young man on the shoulder. When he stands before me Father Lux stops and studies my face.

"I see the light of Havo in your eyes," he says.

"I am doubly blessed, Father," I say.

"Indeed." He seems to think of something else to say, but then he turns and continues on, issuing a short congratulation to the young woman next to me. When he returns to his throne and sits, Mother stands.

"You have all traveled far. You have bid your nearest family and friends farewell. Tomorrow you leave us for Havo, but tonight please dine with us here in our home. You are our most honored guests. Let us celebrate and pray for Havo's grace and wisdom. On one hand, we beseech Havo to restore our fertility. On the other, we wish to understand His greater design. Perhaps you may learn what others have not. Perhaps you will persuade Him we have passed the test."

We go to a dining room off the main audience chamber.

"I want to thank you," Mother says to us all before we dine. "Whatever Havo decides, your sacrifice will show Him our devotion. Havo and Havia be praised."

"Havo and Havia be praised," we say, raise our glasses, and toast.

Over dinner, I notice four of the Offerings, the ones not in the private room earlier, do not speak. I take my first good look at them, and they seem dazed. I remember that every year some Offerings are announced to be overcome with emotion at the prospect of meeting Havo. We all react to everything in our own ways, even—perhaps especially—to the greatest of honors. This is clearly what is transpiring in their case. I would like to calm them, but I am sure I will meet them soon enough.

Though I enjoy my food and talking with the Offerings nearest me, my thoughts are on the morrow and with Havo. What would normally be the highlight of my life pales in comparison with the divine bliss to come. I cannot dwell on it.

The Havican provides us the most opulent lodging for the night, each in her or his own room. I prepare for bed. I sit on the edge of the bed, brush my hair, then take out my mother's prism. My father took it out of its box but kept it in its simple white linen wrapping. I unfold the linen to behold the most marvelous three-sided crystal, longer than my hand, thick and strong.

I hold it up to the light and see the rays of color spread out on the wall. I pray my nightly prayers with my mother's prism, deciding it is a fitting tribute to her after all, on this, my last night on Terra. I cannot thank my father enough. I can never thank him at all, though such concerns fade in importance in the light of Havo and Havia.

I lie in a luxurious bed in a luxurious room and sleep my last sleep on Terra. I allow myself to miss my father, but I rejoice in knowing I will soon see my mother again.

They put us all in grey flight suits. I ask to wear my robes but am denied. I tell myself it does not matter, and we all wear the flight suits.

I am standing on a small platform outside the city with the same five Offerings I first met. We have been driven to the barren, rocky region to the east of Roma, along the Tiber. I marvel at the ship before us, pointing skyward, and the prowess of our blessed rocket scientists. Everyone on Terra knows the ship is stocked with two days' worth of food, its automatic pilot aimed at the heart of the Sun. We squint in the Sun, thousands of Romans listening and watching from a safe distance. The four dazed Offerings from the night before are not here.

I remember other years when fewer than ten stood on this platform. Fewer than ten on display is not unusual, but there is always a video statement to explain. Here, today, the video screens face the audience and are silent.

I hear a fanfare of trumpets, and I look to see a small group of trumpeters dressed in silver and spectra. I see a procession coming toward our platform from our right, headed by members of the highest ranks of the Church. I see eight men and women accompanying the prism-bearer, he who also carries a lantern to symbolize the Sun in the darkness of Space. I see a man carrying *The Book of Havo*. Beyond him I see the Mother and Father of Us All being carried on large canopied chairs, each held aloft by twelve men in the silver and spectra. To either side of the Lead Prisms, two men carry large fans made of peacock feathers. Behind these, armed guards and members of the Havican court complete the procession, which comes to a solemn and stately halt behind us as we turn to face the assembled throng and video cameras. I feel sure my father is watching us all. I hold my head higher and prouder.

I hear motions behind us, during which I know from past years the Father and Mother disembark their chairs, kneel briefly before the statue of Havo constructed to the side of the platform, and receive the obedience of church officials.

I hear one of the Psalms of Terce, number one-twenty, "Custos populi", being chanted:

I shall lift my eyes to the Sun:
where is my help to come from?
My help will come from Havo,
who, with Havia, made Haven and Terra.
He will not let your foot slip:
He will not doze, your guardian.
Behold, He will not doze or sleep,
the guardian of Terra.
The Sun is your guardian, the Sun is your life;

He is at your right hand.
By day the Sun will not harm you,
Nor the Moon by night, reflecting His light.
The Sun will guard you from all harm;
the Sun will guard your life.
The Sun will guard your coming and your going both now and
for ever.
Glory be to the Father, the Mother, and the Holy Spheres,
as it was in the beginning, is now, and ever shall be,
        star without end.
Amen.

At the close of this chant, everyone present says, "Amen." The Father and Mother of Us All come to the front of the platform to speak.

"And now, a short reading," Mother says, "from Titus 2:11-12. 'Havo's grace has been revealed, and it has made salvation possible for the whole Human Race, and taught us that we have to give up everything that does not lead to Havo. We celebrate only what leads us to Havo. We must live good lives here in this present world. Those of us who embark on the journey from this world to the next are the most immediately blessed, and we salute them with all the love in our hearts."

Mother, Father, and everyone else present salutes us, the six Offerings to Havo on the platform. We do not know what the World has been told of the four absent.

"Let us pray." Mother leads the assembly in a call and response.

"Havo, our Father, and Havia, our Mother." The audience here, and, I know from experience, at home, repeats her words. "Our human nature is the wonderful work of your hands, made still more wonderful by your love. You took to yourself your children. Grant us a share in the heat, the life, and the light of your divine rays, which shine and reign for ever and ever. Amen."

"We ask that the Sun accept our sacrifice and show His mercy to our barren world, that we may know the laughter of children in many more homes again.

"Until then, let us praise the Sun. He shows his kindness and faithfulness to us every day.

"Let us praise the Sun."

She allows time for each response before continuing.

"Thanks be to Havo."

Then Father speaks the message he speaks every year:

"Sun Havo, we do not know why in your wisdom you have reduced our numbers these many years, or to what end, but we do know that our children are precious to us. To demonstrate how precious they are, we send them to you every year, that you may see how much we value them, that you might in your mercy take pity on us and grant us the miracle of procreation in large numbers once more. Did we err? Was it a mistake that we grew so numerous? Each year we ask these questions, each year we hope for answers. We search our hearts for the answer, but each year we know not your will. Yet we continue. You told us to go forth and multiply; we thought we knew your will. But our crisis has proved that is never possible to do. We continue living, questioning, always looking for signs from you, Havo, that we may know, or at least try to infer, your will. We will always continue, sure of your light and love."

After turning to face us, Father says:

"Today we commit these Rays, these your children, to You, O Lord. Please welcome them into your hearts and love them as we have. Let them serve you in Haven. Let their joy warm your heart as they have warmed ours. Let our devotion move you, O Sun Havo, we who have suffered much for a long time."

In my mind I see and hear my father saying, "I am sorry." I try to disperse my thoughts of him. I remember the two prisms I am carrying, my mother's and my own. When I am able, I will pray with my mother's prism. I refocus myself.

I whisper, "It is all right." I have no illusions he can hear me or know what I am thinking.

Then something extraordinary happens. One of the six of us begins to sing. I do not know who it was, but the song is swiftly taken up by the rest, and I find myself singing with a full heart a song I have known since I was a child:

Love came down from a star,
Love all lovely, Love Divine;
Love was born of Havo,
Star and servants gave the sign.

Worship we the Sun,
Warmth all warming, Light Divine;
Worship we our Havo:
But wherewith for a sacred sign?

Light shall be our token,
Light be yours and light be mine,
Light in the darkness and confusion,
Light for plea and gift and sign.

"Beautiful!" Father says, clapping. "You have raised a new standard of piety to inspire us all for another year." He leads the audience in clapping for us.

"Producto produxi productum," Father says. "We love and bless you all."

They turn the six of us, four adults and two children, to march into the shuttle.

We file in and pick vertical stasis beds, lining the walls of the small craft. These will render us unconscious for the trip. It will take a little more than six months to reach the Sun, after which we will wake, pray, and move on to the next stage of our existence.

I look about me as the Church assistant issues us instructions and helps us into our beds. I see an equal number of young men and women, as I have always seen an equal number of boys and girls chosen before. I see the four missing Offerings are already in stasis. I take comfort from their sleep. We will all be in Havo's presence soon.

I wake. I am on the same ship. It seems only a moment since I closed my eyes for the journey, but the warmth I feel immediately tells me it is not. I open my eyes to look about me. I see some of the others at the controls of our ship, some still waking, as I am. As the vertical stasis bed turns off, my body begins to heat up. I slide the door open, eager to meet Havo. All is well.

On Terra, the annual games honoring the fifth of Havo's eight lieutenants, Jupiter, must be beginning, underway, or already ended. We always watch them on the Soul River community center video screen.

This year, my father will be thinking of me now. He will know the time is nearing. I try not to think of him saddened. I tell myself that by now he has come to feel proud of me, of what I am doing for us all. I tell myself he is watching the Games, comforted by our friends and neighbors there. I see that eight of us are adults, two of us children.

"Where are we?" one asks.

"We are still a day or two away from the Sun," another says.

"Why? We do not have food."

"Yes, we do."

"We do?"

"We have enough to last us a day or two, until we reach it."

"Why?"

"To pray and purify ourselves."

I see a bridge, a stasis bay, a lounge large enough for six or seven to sit around a table, and a restroom. We are all walking normally, with gravity. How is this possible?

"Artificial gravity. How?" I ask.

"Magnetism," the nearest Offering says. I decide not to ask further.

It occurs to me the ship might not have been built for Offerings. It looks aged, with old scuff marks and scratches on surfaces, but strong and quick.

"What is the name of this ship?" I wonder aloud.

A woman with dark hair asks, "What is the name of this ship? We've been sent here to die and your concern is what is the name of this ship?"

"Do you know it?" I ask.

She snorts with disgust and turns away.

"The *Messenger*," the boy says from the cockpit. "Yes, that is it. The *Messenger*. Right here." He points to a screen showing the layout of the ship. I smile at him.

"Might as well be the *Zealot*," says the woman with the dark hair. "Or the *Naiveté*."

"You speak as if you do not wish to be here," I say.

The woman says, "I do not."

I do not understand.

"I do," the children say. "When do we meet Havo?"

"We do not," the woman says, and the children gasp. Others are still waking. The girl holds my legs. The boy goes to look in the cockpit.

I do not know what to say to this woman. I notice myself starting to feel dizzy.

The woman with the dark hair turns and addresses the rest: "I do not believe in Havo, and for this I was sentenced to death! They drugged me to get rid of me, because that was the easiest way for them to be rid of me! They couldn't brainwash me into being a puppet like her." I see she is pointing at me. The girl holding my legs squeezes me tighter.

"Who else here does not believe?" this unpleasant woman with dark brown hair demands. I start to think of her as Spadix.

"We are here because we believe," a large man, one of the five others at the Havican dinner, says.

"Not all of us," another man says.

"Let's take a vote," Spadix says. "All in favor of turning this ship about and going home, raise your hand."

I cannot believe, let alone comprehend, what I am seeing. I do not understand. How can this be? What is happening?

Everyone stops to vote.

Before I can protest, two others raise their hands. Then another man raises his. With Spadix, that makes four. Thank Havo they are in the minority.

"We are going to die! We are going to burn up in the Sun! For nothing!" It is Spadix again.

I cannot listen to her. My body feels light and ill. I think I may vomit. Even so, this woman's words vibrate my heart and soul the wrong way. Spadix looks about her. She can see she is outvoted, outnumbered. I swallow with difficulty, but a great relief washes over me. The girl and boy do not raise their hands. Havo has saved us.

"Six to four," I say. The two children have provided the winning votes.

"These are children!" Spadix says, stepping toward me, dismissing the children with a wave of her hand. "Four of the *adults* have voted to go home. I'll turn the ship about. Someone else work on restarting the cryogenics." She moves toward the cockpit.

"Four of the adults have also voted to serve Havo," I say as calmly as I can, remaining seated. "We have six votes on our side. We are going to meet Havo." She reminds me of unruly children I have met in my teaching. I will teach her Havo's love.

"You are insane!" the young woman raves. "Would you like to meet Him now?" She throws herself at me, grabs me around the neck, and we fall to the floor. Others, including the children, rush to pull her off me, as the three other men stand back watching. I manage to free myself. I slide backward against the wall, gasping, rubbing my neck. My jumpsuit is now marred, and I am glad I wore it. Those who agree with her take Spadix to the lounge down the short hall. The rest surround me.

"Are you all right?" a woman asks, crouching down.

"Yes," I say, "but achieving purity before meeting Havo is now more difficult."

The woman helps me up. "She was probably disoriented by the cryogenic bed."

The woman leads me to the cockpit, to get me as far away from Spadix as possible, and helps me to sit in one of the chairs there. Fortunately these swivel, so I turn mine around to see the others. I feel I am back in my classroom leading a discussion of deviation angles, dispersion, and reflection.

"We voted," the large man says. "We are going to meet Havo."

"Well, of course," I say.

"Why would anyone not want to go?" he asks in amazement.

"I think she's . . . an apostate," one of the two women says, pronouncing "apostate" as if she were speaking the name of a ghost or a monster. The children look at each other in fright and fascination.

"I did not think there were any anymore," the woman who helped me says. "How could a mistake like this happen?" She looks at us all in confusion.

"Maybe they got lost," the boy says.

"They did," I say. "But we will help them find their way."

"I am hungry," the girl says.

"I am sorry, honey," I say. "We'll find the food that is here." I nod to the other adults to look for it. They begin searching. There are not many places to look, but they approach the aft nervously.

There are no apostates, I think, *and the Church does not sentence people to death.* This is impossible.

The four at the other end must be able to tell what we are doing. They quickly start opening things too. One of the men finds the food in a storage locker between the stasis beds and the small crew lounge.

"Ho, ho!" he proclaims loudly. "Look at what I found here."

The nervous woman from "our" end approaches the man to see what he is holding.

"That is close enough, Theo," the man says.

"Theo?" the young woman puzzles.

"Theocrat. You are a theocrat trying to kill us all for no reason. Well, for a fantasy reason."

The other three in the crew lounge laugh.

Like any good Havian, the young woman is unprepared to be blocked from food by this man. Only children behave this way, not grown men. She does not even know how to respond. Neither do I.

I have taught children, but I have never seen grown men and women behave this way. I have never heard such talk. I have never seen or heard anyone mocking the Day. I am from Sun River! I begin to feel frightened. What are we supposed to do with these . . . doubters? No one told us this could happen. We were sent here without instructions except, "Fly into the Sun." That had seemed enough. But now that I look down the short length of this small craft from the cockpit to the lounge, knowing the engines are behind the lounge, feeling them continue their thrust toward the Sun behind me . . . I do not know what to think, feel, or do next.

The others seem to read my mind. They look past me through the front window. The Sun looms large, filling most of the window. The glass is darkened, so the light is not blinding, but even with the darkening effect, the small ship is as light as day inside.

"Well, Mother of Us All? What are you going to do now?" I hear a voice call from the other end. As outraged as I feel, I do not respond to this call, which I can hear comes from Spadix.

"Names," I say, in an attempt to defuse the conflict over the food. "My name is Cassiopeia."

"Jinx," the nervous woman says.

Magic charm, I think. *We could use some of Havo's magic here.*

"Paula," the other woman near me says.

The largest man on the ship identifies himself as Aetius. In this moment, I must confess, I decide that nothing is going to stop me from reuniting with Havo. Nothing and no one, no matter what it takes. Did not one of the earliest Havians, Augustine, write that war is necessary to prevent greater evil? What could be greater than denying Havo's will? Like children who do not understand their wisdom, these . . . *apostates* do not understand Havo's wisdom. If we must defeat an apostate insurrection, we will. We will do everything not to harm them, only to subdue them. We have Havo on our side.

Down the corridor, the man controlling the food says, "Gaiseric." The name seems vaguely familiar and threatening.

The man behind him says his own name: "Totila."

The man with Spadix says his: "Huneric."

Even their names fill me with a vague fear.

Spadix says nothing. Everyone is watching her.

Huneric says, "Her name . . . is Concordia."

I laugh despite myself. *Harmony. Peace. With one heart.* Spadix/ Concordia growls and runs past Gaiseric toward me. He lunges to stop her. She attempts to fight him off, but he is stronger. He holds her in place.

"Alair," says the boy with us.

"Evadne," says the girl.

"Now that we are all old friends," Gaiseric says, still wrestling Concordia, "let's turn this ship around or no one eats." She wrests free of him and stands still.

My mind races for a word . . . is this what is called "extortion"? I have heard of this . . . I have read of this in ancient texts . . . and this knowledge does not help me. I do not know how to respond. How could anyone use coercion to gain what is desired? Is this how apostates negotiate? If these are apostates, they are as bad as they are described to be.

"Gaiseric, we are here to meet our maker," Aetius says.

"We do not believe in your god," Gaiseric says, "and we are not going to sacrifice ourselves to him."

"We do not have a lifeboat for you," I say. "You are outnumbered, and the controls are here with us. Havo commands it."

"Havo commands nothing!" Concordia states.

But Havo commands everything, even this. I confess I do not understand His will or these people at all.

"She's not very nice," Alair says.

Aetius steps forward. "It is all right. We do not need to eat right now. We need to figure out a plan of what to do." Gaiseric is about to say something when Aetius raises his hand for silence. It is clear he is used to being respected for his size and perhaps more. "We have all voted, but it is clear we still have dissension we need to overcome. We are Havians. We listen and promote peace wherever we go and under every circumstance, and I can think of no more important time to do so than now." I begin to see why he commands respect.

"I do not see why we even voted," I say. "We are here to meet Havo. This is not in doubt. We all know why we are here." I indicate the Sun behind us.

"We know you are all zealots," Concordia says. "And we know we are not participating. We will not go down without a fight."

The more I see and hear this Concordia, the more I feel compassion for her. Is that wrong?

"I think we need one leader from each side to decide our course, by which decision both sides agree to abide," Aetius says. He looks at everyone and receives some nods. "Choose your leader," he says to the other group and turns back to ours: Jinx, Alair, Evadne, Paula, and me.

"Now," Aetius says to us. "We need to choose our leader." He sits and looks at the rest of us expectantly.

"Why should we negotiate with them?" Paula asks.

"We know our mission," I say. "They say they are apostates, but can this be true?" *Why is this happening?* I wonder. *Havo and Havia, is this another test?*

"It is clearly happening," Aetius says. "They say they are apostates, and I see no reason to doubt them, based on their antisocial behavior. And I think we should negotiate with them because they are closer to the engines and can disable them."

I do not know what to do. There seems nothing to negotiate. I find it very hard to believe what is happening—yet it is. These Offerings say they are not Offerings. They say they are here against their wills. They say they are not Havians but apostates! *Havo, how can this be?*

I receive no answer. Evadne looks up at me. I cannot turn this ship around, and I cannot let this woman turn my heart away from Havo. I will not.

"I nominate you," I say to Aetius. The children nod.

"No," Aetius says. "I can enforce, not lead."

Jinx seems even more nervous than before as she looks at me.

"It is clear you are the right choice," Paula says, looking at me.

"Me?"

"You are the most . . . devout and guileless Havian on this ship," Paula says.

"How can you know that?" I ask. "What of Aetius?"

"I am not a leader," he said. "You are."

"How can you know this?"

He looks at the others. The children nod.

"What about you, Paula?" I ask the quiet woman I do not trust.

"Me? No. I can be a diplomat, but I am not our leader. You are, we all know it."

"I only want to meet Havo."

"That is why."

I sigh, stand, and emerge from the group. I walk halfway down the corridor to the place Gaiseric guards a day's worth of food, perhaps two. The other three are still deliberating, but it is clear they have not chosen Gaiseric.

Concordia nods to them, draws herself up, then stands to approach me. We walk to the center of the tiny ship's main corridor. Concordia tells Gaiseric to go back to the lounge.

"For privacy," I say, "I suggest we give everyone else the lounge." She nods. I turn to my group. "Please let us have the cockpit." My group gets up and comes toward us. The children stop at me.

"I want to stay with you," Evadne says.

"Me too," Alair says.

I look up at Concordia. She nods permission. "It will not matter," she says.

Gaiseric comes back to guard the food, leaving five adults in the lounge becoming better acquainted while Concordia, Alair, Evadne, and I sit on the bridge.

"We are not dying," Concordia begins.

"We want to meet Havo," Alair says.

"Alair, Concordia and I are going to talk over what to do, all right?" I ask. "Can you please be quiet while we do that?"

He nods.

"All right. Thank you."

Despite the circumstances, it feels good to be with children again.

"Let's just check our situation," I say to Concordia, nodding at the controls. Concordia reaches for some buttons, seeming to know what she's doing.

"This ship was designed for the Suppression," Concordia says.

"You mean the Day."

"I mean when the Church completed its subjugation of Reason . . . at least on the surface."

Alair climbs onto my lap.

Concordia continues. "It is a good, fast little ship, but it was not designed for the amount of radiation we are currently experiencing. The stasis beds were added for this trip, but that is about it. And of course we don't really have fuel for the return trip. Our best chance is to start back toward Terra then turn off the engines. Newtonius' First Law should keep us on a return course to intercept Terra's orbit, as long as no other force acts on us. We program the beds to wake us in time to prepare for hostile fire. If we are still far from home, we give the ship another fuel boost and ourselves some more sleep, based on how far we've already traveled. It will take us longer to get home than it took to get here, but it can be done — with skill and luck.

"According to these readings, we are already approaching dangerous levels of solar radiation. I predict we will fall unconscious and die within the next few hours, and the ship will survive continuing on its present course for another few hours after that. The heat will fry the circuits and engine. Gravity will pull the whole thing into the Sun."

What about our day or two to prepare? I wonder, but I try not to let Concordia observe my surprise or dismay.

"That is the plan," and she gives me a sharp look.

"If we are going to save ourselves, you'd better give up the religious nonsense soon. Like . . . right now."

I say nothing, still reeling at her news I will not be able to give Havo proper devotion or myself proper preparation.

"I could just kill you. Take the ship back, land it on the other side of Terra, ditch it in an ocean and start a new life."

That gets my attention back. "You would be discovered," I say.

"I would leave the landing site before anyone reached it. No one would ever know which of us it was or where I was."

"I would tell them."

"You might not survive the trip back."

"You strike me as a woman with a conscience."

"You consider that possible of someone who does not believe in Havo?" Concordia emphasizes these last five words.

"I consider a conscience a gift from Havo, not the awareness that it is His gift." That gives Concordia pause. "You would not kill someone for disagreeing with you."

"Why not? The Church does."

"I do not feel very well," Alair says.

"We are not dying," Concordia says. "You will feel better soon." To me she says, "You need to agree to turn this ship around, or we *will* turn it around by force. We are used to fighting. You are not. And we are *not* dying for your god."

I see little hope of compromise. Is it possible that if I agree, the Church will send us back next time? Will the Church realize its error? No, it is not possible the Church made a mistake. I cannot deny the existence of the apostates before me, but I do not know why they are here. I remember the drugged state of the four Offerings, but I cannot ask the Church about that now. I must trust the Church's wisdom. Havo is just. Whatever the truth of her words, Concordia is meant for Havo. The Church wishes it and made it happen, so it must be just. The Church has reasons I cannot know. The alternative . . . that the Church has hidden the existence of apostates and sentenced these to death, would mean that we are no better than those we were told were evil, that Concordia is telling the truth, and that her vile behavior might in some small way be justified. No! That is impossible!

"Why is she so angry?" Evadne asks me in a whisper.

"She is confused," I whisper back.

At this moment, our debate becomes academic. We feel a jarring sensation affecting the whole ship. The children cry out. I let Alair slide down to the floor. "It is all right," I say to them. Of Concordia, I ask, "What was that?"

Concordia is already moving her hands across controls.

"I do not . . . it is not possible," Concordia says.

"What isn't possible?"

"A tractor beam."

"Cool!" Alair says.

"A tractor beam?" I whisper. "That is not possible."

"That is what I said." Concordia reads some instruments, then gives me a look. "We've stopped moving. *I* didn't do it."

"The engines are still on."

"As I said, a tractor beam."

"We are wasting fuel. Turn them off."

"That is the first sensible thing you have said." Concordia turns her head back and calls out, "Brace yourselves, everyone!" I can see in some faces they think she caused the jarring sensation a moment ago. In some faces, I see pleasure at the thought.

Concordia switches the engines off. The ship begins to move faster, its engines no longer fighting against the force holding us. We begin to travel away from the Sun but not toward Terra.

"What about Havo?" Evadne asks.

"Yes, what about Havo?" Concordia asks. "Maybe He'll save you."

"Havo will protect us," I say, standing. "Remain calm. We do not know the answers yet, but losing our heads will not get us anywhere."

"She's right," Concordia says.

I feel as if I am in a dream, unable to believe that any of this is happening, unable to believe that my expected but decreed meeting with Havo should be like this. I also find myself unable to feel surprise at anything this woman says any longer. What can I expect from someone who does not know Havo? She might as well be a savage. She barges past me toward her allies.

One thing is certain: we are no longer moving toward the Sun. *Havo, forgive us!*

A tractor beam. From whom? Why? Imminent danger immediately overshadows our differences, obviating all debate. Even Gaiseric forgets his post as we rush to available portholes. I ask Concordia, who seems the right person to ask for more than one reason, "Does this craft possess weapons?" I am afraid; I have never harmed another human being. I have also never had anything prevent me from meeting my god. I will not be prevented.

"Minimal," Concordia says, "and useless under a tractor beam." *How does she know that?* I wonder. Tractor beams are things of history books.

"Are you some kind of engineering expert?" Alair asks.

"I can be handy," Concordia chuckles.

My heart sinks. The unwillingness of four Offerings to receive the greatest blessing in the Universe is one thing. The *Messenger* being taken by unknown forces fills me with fear. At the same time, I am baffled. What can we do? Nothing.

We wait. We watch. I notice we also fall silent. We listen to . . . nothing. The sounds of the ship remain the only sounds we hear. I am covered with two kinds of sweat now.

Through the windows we see artificial structures surrounding us—grey walls and antennae, lights blinking, bumps, edges, and shadows indicating what appears to be a very large but aged vessel. None of us can imagine what is swallowing us, but something is. I can't read minds, but everyone seems terrified. I look at Concordia, I do not know why. She wanted to kill me a short time ago. Now we are endangered from without together.

"You are an apostate," I say.

Concordia chuckles again.

"You finally get it, huh? That's good. It is too bad you still want to die." Her face darkens again.

"Not when someone else decides it."

"You *already* let someone else decide it," Concordia says. "But that's okay because the Original Crime means you deserve whatever happens to you—even whatever you go along with of your own 'free will' because you're too stupid to see the truth! Havians have an answer for everything." She shakes her head.

I look up at the ceiling of our small craft. We hear hydraulic pressure being released in gusts of air. We feel our ship being grabbed by giant appendages of some kind. Below us, we can see giant hatch doors closing—doors through which we must have just come, into some large hangar bay. Ahead of our cockpit window is a plain metal wall marked with Terran numbers. But this is no surprise: Havo only created Humanity in His image. The Universe exists for Humanity and Humanity alone. Only human beings could make such a ship. Only the Church. And now the Church has come for us?

Apparently Concordia comes to the same conclusion.

"We must be prepared to fight," she says, stepping into the middle of the corridor to reach everyone's ears. "When the doors open, one of us must find a way to get the big doors open. We do not know what to expect, but if we surprise whoever is on the other side of this door, we have a chance to escape. You don't want to be here, we don't want to be here. Is everyone ready?" I agree with her. We come to stand near the ship's side hatch, through which we entered over five months before. "If and when this door opens, do everything you can to disarm and distract whoever is on the other side. I will try to find the controls to release our ship. Do you understand?"

Everyone nods or speaks a yes.

"It may give us the advantage of surprise to open the door first," I say.

Concordia examines the door controls and presses buttons until the hatch begins to open.

"Angel of Havo, my Guardian dear," I say, "to whom Havo's love commits me here, ever this day be at my side, to light and guard, to rule and guide. Amen."

The five other Havians say, "Amen."

The door lifts to reveal a group of men and women dressed in colorful clothes but bearing no weapons, holding their hands high to demonstrate a lack of threat. We are all taken aback.

"Welcome, travelers," a middle-aged man in the middle of the group says. "Welcome to Station Michael." I do not believe my ears.

"We mean you no harm," the man continues. "Yes, we are from Terra, but we are not from the Church. You are welcome to stay with us as long as you like. We will not return you to Church control."

"We accept your invitation," Concordia says, stepping past me. With a pointed look over her shoulder at me, she adds, "Four of us wish no part in human sacrifice. We thank you for your welcome and request asylum."

The man on the hangar floor laughs gently. "You need not apply for asylum here. You see, you are already free of Terra, and this station is free of the Church. We go where we please, and we offer shelter and protection to those the Church sees fit to discard, to incinerate, to show its respect for human life." The man eyes me. "But if it pleases you to call our welcome asylum, your request is granted."

My skin greets the cool air of the hangar with relief, but a change in physical comfort does not change the discomfort my soul feels at being deprived of Havo.

"We wish to continue on," I say from the doorway, the children clinging to me.

"We want to meet Havo," Evadne says. "My parents told me He would be nice."

"Come down, sweetheart," the man says to her, looking at me. "We are nice too. We are not going to hurt you. You can keep going after a little while." That reassures me slightly, but I have no reason to trust him. Why has he interrupted our private deliberations aboard our craft? The children look up to me.

"Who are you, and what assurances do we have you will keep your word?" I ask.

"My name is Gabrielus, and I have no assurance to offer but the word you doubt."

"That's ironic, Mother," Concordia says.

I value words highly. I value the Word of Havo most highly. But I do not know this man. I also understand that a man of his word would not say anything more than what this man has just said. I decide I have little choice but to trust him, as the hangar doors are already closed, and they will not open at my command.

"It is all right," I whisper to the children. "Let's go down. This nice man is going to help us."

I do not know what else to tell them.

I remain on guard, ready to fight for Havo. I try to calm myself by remembering my previous feelings of composure and compassion. We have all been completely blindsided. Would I have fought Concordia for control of the *Messenger*? In my heart, I know I would have.

Gabrielus and his men lead the ten of us out of the hangar down a large corridor with doors at regular intervals. I can see that this ship or station is even larger than we could tell from our vessel.

"Station Michael was lost," I say as we walk, lifting my head to show this man I am not afraid.

"Taken," the man who calls himself Gabrielus says. "Yes, there is much the Church did not tell you. Come out and be free."

"We are free," I say. "Why did you divert us from our destiny?"

"Your destiny has changed," Gabrielus says, "as mine did when I was Offered thirty years ago."

This is a trick, I am sure of it.

"Dine and visit with us until tomorrow," Gabrielus says. "Surely Havo can wait one more day. If you decide to continue your mission tomorrow, we will not interfere. We will help you on your way."

What choice do we have? I am eager for tomorrow. We are prisoners. I say nothing as we walk. The children hold my hands.

"We are not going to hurt you," Gabrielus says to them. "It is the same every year. We rescue the Offerings and they react . . . skeptically, to say the least. But we understand. We were once like you. Let us show you. That will help you to understand."

Rescue? Is that how they see denying us our dearest wish?

"You are welcome to stay with us, even to worship Havo if you wish while you stay here. We have a small Havian church here."

"You go against Havo yet you honor Him?"

"We go against the false church operating in His name."

"How dare you accuse the Church of falsehood?" I ask.

He just smiles at me. I do not like him.

"You are no warrior of Havo," I say.

Gabrielus laughs, offending me deeply. "No, definitely not. But I believe in freedom of belief . . . or lack thereof."

Then he is silent.

We walk to a door, then stop. Gabrielus waits until we are all present and ready to enter.

"I know that you have all been through a great deal," he says. "I cannot promise you will not go through more. What you see next may be hard for you. I am sorry for that. At the same time, it may be helpful." He smiles a half smile, looking at me. For the first time, I feel what I think must be hatred.

I brace myself for whatever torture these kidnappers can devise and prepare to defend myself. Gabrielus opens the door, beyond which lies a large cafeteria, filled with silent faces regarding us. Everyone is standing. I do not understand.

We walk through the door to a cafeteria filled with people, young and old, of every race and description.

"You came at dinner time," Gabrielus says. And then I hear my name. I find this incomprehensible.

"Aunt Cassie! Cassie!"

A child of twelve runs up to me. A child who cannot be alive. A child who lived next to me until last year. A child who died a year ago . . . who is now a year older.

"Aunt Cassie! It is me, Julianus!

"Julianus . . . ," I say, crouching down instinctively to let him embrace me. I am dazed. I cannot believe what I am seeing, feeling in my arms, smelling. "How can this be?"

"They saved us, Cassie! Everyone here was Offered to the Sun! They've been here for years and years! Some of us have even been here their whole lives! They were born here."

I kiss his head, too surprised and emotional to remember my outrage over Gabrielus' effrontery, then embrace him silently. I had thought him dead until now. "I am glad to see you," I say. That much is true.

"Me too, Aunt Cassie."

"Why didn't you go to Havo?" I can't help asking.

"I wanted to stay here," Julianus says. "They're really nice here."

"They're thwarting Havo's will," I say.

"I am not so sure," Julianus says. "I hope you'll stay too."

I stand back up and look beyond my former neighbor's son at the men and women regarding us all silently, somberly, some of them old. Reunions occur with each of my fellow Offerings, even the apostates, several of them tearful. It is clear that apostates have been parts of every Offering ship. I cannot deny it to myself any longer.

"This is how it is every year," Gabrielus says. "Now perhaps you understand a little better, sister."

I had thought this man was kind, but now I am torn between the desire to strike him and the desire to treat all compassionately, even him. "My name is Cassiopeia Ovatio," I say coldly.

"Cassiopeia. And are you eloquent?"

This man's manner is mocking, familiar, as if he has the right to tease me. He has no right. I hate him—and I realize with shock that I have never hated anyone, that I cannot hate anyone, as we are all Havo's creatures. How can I hate him? And yet he provokes me so. There is something about Gabrielus that hinders my tongue, renders me less able to think. I glare at him.

"You have played the cruelest of tricks and will suffer in Barathrum for all eternity," I say. "You are the reason our people continue to suffer."

Gabrielus leans in close to say, "No, we are not. There is no Havo, and we are saving Offerings from an unnecessary death. You and all Havian Offerings are welcome here. We promote freedom of belief here. But that does not mean that in a private conversation I am obliged to hide from you what I think. No, Cassiopeia Ovatio, I will treat your religion with exactly the respect it deserves and no more."

I choose not to debate this apostate. It occurs to me that other Offerings I have known might have chosen to remain here. I remember my childhood playmates who were Offered, who might be here with us now . . . having turned away from Havo, Havia, and their church.

Though I am hungry and some of the others have already lined up for food, I want no part of it. I turn to go.

"Cassiopeia," Gabrielus says. "Surely you have other friends here."

I run my fingers through Julianus' hair one more time. *It is not his fault*, I think. He's just a boy. But what of these others? What of those who achieve adulthood here? "What is *your* history?" I ask Gabrielus sharply.

"I was Offered thirty years ago," he says. "That is when I learned the truth."

"What truth?"

"As I told you, there is no Havo. The Church is a lie."

"Stop," I say. "Stop. You have gone against Havo, and you speak with Scar's forked tongue!" Any shame or remorse I felt over my previous reactions has now been removed by his attacks.

This man named Gabrielus bows his head and withdraws, which surprises me. I decide I will have to watch him more carefully.

Despite myself, I am tired and hungry, but I will not give that man the satisfaction of seeing me seek his help.

"Cassiopeia," I hear.

I turn sharply, prepared to fight, and find Octavius de Haricuria standing before me. I am speechless.

"This is a fine way to greet a friend."

"Octavius!" I embrace him. I cannot help myself. The sight, the sound, the smell of him are overwhelming. It is really him.

"It seems Gabrielus told the truth about at least one thing," I say.

"He usually does," Octavius says.

I say nothing. All I can do is stand still.

"Most Offerings continue on to meet Havo," Octavius says. "But many chose to remain here."

"Why did you?" Octavius' family is devout. I never would have dreamed this possible.

"The people here showed me some things."

"What could possibly turn you from Havo?"

"Nothing. I still worship Havo. The Church on Terra, however, is false, Cassie. Do not die for it."

"Gabrielus called this place Station Michael."

"That it is."

"Station Michael was destroyed in the war, during the struggle for Day."

"No. That is what they want you to think. They didn't want to admit they had lost control of it, so they claimed it had been destroyed—by us, no less."

"Us?"

"The Resistance. Station Michael was taken by the rebels during the war, and it is true the Station was badly damaged by the fighting. But over time, it has been repaired, even extended. It is now bigger and can accommodate more persons than ever before. As you can see, it can even travel millions of miles."

"Where do you get your fuel?"

"We run primarily on solar power. Fortunately we only use fuel to hide from Terra."

My eyes flashed to his. "And the Offerings?"

"The year after the Church began making Offerings, the Station began intercepting the Offering ships. The Offerings from the first year . . . could not be saved. They were lost, regardless of their true beliefs. We remember them even as we give every Offering since the choice whether to continue. We honor all choices. We will honor yours. I fail to see how giving and honoring choices could offend Havo."

"You are tempting Offerings away from Havo—and succeeding. And do you mean to tell me this apostate operation has been stealing Offerings for a hundred years?"

"Again, there has been no stealing, no coercion. All we do is provide an opportunity to serve Havo a different way. Every year some accept."

"And what do you do with those who decline your invitation?"

"We let them continue on to Havo."

"This is why Havo has not yet lifted his curse."

"The Church told the public the Station had been destroyed rather than admit it had been taken. They do not know what we do with it, and they wouldn't be able to harm us if they did."

"Havo knows!"

"We hide behind the Sun in its radiation shadow most of the year and only come out to give Offerings the choice to live."

"You hide because you know it is wrong to brainwash them!"

"No."

"Gabrielus has already committed heresy against Havo. He told me Havo doesn't exist."

"It is true, Havo doesn't exist, but he cannot make you see that any more than I can. Only you can do that."

"You call such statements 'not brainwashing'?"

"I call them 'my view, not yours'. I feel no obligation to keep my view a secret, if that is what you are hoping."

I suppose that is what I am hoping, as I am beginning to doubt my church. How could any of this be happening? How could the Church have lied about Station Michael? All schoolchildren know it as one of the biggest losses in the Havian struggle against the evil rebels.

"What happened to the Havians posted on this space station before it was, as you say, 'taken'?"

"This station was taken by Havians who saw the opportunity to renounce Havo and the Church. They became the forebears of these people you see before you. The Church, of course, presented their betrayal as martyrdom, rather than admit the truth. Any lie to serve its propaganda, of course."

I can stomach no more. I turn to find a place to sit.

"Here, let me help you," Octavius says.

"Get away from me!" I say, surprising myself with the first unkind words I have ever uttered. I sit on a table bench and lean back against the table. "I cannot . . . I am sorry." I hold my head and close my eyes.

"I understand," he says and withdraws.

A few minutes later, I rise and walk out the door of the cafeteria. No one follows me. I wonder why. Surely I am being watched, not trusted.

I stay just outside the cafeteria door so as not to become lost myself. They might fear me a *saboteuse*. I think impulsively of taking the *Messenger* back to the Sun by myself, but first I will have to learn how to open the hangar bay doors.

I am tired. I hope my captors provide me a bed soon. Gabrielus comes out, sees me, and smiles.

"I thought you would have crashed your ship through the hanger doors by now," he says and chuckles.

"I am not violent," I say with perhaps more pride than I should.

"No, you slay me without lifting a finger."

I am not affected by his attempts at charm, except in that I feel surprise at them. Why should he speak to me thus? He is an apostate, so he possesses no morals. He is as liable to pick me up, take me to a secret room, and violate me as look at me with a smile and charming words. He is trying to trick me, so I shall be direct with him. I look him in the eye.

"I want to meet my god," I say.

"Your god is a loving, merciful god, yes?" he asks.

Despite my distrust and unwillingness to agree with anything he says or asks, I am forced to nod.

"It is possible that your loving, merciful god wishes you to live another night and day. Is that possible?"

I am forced to acknowledge that it is possible. Havo controls all things. It is possible I am here on this station due to His conscious will. It is possible this is a test. I will not fail Havo.

I nod again, curtly, and look away.

"Havo works in mysterious ways," Gabrielus says, again mocking.

"Yes, He does. I saw an old friend of mine in there, someone I thought dead."

"I am not surprised. Every year at least one Offering has accepted our invitation. You might find more from your province in there, though not from every year."

I consider this and allow myself to remember the Offerings from the past several years. I did not know most of them, but there were some I would enjoy seeing again, if they chose to stay here.

"I hope not," I say.

"Well, I am sure you are tired," Gabrielus says. "And I know you wish to continue on to Havo tomorrow. Would you like me to show you to your quarters for the night, not that we have night here?"

This is it. This is when he is going to attack me, when he gets me alone in some secret place. Though I would desperately love a bath and bed, I say, "No. Thank you. I will wait for the rest of my companions."

Gabrielus raises his eyebrows but says only, "As you wish."

He goes back inside the cafeteria, leaving me more surprised.

Eventually, everyone comes out, the greetings over. Concordia and the other three apostates from the *Messenger* are laughing and smiling with new friends—or perhaps old ones thought gone. The faithful come to me rattled and confused.

"What are we going to do?" Jinx asks.

"I do not understand your question," I say. "We are going to meet Havo." She continues fretting.

Gabrielus, who seems to be the leader of the people on this station, takes us personally to show us quarters. "Back home, you had a lot of space. Here we do not have that luxury. Despite all the space outside, space is at a premium inside. Every year we welcome more Offerings, and some babies, and we do not subtract as fast as we add." He leads us to an unremarkable metal door. "This is for Jinx and Cassiopeia. Not very private, but not as bad as six or eight. The engineers all sleep together." He opens the door to reveal a room with four bunks, two enormous lockers, and a metal pipe cutting through the space next to the bunks at left. "We'll provide you toiletries. The showers are down the hall, over there." He points to our left down the main corridor, which I notice curves like a giant ring. "Here are some night clothes, and one towel to share." He hands folded night suits and a towel to Jinx. "Sorry. We have to conserve everything. At least we have artificial gravity."

I nod. Two enormous lockers divide the small room and its four unremarkable bunks. I am afraid to consider what might be inside the lockers, but I dispel fantastic notions by looking back to Gabrielus' face. "Your bunkmates, Urban and Leo, are on duty, but they'll be back after their shifts," he says. "If you decide to stay, you will be asked to do work on the Station, work related to your particular gifts."

"Thank you," I say. Jinx and I wish everyone a good night and go inside. I dread sharing a room with two strange men.

"I am sorry," Jinx says after the door closes.

"For what?" I ask.

"I am sorry we are not with Havo."

"I am too," I say and embrace her. I kiss her forehead.

I consider not showering, fearing someone might attack me, but I wish to present myself well for Havo tomorrow.

I take the towel and go down the hall to the shower, not sure what to expect. I find a room with three shower heads, much like the showers at my teaching school, where I lived in a dormitory, but smaller. Fortunately, no one else is there. I marvel at the science behind the artificial gravity catching all the water droplets.

I think about the shower at home and how different it is from this station's large, cold room as I take my first shower in over six months. I put on the Station's night suit and go back the short distance to our cabin, where I find Jinx kneeling on the floor, praying. I decide to pray after her. I move past her, crouch down, and, with effort, find my way onto the bed she has not chosen, the lower bunk on the left, when one is facing the lockers. Of course I bump my head on the bottom edge of the bunk above, out of practice. I watch Jinx rock back and forth, intent in prayer, thinking I will be glad to sleep if only to stop hurting myself.

I am torn by my love for Havo, my desire to see Him, and my dismay over what has happened since we awoke in the shuttle. How is it that apostates were sent on this flight? How is it that we arrived with so little time to prepare ourselves? Were these two facts related? Did the Church think the apostates might cause trouble? Did the Church wish them dispatched faster than usual? What if this was usual? Was this fair to faithful Offerings? I suddenly realize I can ask the previous Offerings about their experiences.

And what of Station Michael? How can this be true? I am here, and yet this is impossible. The Station was destroyed by apostate rebels over a hundred and thirty years ago. Would the Church lie about something like this? Would the Church lie at all? How can this be? I decide the Church was at worst misinformed; the apostates must have falsified the Station's destruction. I will ask Gabrielus to confess this before I leave the station.

A sound interrupts my thoughts, the sound of soft knocking on the cabin door.

I open it to find Octavius.

"Come in," I say, feeling remorse. "I am sorry I cannot offer you a place to sit."

"Nonsense," Octavius says. "I am used to sitting on bunks and floors."

I look at Jinx, who has just finished her prayers. She raises her eyebrows but leaves the room. I am grateful to her. Octavius sits on the floor and crosses his legs. I do the same near him in the small space.

"Cassie, you cannot go," Octavius says the moment after the door closes behind Jinx.

"I must go to Havo. You know this."

"I know there are things you need to see and hear."

"I will not consent to brainwashing."

"Cassie, they do not lie here. You can believe what you want but only *after* they show and tell you the truth. Then it will be up to you."

"Is that a threat?"

"Only if the truth threatens you."

"I fear no truth."

"That is what I always liked best about you. Tell me, have you ever seen little things that did not quite fit what the Church said? Haven't you ever wondered why they said what they said but some things you saw or knew to be true did not line up with what they said?"

I shake my head no, and then I remember Mother's death. I look down.

"You have."

"Some things are mysterious. That is why we call it faith."

"Faith doesn't—or shouldn't—mean denying contradictions in Reality. It also shouldn't mean ignoring them. There is only one truth, and the truth is that the Church lies to you to get you to believe what it wants . . . to get you to *do* what it wants, which is to stay quiet and obey. Those who do not are punished, some most severely."

"How?" I ask.

Octavius gives me a pointed look. "They aren't all sent here. Some are killed back home. Of course, this is the easiest way. I was sent here because my father questioned doctrine."

"He did *what*?"

"He stood in church and asked why nonbelievers went to Scar. He said if they were good people who simply did not believe in Havo otherwise, Havo wouldn't punish them, and if He did, then that is not the kind of god my father could accept."

"Heresy!" I rise to my feet without even thinking.

"Yes. The idea that Havo required my father's approval overwhelmed the congregation—and yet of course He does. We must find our god *worthy* of praise and worship to praise and worship Him, else our minds and hearts are good for nothing, and why would a good god want that? No, a good god rejoices in—wishes nothing more than—the free approbation of a good worshipper." Octavius smiles. "I am proud of him to this day. I just miss him." He looks up at me. "I told you—we do not spare or deny the truth here.

"But have not *you* wondered about Havo's love for nonbelievers?"

I have.

I nod, almost imperceptibly.

"I knew you were too smart not to."

"What did they do to him?"

"They told him to leave the service. Then they spoke with him after, behind closed doors. They told him to stop questioning. He said no. But they did not kill him. They did something far worse. They sent me here to die, to destroy his spirit. I hope it did not work. He still does not know I survived." Octavius pauses. "At the time, I told him to protect himself, to stay quiet. But now I hope he did not." Octavius looks at me with a very odd look.

"How could you?" I ask.

"Do you think a child should be punished for the heresy of his father?"

"I am sure there is no relation between the two facts."

"Do you think his question deserving of any sanction whatever? You have wondered it yourself!"

I find it hard to breathe.

Octavius leans toward me. "I hope he kept provoking thought because he was *right*. The truth should not be feared, if it is the truth. What kind of a god—or church—fears the truth? Only a false one."

Octavius leans back and regards me. He can see my doubt.

"You are a heretic," I say.

"And you will be a great force for justice once you learn what it is," Octavius says. He regards me for another long moment, then stands. "Stay here. You must learn the truth. You must spread the truth. We must liberate Terra."

"What?"

"You heard me."

"I heard you, but I do not believe you."

"You *are* a skeptic, after all. But you may believe me. *I* will not lie to you. Terra needs you, Cassie. I have been urging Gabrielus to return us to Terra for some time now. But now that you're here . . . I really think we should do it."

"Me? Why?"

"Because you are a great leader. I have always thought so." He pauses. "I have always looked up to you."

I am almost overcome.

"Octavius, I know you have been here for three years, but none of this sounds like the boy I knew. What have they done to you? What have they said? How could you possibly become a rebel against the Church?"

Octavius crouches down in front of me. "I am *not* the boy you knew. I am a man now. And what they have done is show me the truth, which I am now trying to do for you. I have not rejected Havo. We are talking about what the Church has done in His name. If you love Havo . . . defend Him from the villains perverting Justice in His name. You will find in me an ally, Cassiopeia Ovatio." I find myself affected by his eyes as he speaks, his face near mine. His using my full name hypnotizes me.

I do not look up as Octavius stands again and leaves. Jinx comes back in, but I answer her questions and comments absently. I return to my bed and pray to Havo. I hold my mother's prism, whispering, "O, Holy Spirit of Havo, abide with us. Inspire all our thoughts, pervade our imaginations, suggest all our decisions." Jinx looks down at me and climbs up into her bunk. "Be with us in our silence and in our speech, in our haste and in our leisure, in company and in solitude, in the freshness of the morning and in the weariness of the evening; and give us grace at all times humbly to rejoice in Thy mysterious companionship."

When I arrive at the Sixth Mystery of Havo, "Let us honour the wonderful operation of the Holy Light creating within the Church that other Sun—the Prism—and conferring the plenitude of the Prisms on the Rays," I pause. I find myself feeling doubts of my church. What am I becoming? Am I becoming corrupted?

"Amen, amen, amen," I say.

Jinx turns off the solar lamp hanging from the ceiling, and I fall into a troubled sleep. My future might be empty, but my mind is full, and I realize I forgot to ask Octavius about his experience coming here.

A few moments later, or what feels like a few moments later, I am awakened by the door of the cabin opening. At first I do not remember where I am. The cabin is dark; only the light of the corridor behind the man coming in reminds me. Though I am wearing the night suit provided by Gabrielus, I instinctively draw my blanket up to cover myself. The man activates the overhead lamp and notices us in its pale light.

"You must be from the Offering ship," he says. "Gabrielus told me to expect new bunkmates. But only for one night, right?" He chuckles.

"You are correct," I say.

"Well, it is your funeral," the man says. "I am Urban."

"Cassiopeia."

"It was nice knowing you, Cassiopeia." He laughs. I feel a chill of horror go through me. How could anyone be so callous, so cruel, so wrong to someone working to save Terra? *To save Terra.*

I turn away and recite the nightly thanksgiving prayer to myself. "I adore You, my Sun, and I love You with all my heart. I thank you for having created me, for having made me a Havian, and for having preserved me this day." He did—He did preserve me this day! "Protect me while I take my rest and deliver me from all dangers. May your grace be always with me. Amen."

"How sweet," I hear from Urban. "I love prayer—the most useless thing ever."

I say nothing and, despite my hunger, go back to sleep, grateful that the sleeping Jinx has not suffered this horrible man.

I note that he must work hard, judging by his smell. I do not begrudge this, but I do not enjoy it either.

Of much greater importance is the question: does Havo want me to stay alive?

In the morning, a gentle knock at the door awakens me, and for a moment I think it is my father calling me to breakfast. Before I even open my eyes, I remember where I am. Then I wonder who it could be. Is it Octavius come to tell me more, to challenge me again, to whisper my name in my ear? A part of me hopes it might be. "Who is it?" I call out.

"Gabrielus." My heart sinks.

I rise, still in my night suit, and answer the door. "Good morning," I say.

"Good morning," he says. "I came to invite you to break your fast. In your case, you have not eaten in over six months, have you?"

"I have not."

"The rest of your companions ate at the welcoming dinner last night, while you waited outside."

"That is true."

"You are a proud one, Cassiopeia Ovatio."

My father used to say that, in the years when he was happy.

"I am a true follower of Havo."

"So you are," he says.

"That is why, hungry though I may be, I must first give morning praise before I accompany you."

"Of course. I'll wait outside." Gabrielus steps back out into the corridor.

There are more than one prayer for each time of the day. This morning I give this one:

"My Sun, I adore You," I say, closing my eyes, "and I love You with all my heart. I thank you for having created me, made me a Havian, and preserved me this past night. I offer You the actions of this day. Grant that all of my actions today may be in accordance with Your holy Will and for Your greater glory. Protect me from all evil. Let Your grace be always with me and with all my dear ones. Amen." *Especially my father*, I allow myself to think.

I wish I had brought my robes. I step outside, and we walk to the mess hall.

"How are you this morning, Cassiopeia Ovatio?" he asks.

"I walk with Havo. I am always well."

"How fortunate you are," he says.

"Indeed," I say. "You are the head of this station, if I understand matters correctly. Surely you have more important things to do than take me to breakfast."

Gabrielus chuckles, surprising me.

"I have to eat too," he says. "And I want to make sure you are treated well while you are with us, however briefly. I wish to honor your faith and you."

"If you wished to honor my faith, you would not have violated it in the first place. You would have let us go once you met us. You would not have subjected my faith to your ridicule and contempt. And you would not give me political advice regarding my clothing."

"I could have been more kind in my words," he says, "but I imagine your faith and relationship with Havo are strong enough to withstand any political difficulty." He pauses. "My mechanics have been looking over your ship. Your fellow Offerings and you may depart any time you like this evening. We always have a small ceremony to see Offerings off."

I seem to have no choice but to accept the unacceptable and hope Havo will forgive us.

"In your respecting those Offerings who wish to continue, you are indeed touched by Havo," I say. "He and his consort are filling you with their love. Is there no chance you will join us and return to them?"

"No," Gabrielus says. "We are not touched by anything but the desire to be moral human beings. If you wish to die, despite knowing that your church has lied to you about our existence for over a hundred years, despite knowing that many of the Offerings chosen each year are apostate prisoners sentenced to death for no crime but their views, despite knowing the truth that every single person living happily on this station does so *voluntarily* yet the Church controls and coerces almost every aspect of daily life on Terra . . . then I think, yes, I would prefer not to have you on my station. If you wish to die, I cannot stop you, and I would consider you dangerous were you to stay here. Those who are *not* suicidal tend to make easier guests."

"I do not want to die," I say. "I want to serve Havo."

Gabrielus shows the effrontery to place his hands on my shoulders. I do not fight him, as I do not know what he might do if inflamed. I try to appear unafraid.

"Cassiopeia, you can leave here and fly into the Sun if you like. But did it ever occur to you that you could be of greater use to Havo alive? Look at all the evil and corruption on Terra. You are good, that much is obvious. Do you really think good persons should shoot themselves into the Sun for nothing? Have all previous Offerings earned Havo's forbearance? Has the Inopia ended? Has Offering done any good whatever? Hasn't it harmed matters? We suffer a lack of children so we kill those few we have? And now we have so few we also kill young adults? Soon there'll be no one left to sacrifice!

"You are barely an adult yourself," he continues. "Live longer. You may do as you wish, but I would be grossly remiss if I did not say that in my opinion—which does not come from Havo or anyone else but me—your death would constitute a great loss to the World . . . and to Havo."

I shake free of him wordlessly and stare in the direction we were walking. I will not address him further for his apostasy . . . but his words gnaw at me. He is not allowed to decide for Havo what would be a loss to Havo! The arrogance, the pride!

Gabrielus leads me to the cafeteria without attempting further conversation, which is a good thing. I have been through more conflict in the past twenty-four hours than I have ever experienced before—even the idea of having to debate him in the corridor is disturbing to me. Why does he care so much what happens to me? Why does he want me alive? Does he want to use me for some evil purpose? What could it be? Not only do not I ask him about the Station's history, I am now the most upset I have been since arriving.

I walk into the cafeteria. My grey flight suit stands out among the sea of dark green jumpsuits. Gabrielus and I pick up trays and go through the line. I take water and an orange.

"That is all?" Gabrielus asks.

"I am not hungry," I say.

The Station residents before and after us on the line seem uncomfortable, though some welcome me.

"We're glad you chose to stay," the person serving the food says to me.

We come out into the large dining hall. I see Aetius, Paula, and Jinx in their grey flight suits. They invite me to sit with them. Gabrielus comes with me.

"You do not have to sit with us," I say.

"Yes, I think I should."

We sit, eat, and speak of small matters. A man comes up and asks me, "Do you believe in Havo?"

"Yes, of course."

"I hope you join Him today!"

"Easy, son," Gabrielus says.

"I will be glad to join Havo," Aetius says.

The man withdraws.

"I'm sorry about that," Gabrielus says.

I see Concordia and the others from the *Messenger* sitting together with other residents at another table. I catch Concordia looking this way. Now they are talking about what happened. I cannot decide whether to wish they would join us on the *Messenger* or stay here. They all need Havo more desperately than believers do, but a part of me thinks they should be free to reject Havo if they wish. What do I care if they join Scar forever? I realize this is anger, grief, and hunger talking. Of course I care about them, as I care about all souls. With shame I remember my vow to treat nonbelievers with compassion and love. I failed to do that yesterday. I have disappointed Havo and myself. I will succeed today.

Havo created the Universe, the Planets, and the first human beings from photons, placing light inside all of us. The early Havian prophets and then the Church went through centuries of debate on the subtleties of doctrine. I know that Havo created good and evil as equal gifts, that the benefit of good is obvious but the benefit of evil is less so. I know that evil is necessary for us to enjoy the gift of free will. I remember my father saying that we all enjoy Havo's love, even those who turn from Havo.

"*We even have the right to rebel,*" *he said.* "*Remember that, because it is very important. It shows how much Havo loves us, even those who stray.*"

"*Who would want to do that?*" *I asked.*

"*Well, no one nowadays, but it did happen in the past. To stray is to suffer, but the bad things that happened to those who strayed were lessons from Havo designed to remind them His love is beneficial. Havo loves us all, but like a parent, He teaches us lessons. He just wanted the rebels to return to Him—and they did. But forcing them would have denied their free will. They had to come back on their own. That is how great Havo is. And oftentimes good comes from bad, which is just another sign of Havo's love for us.*"

I also know that to the extent bad things happen to good persons who do not stray, this is Havo using Scar to test us.

"*What about evil persons?*" *I asked him.* "*We do read of the occasional crime occurring.*"

"*Evil persons do exist, but most evil is caused by otherwise good people who are confused. We do have places where we help them to be better again. You have to remember also that evil exists to test us, to help us remember our own goodness and, above all, to show it. Evil might test us, but we must rise to the test, as Havo wills.*"

This is how I should treat the apostates here.

I stand and approach their table.

"I couldn't help but notice your new friend, Mother," Concordia says, leaning forward. "The Church has generated quite a bit of ill will, and I'm afraid that one little Havian cannot erase that." Even Gaiseric stops eating.

"I am sorry," I say. "I am sorry for the conflict between us."

"But you're still right, right?"

"I am glad we are here, that you may live. I do not want you to die." I turn to leave.

"And what are you going to do? Are you going to die?"

I turn back and see that the person asking me is Huneric.

"I still feel Havo calling me," I say, "but I am not sure in what direction now."

I do not know why I say this. They make sounds of surprise and amusement.

"Somebody's faith is not complete!" Huneric says.

"Let me know if you need help jumping out an airlock," Gaiseric says.

I turn and walk away. The cruelty of the apostate has not been misrepresented. I return to my table in silence.

"What did you say to them? What happened?" Jinx asks me.

I shake my head no and keep eating. I cannot shake from my mind Gabrielus' words: " . . . *Your church has lied to you about our existence for over a hundred years . . . many of the Offerings chosen each year are apostate prisoners sentenced to death for no crime but their views . . . every single person living happily on this station does so* voluntarily *yet the Church controls and coerces almost every aspect of daily life on Terra . . .* "

No, no! my mind screams to itself. As hungry as I was, I barely eat an orange then push it away. The others do not press me.

After breakfast, we are permitted to explore the station with guides. I am in no mood to do so. I go back to my cabin. I think long and hard about Havo and Havia, the Church, and the nature of things.

I am considering not flying the *Messenger* into the Sun. I feel my heart is neither pure nor true. I cannot believe I am considering these things. Alone in my cabin, I begin to cry.

Is Havo redeeming me and this situation? Could it be possible that Gabrielus is right? Could the Offering be the bad event from which Havo is trying to rescue me? There is no Havo, Gabrielus said. He is clearly wrong, but could Havo have another purpose in mind for me? Why else would He have saved me—and the rest of us for that matter?

What of Octavius? I cannot bear the thought that he has been brainwashed by these apostates, but he knew me. He knew my heart, then. If what he says is true now . . . but this cannot be.

I tell myself that back on Terra, everyone is happy. There really isn't anything for me to do. I can just meet Havo with a clear conscience. But everything I have experienced since waking in the *Messenger* has suggested to me a world of conflict and problems of which I had been unaware before. In Soul River, I taught and ran the house after Mother died. I had not really had time to decide what to do with my life when she died. Father worked on computers for the Church and local businesses. He saw and spoke with almost everyone in town. Now that I think about it, he told me very little about his interactions with the town. Was he protecting me? From what? From apostates like Concordia? Who else in our town was an apostate? And why was the Prism so uncomfortable speaking with me? If I die, I will never know, and a part of me wants to go back to find out. A part of me thinks Havo wants me to do this. That part of me starts to form a plan.

I leave my room and seek out Concordia.

I find her in the Station corridor with the other apostates from our ship and another man I do not know. They are looking out a darkened window discussing the Sun's features. Concordia seems to be becoming friendly with the man. I wait a short distance from them until they notice me.

"Hey, if it isn't the crazy bitch!" one of them says. I ignore this and stare at Concordia.

"Hey, she's starting to scare me," another says. "Do not you have an appointment with Death, sister?"

I disregard these comments.

Concordia says, "It is fine," and comes over to me. We walk to a private place farther away from the others, where Concordia leans against the wall. "Well?"

I do not know what to say.

"You already said you were sorry. Have you had another epiphany, Mother?" Concordia asks, mocking me.

"Yes." I look down and hesitate. "I think . . . maybe this is Havo's will."

Concordia drops her arms in surprise.

"I mean . . . I think maybe Havo wants us to do something with this. Maybe there's a *reason* we were rescued—all of us." I wave my hand to indicate the past Offerings, the entire Station. "But I do not think that reason is to spend the rest of our lives, living out generations on this ship."

"What do you think it is?" She peers at me so intensely I cannot meet her gaze.

I swallow hard.

"I think . . . we need to go back."

Concordia laughs. I am crushed.

"You *are* crazy!" She keeps laughing.

I can barely ask her, but I manage: "Why?"

She pokes her finger into my chest suddenly and painfully. "The Church is the Worldwide crime syndicate. I got sent here because I got caught. Do you know what I was doing when I got caught?"

I shake my head no.

"I was trying to *burn the library* in Eboracum Novum, to prevent *stulti* like you from reading more of the Church's propaganda. I want to put an end to your church. I want it gone. Dead. Done."

I feel dizzy and ill.

"I need you," I whisper.

"You finally figured that out, did you?" Concordia snorts. "You are a pathetic, useless, sniveling little sheep. You hear and obey. They say pray and you ask how loud. You never think, you never question, you just live in your little fantasy world while others fight and die to free you from a slavery of which you are not even aware! You disgust me, Cassiopeia Ovatio!"

I feel ashamed. I look down and say without raising my eyes:

"I want to take this station back home."

Concordia stops berating. I hear, with dripping sarcasm and perhaps even a note of pain:

"To give it back to your 'theocratic socialism'?"

"No," I say. "To show the World the truth."

"Why? Since when have you been concerned with the truth?"

"That is all I have ever been concerned with." I look back up at her, tears in my eyes.

"I see. We just have different truths, eh? Well, what if we do that and your Church does something that shocks your conscience, Sister Cassiopeia? What are you going to do when it turns out the truth is not what they told you?" Concordia laughs. "They've already tried to *murder* you, for Goodness' sake!" She hardens again. "And you *went along*.

"You've got some thinking to do. You sound confused, which might be the first step forward in your life. Good for you, Cassopeia Ovatio." She turns to go, then turns back. "Here's a hint: do *not* get on that ship today." She walks away.

Do not get on that ship today. I am not sure what I should do, but a little voice inside me grows increasingly loud saying the same thing. I watch Concordia and her friends walk away, some of them laughing and casting mocking glances in my direction. I begin to feel that perhaps I deserve those laughs and glances. I turn away, unsure, not knowing why I am unsure, and not knowing how to regain the surety that both guided and comforted me until now.

I seek and find Aetius's room. He strikes me as the most calm and secure member of "our" team on the ship. He opens the door and lets me in.

"I was just praying," he says. "Would you like to join me?"

I shake my head no as he shuts the door.

"Aetius, I am having doubts," I say.

"About what? About Havo? Are these apostates getting to you?" He frowns. "Please sit."

I do, on the edge of one of the bunks. I shake my head. "No. Absolutely not. I am starting to wonder . . . if maybe Havo saved us for a reason."

"The Sun works in mysterious ways, eh?" He smiles.

"Yes. I was thinking . . . what if He intends for us to live?"

He says nothing, so I continue.

"What if we were not only meant to live but to perform a duty, for Havo and our world?"

"What would that duty be?" he asks cautiously.

"That is what I have been asking myself, and the only conclusion I can reach is that I think Havo wants us to take this station back to Terra."

"It could just as easily be to destroy the station before it causes any more harm."

"Havo could destroy this station without anyone's help, and without anyone on Terra knowing about it. The only reason He would involve *us* is that He wants people to know about the Station. That is the one lead here. And if we do bring this station back to Terra, we will be helping everyone there in more than one way. Our doing so would provide both knowledge and a big tool for Humanity to use in the future."

"I notice you have not mentioned the Church," Aetius says.

"I serve Havo," I say, "even more than I serve the Church, as the Church teaches."

"It is rare that anyone thinks the two do not coincide," Aetius says.

"It is, yes."

"It would also expose the Church to accusations of falsehood. Remember, we were all taught this station was destroyed."

"Yes, it would, but I think Havo's truth is more important than human error, which is surely all it was—a long time ago at that." The current Church leaders were not responsible for the errors of the past and would like to be corrected. Anyone interested in the truth would.

"Well, I'll think on it, but right now I am going to get back to preparing myself."

"Of course."

I leave feeling disappointed and something else I have never felt: disconnected, removed. I feel apart from Aetius and his goal of sacrifice. I fear what I am becoming.

I feel enough doubt that I realize and decide I cannot leave the Station. I seek Gabrielus out and ask for a private word in the corridor.

"I have decided to stay," I say.

"That's wonderful! I am very pleased."

"*I* am not entirely pleased," I say. "I am suffering from doubt. Your intervention—your existence—has thrown my faith into jeopardy. So I am not entirely happy with *you*."

He laughs. "I'll take it. Your anger is better than your death."

"You are *staying*?"

I spin around to find Jinx coming toward us.

"Gabrielus, you remember Jinx," I say.

"Oh. It's 'Gabrielus' now. These apostates have really gotten to you, have not they?"

"The truth has. There is some reason Havo is orchestrating these events, and I want to learn what that reason is."

"Well, while you study the Stars and read the omens, some of us are still going—tonight!" She sounds as if she might cry.

"I would say do not go, but that would be hypocritical of me," I say. "You should do what you think is right."

"That is the problem, Sister. You've got me not knowing what I think!"

"I understand," I say, embracing Jinx and trying to soothe her. "This is hard for all of us—the Offering, the apostates on our ship, then the Station taking us, and everything we've seen and heard since."

"Speak for yourself," Jinx says. "The only thing hard for me is you not going."

"Why?" I ask her.

"You were the rock, on the ship and after. What did they do to change your mind, in just one day?" Jinx chokes up.

"I changed my own mind, Jinx," I say, holding her head and looking her in the eyes. "I have my own mind, it is mine, and I control it. No one can change my mind against my will. I still believe in Havo. I am just not sure what He wants from us, what his purpose for us is. I think He might want us to live." I look around for a moment. "I mean, it sure does look it, doesn't it?"

Gabrielus nods.

"I do not know," Jinx says.

"Stay here and figure it out with me. We can always take the next ship, next year, if we need to, right, Gabrielus?"

"Absolutely," he says.

It is not self-preservation motivating me, it is belief. If I believe it is Havo's will for me to die, I will die. If I believe He wants me to live, I will live. I am not afraid to die. I am afraid of not serving Havo's will, whatever that might be.

For the first time in my life, I am not sure that I believe the Church's will is Havo's will.

Jinx and I embrace, and I cry a little too.

Here, on this station, the Church has no reach or sway. The Church claims to be universal, but it is not even solar. It is clear to me now that, in this solar system, apostates run rampant, doing as they please—or, if not doing as they please, at least moving freely on Terra and in Space. They *have* touched me, and the Church is looking smaller as a result.

My cabin is my only refuge, and I return to it. I lie on my bed and wrestle with my thoughts some more. Alone on a bed on a station on the other side of the Sun, I felt connected to the Church until today. I still feel connected to Havo, and this will sustain me, no matter what happens.

How will I feel about the Church when I return to Terra? How will the Church feel about me?

I will explain myself, and the Church will understand—*if* I can persuade these apostates to take us all home. But what of those who have no home but Station Michael?

At 1700 hours, the *Messenger* will depart. I do not know who will be aboard, but I feel anxious. I no longer plan to go, but I cannot help feeling that each and every soul planning to do so should rather stay and work to serve Havo in a different way. A part of me envies those who still possess faith in the sacrifice, but I am mainly afraid to see who will participate in it. At the appointed time, the rest of the faithful arrive in the hangar deck: Aetius, Jinx, Alair, Evadne, and Paula. I stand with Gabrielus and a few others who wished to attend. As they pass me, they say farewell.

"Well, Aetius?" I ask him as he stands to face me.

"I understand your decision, and I wish you peace," he says. "I thank you for trusting me. I hope you find the answers you seek and join us next time." He turns to the ship and boards it. I sigh with sadness.

"Jinx, I wish you peace," I say.

She grasps my hand. "I wish you the same. I am sorry, but I need to go," she says.

"I understand. I envy you."

"I will hope to see you again."

"And I you. Vale."

I embrace her.

Alair and Evadne come before me.

"Cassiopeia!" they say.

"Beloved children."

"They say you're not coming!"

"That is true. Havo has a different plan for me."

"Is it a secret mission?"

"I honestly don't know."

"Ooh!" Alair says. "That *is* a secret!"

"We're going to miss you!" Evadne says.

"We will meet again," I tell them both.

"You promise?"

"I am sure of it."

We embrace, and I begin to cry.

"Do not cry, Cassiopeia Ovatio," Alair says. "Praise Havo."

"I will," I say, wiping my tears away, remembering my speeches to my father and Prism Arcturus.

"You remind me of my mama," Evadne says.

"I do not have children," I say, "but if I did I would want them to be just like you.

"Remember, you are good and holy. You are almost there."

Evadne smiles. They both hug me again and move on. I stand, still wiping my face.

"Paula," I say, when I have composed myself.

She nods.

"I wish you joy," I say.

"I feel it," Paula says. "I am staying here."

I am stunned.

She smiles at me.

"You do not wish to join with Havo?" I ask.

"You clearly do not," Paula says. "Why question me?"

"I am just surprised," I say.

"We have both decided to take advantage of the opportunities this station affords," Paula says, amused. "Havo be praised." She stands next to me to watch the others board.

I am bursting with the desire to rebut her suggestion I am taking advantage of opportunities. I am only trying to serve Havo's will! But I master myself, deciding that now is not the time to argue. We are standing solemnly, watching as the four Havians board their shuttle home to Havo. I should be filled with joy. Instead I feel surrounded by questions, tainted, damaged.

I have lost almost all my allies from the *Messenger*. Paula is the exception, but she provides little comfort. Paula's presence and the prospect of her continued survival on this station alarm me, though I couldn't say why if asked. I just do not trust her. Then I realize in the span of two short days I have become cynical and distrusting, a person I do not even recognize as myself. Of course Paula's motivations are as pure as my own—she is probably suffering similar doubts. If she had not been sincere, she would have sided with the apostates on the ship. And what would we have done if the vote had been five to five? With her vote, Paula had given victory to our side. I do not want to speculate the outcome, however, if Aetius, Jinx, Paula, and I had to fight the three large men and Concordia. I have never fought anyone in my life.

The hatch closes, the small craft's engines start. Those of us in the hangar withdraw to a safe viewing area behind glass, then the large hangar doors open. Gabrielus gives the order for the docking clamps to lower the ship out into Space. The ship heads forward out of view under its own power.

We watch the ship's progress on a video screen. It turns toward the Sun and makes steady progress.

"They are doing well," Gabrielus says. "They will likely lose consciousness in the next several hours and die thereafter." I feel uncomfortable. I feel the loss of the children.

"This happens every time," Gabrielus says. "Some choose not to stay here, and we respect their right to self-determination, as much as we may disagree with their choice. We are not tyrants, contrary to what the Church would tell you. That is why we wait until after this happens to hold a certain ceremony." A part of me is filled with dread. I have heard my whole life that apostates were known for their cruelty, torturing Rays to the point of begging for death. Is this what they will do to us? Have I made the wrong choice?

I master my facial expression as Gabrielus leads us to another room, where, to my surprise, I find Concordia, Huneric, Gaiseric, Totila, and others I do not know. Is this their revenge? On a table in the center of the room is a small assortment of items ranging from clothing to jewelry to books.

"All who have chosen to stay here are now welcomed," Gabrielus says. "There are a few hundred of us on this station, and every year in advance of the Offering, some of us make gifts to present to those who choose to stay. These gifts symbolize your new home and your new life. Each of the six of you has chosen to stay, and we invite you to take something that suits you." The six? Of course!

I relax greatly, then, with the others, regard the tabletop more closely. I notice an ancient book, tattered and worn, the title of which is hard to make out . . . *Havo is Not Great*. The moment I decipher the title Concordia snatches it out from in front of me. "I'll read it to you," she says. I find it hard to feel compassion and love, but I study the jewelry and select a small medallion reading, "A New Birth of Freedom." It shows human beings holding hands and cooperating.

As we leave, a woman by the door hands each of us a dark green jumpsuit, matching those worn by the others here. Paula takes one, but I decline. The woman looks at Gabrielus. He thinks, then nods to her that it is all right.

"The believers sometimes wear something different to mark themselves," he says. "If you wish to stay in your flight suit, it is fine."

"I wish I had my robes," I say.

Then I notice Concordia is already wearing a dark green jumpsuit. She somehow obtained one before this meeting. I suspect her new friend assisted with that, then find myself wondering why I should care.

"Well," Gabrielus says to us all back outside the small room. "Welcome to Station Michael, your new home."

We all thank him.

I am still not sure I have done the right thing. A part of me still envies those who have just departed, but I find myself accepting my new course. *As Havo wills*, I tell myself.

Now I am on this station, surrounded by apostates, still trying to learn what Havo wishes of me. I know only this: Station Michael needs to go home.   Rather, those on Terra need to know it exists . . . to learn the truths I have exposed, perhaps more.   But where will I go, if we do return to Terra?   What will I do, on a world where I was told to die?

At supper, I am silent.   At bedtime, in my own new quarters with former Havians, I pray not only for those who have gone on but for myself. What will become of me?   Why did I stay here?   What is your purpose for me, my Light?

"Have all previous Offerings earned Havo's forbearance?" Gabrielus asked me.   *"Has the Inopia ended?   Has Offering done any good whatever?"*

I stare at the ceiling until I fall asleep.

I walk the station both afraid and depressed, ignoring most of what I see or hear, my foundation slipping out from under me. Gabrielus takes enormous personal interest in my case but is unable to stay with me at all times. He assigns me a guide named Lucretia. I do not want her with me, but Gabrielus did say he would consider me dangerous if I stayed. Perhaps he wishes to monitor me. I will not give him the satisfaction of engaging in anti-social behavior that would only confirm him in his prejudices, and these apostates did and do consider their interception of me a "rescue", so in their minds I owe them a debt of gratitude. Though I do not feel grateful to them for destroying my holy certainty—for damaging my faith in the perfect alignment of Havo, Church, and State—I know this is how they feel. Because I consider myself a guest more than a resident, despite their words of welcome, I need to abide by their rules—at least until I decide what to do with myself. I also know my decisions are limited on Station Michael. If I refuse a guide, I might find myself in the brig or out an airlock. I cannot trust them, but they cannot trust me. A part of me understands all these matters.

I want to see Octavius, but he too is working.

I did not sleep well. I resolve to eat today.

"You are not the only believer here, you know," Lucretia says after watching me stare out a window.

"Yes, Octavius told me."

"It's true. We rescue Offerings whether they believe or not. Some go, like your friends, but some stay too. You might like to meet some of them."

"All right," I say, to please her more than myself.

"I can introduce you to some at breakfast."

Lucretia escorts me to the cafeteria.

A mural in the Ring near the cafeteria depicts a scene I find disturbing. It shows the Station leaving Terra at the end of the Night, the beginning of the Day. Above the image of Terra and the Station float faces I do not know, of smiling apostates and scowling Church leaders. To the right of this is a scene showing the struggle on Terra, with pitched battle between the Prisms and the apostates. The apostates are uniformly depicted as heroic, almost divine, whereas the Prisms, both men and women, are shown as intolerant villains. I cannot bear the sight of those Prisms wounded and dying in the image. Whenever I pass the mural, I do not look at it and walk more quickly.

I do not understand how anyone could hold such hatred in his or her heart. What could the Church have done to them? I note that the mural is old and cracking, so perhaps it is kept as a relic of a former time.

The images depicted are clearly making Lucretia uncomfortable. "I am sorry for this," she says. "We should paint over it. I will mention it to Gabrielus." I say nothing. I am the enemy.

Lucretia and I walk through the door into a sea of dark green jumpsuits. I feel out of place in my grey flight suit, but I know this was my choice. I catch a few residents giving me surprised or sidelong glances. I ignore these as Lucretia and I pick up trays and receive eggs, vegetables, and soy milk from the workers behind the counters, workers who also wear dark green under their aprons, gloves, and cafeteria hats.

We come out of the line, and Lucretia leads me to a long table with three former Offerings who remain true to Havo, sitting with a red-haired girl. I am both uncomfortable and eager to meet and sit with them. They all wear dark green jump suits. The first is a tall man with thin white hair and dark eyes named Mattheus. The second, a tall, thin woman with short brown hair named Iulia. The third is a middle-aged woman with dark brown hair and a compassionate face named Klarcia.

"You are Rays?" I ask.

"We are," Klarcia says.

"Why do you wear the jump suits?" I ask.

"Beats being naked," Mattheus says, then chuckles at his own joke. Seeing no one else laughing, he becomes serious: "Wearing the jumpsuit does not mean we reject Havo." He takes a bit of food.

"Where are you from?" Iulia asks.

"Pax Occidentalis, Provincia Cascadia."

They nod. "Oh, I hear it's nice there," Mattheus says.

"It is," I say. "And you?"

"Pax Romanus." The Heart of Havo. I see Iulia look at Mattheus. I cannot help but feel respect for them, as they were closest to Havo of all, and yet I am all the more baffled by their adoption of this life.

"And you?" I ask Klarcia.

"Cascadia."

"Really?"

"Yes. Vir Sanctus Francisco."

"How long have you been here?" I ask them all.

"Twenty years," Iulia says.

"Thirty glorious years!" Klarcia says and laughs.

Twenty years. Thirty years. Am I really going to be here for the rest of my life?

"And what do you do here?" I ask. "How do you survive?"

"I run the music program," Iulia says.

"Music program?" I ask.

"It's simple and small, but we do have instruments, and it's good for the soul—young and old. Do you play an instrument?"

"I do not, but how wonderful!"

"You can learn."

"Yes, perhaps I can. And you?"

"I am in charge of our communications," Mattheus says. He takes a sip of his drink. "That means making announcements, sending messages and memos to departments, duty schedules—everything it takes to run a small society."

"And making bad jokes," Iulia says.

"I have a bad sense of humor and I'm not afraid to use it," Mattheus says. "It keeps life interesting."

I look at Klarcia.

"I run the child-care center," she says. "We call the kids in there the Paraxials." I smile. "As you can imagine, this station is a self-sustaining society. We have children here—both the Offerings from the last several years and new ones who are born here. We have a lot of little ones, and, because we do not kill them, the population keeps expanding. Gabrielus is going to have to add some more living space to the Ring."

"Or start culling the herd," Mattheus jokes, but his joke sends a shiver down my spine. I wish to run, but I stay in my seat. This man is a Roman Havian?

"Mattheus, stop," Iulia says. "She's nervous enough. Look, she's turning green."

"The center is a beautiful place," Klarcia says. "Full of energy. I hope you will come visit."

"I would like that," I say. I have never seen many children playing together. In Soul River, children are rare, and parents keep them hidden. You said you have a lot of little ones?"

"Yes, we don't suffer the Inopia. We don't know why. Our doctors say everything—and everyone—is normal here. It must be because we have been separate from Terra since before the crisis, but even the Offerings that have come here have never contaminated us. Some have even had children after arriving, with no trouble."

How can this be? Why is Havo blessing them but not us, I wonder? Then I realize I have said "them" and "us". I still consider myself on the outside, though I have been accepted here, and though Terra sent me away. I wonder if that will ever change. This is all foreign to me. But Havo is clearly blessing the people here.

"This is in addition to our regular work," Mattheus says. "We do these things because we love them, but everyone has to do repairs and maintenance work as needed." I nod, then pause to consider how best to ask my next question. I see Iulia touch Mattheus' arm in a bid to get him to slow his talking for my sake.

"I'm all right," I say. "I have a question."

"Anything," Klarcia and Iulia say at once.

"How do you live here? How do you reconcile it? Didn't Havo want you to join him?"

"We believe in Havo," Mattheus says, "but we do not believe He wanted us to die, which is made clear by the fact that we did not. If you truly believe that Havo controls all things . . . well?" A playful expression lives around his dark eyes, always on the verge of appearing. "As for the human side of things, we also believe it makes no sense to sacrifice children when you are running low on your ability to make more. You should keep all you have got, right?" He smiles. "We feel that the Church goes against Havo by sending Offerings, and that this station is Havo's way of responding. Think of all the Offerings Havo has saved and allowed to thrive here for over a hundred years, all the children they have made. We are grateful to Havo for this. And we may not be on Terra, but at least we are doing our part to preserve the Human Race. This is our daughter, Livia."

I regard Livia, who sits and eats quietly.

"How does she feel about all this?" I ask.

"How do you feel about all this, Livia?" Iulia asks her daughter.

"Fine," Livia says sincerely. "The Church is crazy."

"Livia," Iulia admonishes. "Cassiopeia is still new to everything here. Right now I suspect she just misses Terra—and the Church."

"Sorry," Livia says.

I wonder if the child wishes to return to Terra, but I decide not to ask. I realize she has never been there to return to it. This is her home.

"You do not think Havo is angry with you for your choice to stay here?" I ask the adults.

"If He is, He's got a funny way of showing it," Mattheus says. "Our life here is a lot better than it was on Terra."

"In Pax Romanus?"

"Things are not always as they seem, my *amicus nova*."

"But you could have united with Havo."

Iulia explains hastily, "We make a distinction between Havo and the Church. Havo is infallible, but the Church is ruled by human beings, and sometimes we—human beings—make mistakes. The Church sent us here, but we cannot know if this was in accordance with Havo's will, and the Station taking us . . . we were as surprised and disconcerted as you must be. Though we chose to stay, it took us a long time to fully accept this was Havo's will. We were tested every year. I still feel a pang of doubt."

She seems ashamed, or at least unaccustomed to having to explain herself.

Though I am equally unaccustomed to hearing such talk, I force myself to nod. I know that it is heresy, though I also know I am beyond the reach of the Church here. Everything I have done since the hatch of the *Messenger* closed has been heresy.

"Where do these foods come from?" I ask.

"We have a small population of livestock, and of course a hydroponics bay," Mattheus says.

"Livestock? Hydroponics? That's amazing," I say.

"That's luck—or the Will of Havo," Mattheus says. "That's good planning on the part of those who first served here. We consider ourselves very fortunate."

I thank them all for making me feel less alone.

"You will be fine," Iulia says. "Let me know if you need someone to talk to—other than Havo. And definitely not Mattheus."

"What?" Mattheus asks helplessly. "Did I say something that was not true?"

Iulia rolls her eyes.

I thank them again. As Lucretia and I walk toward the cafeteria doors, Klarcia comes after us. I stop, as does Lucretia.

"It is clear to me you love children," Klarcia says.

"That is true."

"After you've been here a little while, you would be welcome to come work with us in the care center."

"You are most gracious," I say. "I do love children. I was a teacher on Terra until a month ago. But right now I do not think I can work with children. I need to do something else. I find it too . . . difficult. Perhaps later."

"I understand."

"Gratias tibi valde," I say.

"Oh, you're welcome! We're glad you're here," she says.

Lucretia and I depart for a tour of the Station.

The exterior Ring of the circular station contains the living quarters. The interior contains the command and control center, the engineering section, the reactors, and the engines. After we walk half the Ring, Lucretia regards the arched entrance to the nearest Strut leading to the interior.

"Let's go someplace new," she says. I have not entered a Strut before, having spent my first two days on the Station between two Struts, going from my room to the cafeteria and back without venturing farther. Now I am heading to the center of the Station, a central tube connected to the outer Ring by four thick Struts, making the station resemble a giant child's top or clock gear in Space.

"Where is the hydroponics bay?" I ask.

"In the Central Spine," she says. "Would you like to go there first?"

"Yes."

We enter the Strut, which, like the *Messenger* and the Ring, contains artificial gravity. I remain amazed by the innovations of science. To our left, the Ring and a Strut at a right angle to this one, leading to the central tube called the Spine. From our left and below, the Sun blazes through the windows of the Strut's wide walkway. To our right, the Ring and another Strut at a right angle to this one. The glass windows consist of the same dark material we found on the *Messenger*'s front windows. We walk illuminated by the red, orange, and yellow of Havo's Sun, casting long shadows above and to our right, except on the opposite windows.

"Breathtaking, isn't it?" Lucretia asks. "I never tire of it." The entrance to the Spine lies ahead. The Station is so large that I estimate it will take us at least five minutes to traverse the distance.

"Yes," I say. "And a little intimidating."

"Of course. I am sorry."

We arrive in the Spine, which on the inside appears much like the rest of the Station: old, worn, patched, rusting in places, but functioning. The style of the architecture Station-wide is old, but generations of repairs have changed the character of what must have been a much sparser station.

I do not think I will ever become accustomed to the hatched doorways, lifting my legs so as not to trip, or going down steep ladders backward from one floor to the next. The main corridors of the Station and Struts are wide, allowing foot traffic both ways, but the rest are cramped and narrow. Every moment in the majority of corridors requires that I watch my step and my head.

"Sorry," Lucretia says the first couple times I hit my head in her presence.

"It is all right," I say. "I am becoming accustomed to it."

We walk through the hydroponics bay, which lies above the command and control area and makes me feel as if I am connected to home. I see tomatoes, carrots, beans, and other vegetables growing.

"We grow nuts, seeds, berries . . . everything we need," Lucretia says.

"How did this come about?" I ask. "I do not remember hearing about this in school."

"The records of the time are incomplete, but we believe this was created by the Church, to provide food for the original Havian crew," Lucretia says. I can't help but feel I am looking at food stolen from my people. "After the change in allegiance the rebels augmented it for long-term survival. They just did not know how long-term it would become.

"The believe the hydroponics bay was here at the beginning, but we know the greenhouse was added later."

"Greenhouse?"

Lucretia nods. "This station is *much* more than it was a hundred and thirty years ago."

"I am sure," I say.

"And that's a good thing, in case the Church ever attacks us. They don't know what we've got, so at least we will have a fighting chance. I probably shouldn't say such things to you."

I still don't know how to respond to such comments. They speak of my beloved church as if it is the enemy. I have questions for my church, but I do not consider it the enemy they do.

It already know, though I do not like to think of it, that from their point of view I represent the enemy. I wonder why they are being kind to me.

"I promise not to give away Station secrets," I say.

"Good," Lucretia says. "I often think about those rushed, early days. They grabbed whatever they could and threw it in here, hoping it would be used later. Many of them never got to see what was done with it, and every little thing someone thought to bring on was fully exploited. Thanks to one person back then, we even have an orange tree now." Lucretia indicates a small tree in the corner, planted in a large box of soil. "We trim it to keep it from getting bigger, but, as you see, the trunk is fairly thick." She walks over to it. "Whoever gave us oranges did us a greater service than he could ever have known. Unfortunately, we do not know who it was. Some records were lost during that time." Lucretia sounds genuinely sad over the lost knowledge, the chaos of a war neither of us can fully imagine.

For living—for agreeing to live—, for helping these apostate rebels, am I going to Barathrum, the cold pit of eternal torment reserved for the unrepentant, the irredeemed? Should I be on my knees begging forgiveness from Havo? I know I should be. I know the Church would condemn me utterly, excommunicate me . . . and yet I do not feel I am committing a crime.

I know that Havo punished Humanity for Marcus and Ursula stealing into His Library and reading the Book of Knowledge without permission. I know we all carry the burden of this crime. Like most Havians, I dread eternal punishment, but yet I cannot help but continue wondering why Havo would leave lying about a book He had instructed them not to read, knowing human nature, and why He would punish them for the nature He Himself had created. He knew in advance what they would do, since He knew everything that would ever happen in advance—yet He punished them anyway. Why? Not only "why did He punish them", but why did He knowingly set in motion the whole chain of events? Marcus and Ursula found and read the Book, which led to their awareness and independence.

I wonder why Havo would allow Ennius to summon bears to kill those who taunted him. I wonder why Havo would allow the Lissians not only to win a battle but to kill all the enemy men and "keep the women for themselves", as if they were property to be disposed. I wonder why Havo would want slaves to obey their masters. These are stories that I had placed out of my mind, had forgot as absurd, but they have come back to taunt me in my free moments, thanks to these apostates.

"Our greenhouse requires the Sun," Lucretia says, interrupting my thoughts. "Would you like to see it?"

"Yes," I say. At the back of the hydroponics bay is a door to a shaft with a ladder bolted on the wall. We take the ladder up, and Lucretia opens at a trap door at the top. I am unprepared for what I see when I emerge: the Sun itself filling half the dark-glass ceiling of a small greenhouse.

"At this distance, the glass needs to be extremely thick, and it is— all over the Station," Lucretia brags. "We take the occasional trip away from the Sun to reinforce the glass and of course the entire station structure."

"Where do you get the raw materials?"

"Believe it or not, the cargo bays were full at the time of the separation, but we have sent the occasional shuttle back to Terra on covert missions."

"Really?"

She nods.

Row upon row of boxes of plants that would not thrive in a hydroponics bay are here.

"We use our own waste to keep the soil fertile," Lucretia says.

"Amazing," I say.

I am impressed most of all by the view.

"We'd prefer just to see the Stars, but we spend most of our time next to the Sun, I am afraid," Lucretia says. "We do get more Sun than any other greenhouse in the solar system." She chuckles.

"Why do you stay so close?" I ask.

"As you know, we stay hidden from the Church. We usually only come out from the blind spot long enough to rescue Offerings."

"You can't back away from the Sun while keeping Terra directly opposite?"

"The farther out from Sol, the easier it would be for them to see us. They hide it, but their science is advanced. We know they'll spot us eventually. Actually, we are surprised we've been safe this long. I fear they are preparing something for us—but I've been fearing that for years now."

I nod. I am becoming a part of their conspiracy. What would Arcturus the Prism back home think or say? What would my own father think or say?

"Are you all right?" Lucretia asks.

"How do you know the Church is your enemy?" I ask, then immediately regret it. "Have you even been to Terra?"

"I have not," she says, then gestures back toward the way down. I feel I have offended, but I cannot help but ask questions. Yes, I know the Church defeated the apostates in a war, and both sides must have engaged in killing, but this painful episode is long past. Surely each side feels right and justified. The Church has made clear it only killed as a last resort, to protect lives, and yet these apostates act as if the Church is their enemy still. This frightens a part of me, since I have never heard any Church mention of apostates still existing. This entire situation could be all in their minds.

All her life, this apostate has been indoctrinated by those around her, including disgruntled Havians with personal complaints against the Church—the Church that cannot explain or defend itself here. I must keep that in mind and not think less of those who only know what they have been told.

We go back down, and Lucretia leads me to a small, quiet room. "This is both classroom and museum," she says. "It is usually only available by appointment, but Gabrielus has told me you are to see anything I deem fit." We walk inside a room filled with artifacts.

"The Church of Havo was once called the Roman Catholic Church," a recorded voice says calmly.

The Roman Catholic Church? What is this?

"It is a Church recording," Lucretia says in response to my expression. "Reserved for senior Church leaders. We intercepted it in the past few years."

If what she says is true, everything we are told about the Church by the Church is a lie. I cannot believe it. I will not believe it.

I look in great skepticism at the items on display: weapons, papers from long ago, flags, uniforms on mannequins, photographs. "Its god was named Yahweh," the voice continues.

Yahweh?

"When it was discovered that ancient translations had been in error, that our god's name was truly Havo, this error was brought to light. The entire Church and Scripture were reformed to reflect the truth. The role of Havia, formerly called Mary, was brought forth to reflect the importance of women. This news was not immediately accepted by all Terrans. Many clung to the former errors. Sadly, many original documents were lost in the ensuing struggle, but we know from Havian records that after centuries of repression, Havo, Havia, and even Diab were correctly named and their false names and idols were destroyed. When at last the forces of error were defeated, Havians were educated—and now, decades later, Havo's light has been revealed to us all. Of course the ancient texts had to be corrected in more than one way. Not only names but entire books of the old text had to be discarded for their errors. Shortly after our final victory over darkness, several new books were found in an ancient cave due to the miracle of Havo's grace. Together the old and the new form the backbone of our civilization today in the *Book of Havo*. We celebrate Havo's wisdom on its every page."

Instead of the eternal, timeless, divinely inspired Word of Havo, the Church is admitting its sacred text is cobbled together from different human sources? Our deities had different names before? All we were taught is that Havians overcame previous errors, never in detail, always under the pretext there were few records, but even this is much more than I have ever heard before. I wish to dismiss this recording as a forgery, but its words, its tone, its delivery are too accurate to be false. I do not know how to react except to think—again—the Church has been lying. This recording is meant to educate the Church elites, but it has the effect of horrifying me.

I do not hear the recording start over, for as I glance about a photograph strikes horror in my soul, rooting me to the spot. It is a photograph of a Prism about to murder a group of apostate prisoners. The prisoners kneel on the ground, and the Prism holds a pistol in his hand. Other church officials stand about accepting what appears to be the inevitable.

This cannot be true.

Lucretia points at another photograph, next to it, showing the Prism shooting one of the prisoners, half of the others lying on the ground, apparently already dead. Next to that, a third photograph showing all the same prisoners on the ground dead, the Prism standing talking with the other church officials. I gasp and recoil.

"This series of photographs was taken by a double agent shortly after the 'Day' was declared," Lucretia says. "She was killed when exposed." I look at the photographs again, at the faces of the apostates, the rebels on the ground in their last moments. I feel ill. I cannot look at any more.

I walk out of the room. Lucretia follows. I recover against the wall outside.

She says, "This is how I know the Church is my enemy. We do not kill defenseless people."

Neither does the Church, I think, but what I have just seen goes against everything I believe. Could the photographs have been forged? Yes. I do not know if they were, and the fact that I can allow for the possibility they are genuine alarms me. Could a man of Havo, a Prism refracting Havo's Light into Rays, do such a thing?

How?

Perhaps to honor the Terran day, the Station's schedule is divided into twenty-four hours, and each day is divided into three eight-hour shifts: sleep, work, and leisure (punctuated by a mid-shift meal served by the cafeteria workers, with cold foods always available). At first this surprises me, but then I remember that when one passes one's entire life aboard a space vessel, one must schedule one's leisure time as well as one's work. I choose to sleep, work, and play on the same schedule as Octavius and Gabrielus. Concordia sleeps when I work, works when I play, and plays when I sleep. This last makes me slightly nervous, but I tell myself Concordia does not wish to harm me.

I am not interested in teaching in the Station's school or working in its childcare center right now, but even if I were, I am an unknown quantity, so I would not be allowed to do either until I have been deemed trustworthy. This explains Klarcia's words "in a while". Gabrielus tells me that as I prove myself I will be trusted to do more and more. "You became less dangerous when you decided to stay—I hope," he says. "Do I have to worry about you?"

"No," I say.

"I didn't think so," he says.

I understand and accept this. I do not know these apostates very well either, and as of now I am grateful each day not to be murdered. I do not really know why they stole me from Havo, and a part of me continues to feel I have failed Him.

"Do I have to worry about you?" I ask.

"No," he says.

I ask for and am given a supervised job in the hydroponics bay and greenhouse, in which things go smoothly. I learn how to monitor progress, respond with more or less food, more or less light, more or fewer nutrients. I learn how to predict crop yields and increase them, and how the proximity of the Sun affects growth. It feels good to learn, to help myself and others at the same time. My mentor in the bay, Cymus, while monitoring me as a security threat, praises my gardening knowledge, such as it is, and my aptitude. He likes my learning quickly, not because we have a deadline but because he doesn't have to explain things many times.

"Thank you," I say. "I just want to take my mind off the past."

Cymus nods with understanding. "You are fortunate," he says. "You are alive after being shot at the Sun. That is a good thing."

I tell myself he means well.

Days go by. I do not speak to the Havians with whom I share a cabin. I eat just enough. I do not speak with others. I miss Terra. I miss

Jinx and Aetius, who are with Havo. I find it odd to work in the greenhouse, so close to the Sun.

Gabrielus comes by the hydroponics bay to check on my progress.

"You seem to be fitting in well," he says. "You seem not to be on the verge of jumping out a porthole or poisoning us all for Havo."

"I am not a violent person. I believe Havo protects and preserves us all. I am still trying to learn his reason for preserving me. It is not to harm you or anyone else."

"I am glad. You are a welcome addition to our station," he says.

"Thank you."

He turns to go. "Gabrielus," I say before he can. He turns back. "You have saved my life and instilled doubt in me, doubt of my faith. You have done quite a bit. Believe it or not, right now my thoughts are with my father. I want to see him, and I want to know how soon I can return to Terra."

This surprises him visibly. He says, "If you go back, the Church will kill you."

I am frozen. I do not know if he is right or not.

"You already know far more than they wish. You already know they have lied, repeatedly, to you and everyone else. Now you are dangerous to *them*. No, they could not permit you to live longer than a few minutes, and then they would hide your body forever. They would never utter your name, and they certainly wouldn't allow you to reveal yourself to the public. You do understand they could track your approach before you even reached Terra, yes? If you went there in a shuttle, they could shoot you down before you even landed and saw your father again. He would never know you survived your Offering. Your father would not even see your grave."

"What's the alternative?" I ask. "Living the rest of my life here, giving up? If my father already thinks me dead, then it doesn't make a difference to him if they kill me before he knows the truth—but it makes a difference to me if they don't. If I have even the smallest chance of reaching him and telling him the truth—and not just him, everyone else—I have to try."

"Tell . . . everyone else . . . what, exactly?"

"The truth to which you and everyone else here has been subjecting me since my arrival: that the Church is evil, that we are all pawns being controlled, that the Church lies to control everyone."

"It does."

"So why wouldn't you want to tell everyone that? You just said that my revealing myself would cause the Church big problems."

"We are just one station. The Church controls the entire planet."

"We have the truth on our side, and my soul rebels against falsehood, Gabrielus."

I see a change in him. He regards me anew and studies the determination in my face.

"You said, 'we'," he says.

"I suppose I did."

"How do I know you don't simply wish to betray us to your church?"

"The Church that would excommunicate me for disobeying it to join you?"

"You could be a plant."

"What if you hadn't intervened? Does the Church engage in such gambling?"

"Not that I have ever seen, no."

"And to what purpose when the Church could just as easily attack you here, if it knew of your presence?"

"It might prefer capturing this station to destroying it."

"And suppose it captured this station. Then it would have to admit to the world it had been lying all along. No, it would not do that to itself—and I would not help it do so. I am no spy. I am a teacher."

He seems stymied by my logic.

"I still believe in Havo," I say, "but it is clear to me now that it was Havo, not you, who spared me for a purpose. You may not believe yourself a part of that purpose, but it *is* all a part of Havo's plan, and I believe that His plan is for us to reveal the truth to the World, to *expose* the Church that has betrayed Him. The alternative is a living death here. Yes, you have food and society, but you are in exile, and you know it."

"I was brought here, and I continue to thank my lucky suns for that," Gabrielus says. "This is my home now. I did not like Terra then, and I do not wish to go back there now. It is an evil place, dominated by tyrants."

"Did you walk among trees?" I ask him. I see a look of sadness and longing pass across his face. "You cannot do that and consider the planet evil. Some persons might be evil but not the planet. Help me reclaim it. Give me a ship," I suggest.

"For Havo?" he asks, jesting.

"For Humanity."

He walks away, leaving me to my work. I start making plans to steal a small ship, whether Gabrielus agrees with me or not. But I am no pilot. I will try to persuade the one woman on the station I think can do it, the one woman I feel I can trust, but I know it will not be easy. Terra is the last place in the solar system to which she would willingly return. Havo, give me strength.

Concordia has apparently ingratiated herself with the engineers, and her new male friend is apparently one of them. Still officially not allowed to go exploring by myself, I express an interest in the engineering section to Lucretia, so she leads me there to see the reactors, the equipment. Dark and confusing, this area reminds me of stories of Scar's underworld. Metal girders strike across the space. Turbines, tanks, pipes, and other inexplicable machines hum loudly, making it hard to hear speech. It is warmer here than in the rest of the Station. Workers walk to and fro or concentrate intently on their instruments and control panels.

"Too much pressure here," one says.

"Compensating on Valve Four-Thirty," another says as we walk past.

Lucretia introduces me to everyone there. Concordia is not pleased to see me, though she reacts with less hostility than before. She seems merely to be evaluating me.

I do not succeed in finding a moment alone with Concordia to ask her for help. I realize I should not have expected to do so. My plan is a failure. I try to salvage it.

"Concordia, I would like to invite you to dine with me this evening," I say as casually as I can, trying to make it sound as if I do not have an ulterior motive and only just had the idea. She raises her eyebrows skeptically. I look about me, and no one else seems to notice my words at all.

Lucretia does say, "That would be nice. For you, I mean—to make friends."

"What's that supposed to mean?" Concordia demands of Lucretia.

"It means I know the two of you have clashed, I think Cassie is attempting to foster *concord*, and I think it would be good if the two of you could get along," Lucretia says. "For the greater good—the greater good of the Station but also the greater good of the two of you."

Lucretia eyes Concordia sharply. At that moment, the matter becomes a personal challenge.

"I accept," Concordia says. "May I bring friends?"

"I would rather just get to know you better," I say, attempting with my eye contact to indicate another, larger purpose. Concordia seems to get it.

"All right," she says, "*Cassie*."

"Excellent," Lucretia says. "I'll enjoy this."

"That means just her and me," I say. "Sorry, Lucretia. If you need to chaperone me, you can sit at the next table over."

"Really?" Lucretia asks. "All right." She harrumphs. "Well, I understand. Sometimes we all just need some privacy. I will not let anyone else come near you as you try to patch relations. I still applaud you for doing so. You are a peacemaker, Cassiopeia."

At supper, Concordia and I sit at the end of a table, several feet from others, our low voices unheard by anyone. I spot Lucretia a couple tables away, dining and talking with others. For all intents and purposes, Concordia and I are alone. I wear my grey flight suit as a diplomatic gesture.

"You've done some thinking," Concordia concedes, when I tell her of my hope to take a ship back to Terra. "But you have thought the wrong things."

"What do you mean?" I ask.

"First of all, I like my new life here. This is the first place I have ever felt accepted for who I am, not for what I believe or do not believe, after a life of persecution and fear under the Havians." She pauses. "But you wouldn't know about that." She takes a sip of her nutrient drink. "My point is that, as a new member of this society, I have every reason not to want to break its rules. I wish to be accepted. I wish not to show my gratitude for having my life saved by spitting in the eyes of everyone who saved me — which means everyone here except you. Everyone on this station participates in saving those your church casts off. Even the Havians already here did not try to kill me. Only Paula and you did."

I begin to respond. Concordia cuts me off:

"Second, there is that little 'life saved' part. I do not want to die. I am safe here. I have no reason to go back and every reason to stay here. If I were to go back, I would be killed immediately, no questions asked, or worse, tortured then killed. No, I have very little — correction: *no* — incentive to go back." She takes another sip.

"Third, I should think you would have become smarter by now, Sister Cassiopeia. If you go back, you are marked for death too. Oh, I forgot: you already have a death wish."

"I do not," I whisper.

"What was that?" Concordia demands.

"I said I do not have a death wish. If I did, I would hitch a ride on next year's Offering ship."

"Then why *do* you want to walk back into the lion's den?" I remember the photographs of the Prism murdering apostates. "The Church" — Concordia pins me with her gaze — "is your enemy."

"To show everyone the truth."

"The truth!" Concordia roars with laughter, drawing glances from other tables. She whispers again. "The truth! Since when have the majority on Terra cared about the truth? You've come to the game late yourself, if you recall. You still believe in Havo, which you make painfully clear with everything about you.   Thank the Universe you've started to wake up."

I am becoming accustomed to being insulted, to feeling shame, to not feeling shame at all. I answer calmly, "Yes, I still believe in Havo. And it may surprise you to hear this, but I have always believed that Havo cares about the truth. *I* certainly do. I think our people—yours and mine, back on Terra—do too. Are you going to help me change the World or not? Do you care more about Terra or about your own hide?" I shock myself with these words, but a part of me feels I must speak this way to reach her. "Is being an apostate about safety and comfort, then?"

Concordia regards me with a cold, dead look on her face.

"I congratulate you," she says. "Oh, don't give me that innocent look. It's nauseating. I knew the Church had trained Havians to sway others with emotional appeals. But *you* have appealed to my morality and integrity, which I did not expect, since you do not think I have any." She pauses. "The fact is, there are still some people there very dear to me." Concordia looks off, then back at me. "The fact is, it has been crushing me that I am here and they are there, completely unaware of my fate." She holds her lower lip inside her mouth in thought. "The fact is, we might be able to bring them back *here*, if we steal a ship and extract them from Terra." She makes fists and looks at me in helpless pain. "The fact is, I hate you and everything you stand for."

"I hear you with sorrow," I say. "I love you even so."

"Do *not* say that!" Concordia throws her drink in my face and gets up. "*And* the fact is, I want to see *you* learn the truth!" She storms off, as everyone in the cafeteria gasps and stares from one of us to the other and back.

I take this as a yes.

"Cassie!" I hear Lucretia say. She comes running over to assist me wiping myself off. "Are you all right?"

"Yes," I say. "I needed a bath."

"Very funny," she says, wiping off my face, my shoulder, my sleeve. "I am sorry that happened. Concordia is not very concordant. I will speak with Gabrielus about this."

"There is no need," I hear Gabrielus say. "I will have a word with her."

"No, it is all right. I offended. Out of habit I wished her the peace of Havo, and she reacted understandably. The fault is mine."

The two of them are surprised. "All right, Cassiopeia," Gabrielus says. "As you wish."

It does not occur to them that I could be lying to protect Concordia, which works in my favor. It occurs to me that I am lying for the truth.

"You tried," Lucretia says. "Some people just aren't very friendly. At least it is a big station, right? You will not have to see her very much at all, really. She works in engineering, and you have different shifts."

"Yes," I say.

"Are you all right?" Lucretia asks.

"Yes, thank you."

"Would you like company?"

"No, thank you," I say. "I am just finishing up."

I want to be alone, but it is clear she will not allow that, so I bolt down the rest of my food. She walks me back to my room, the only place I am allowed to be by myself. I wonder when they will trust me enough to let me wander freely. The times I have seen Paula she too has had a chaperone, so at least I know it is not just me. They must do this with all believers. They did not do it with Concordia and the other apostates. But that is because they are apostates. They must trust apostates more than they trust Havians. The whole world is backward. Is this what it is like for them on Terra?

"Thank you," I say to Lucretia at the door to my cabin. "Good night." I close my door and lie on my bed. I am alone. It is not yet my sleep shift, when my new roommates—Arista, Dea, and Prisca—will be working, yet they are not here. I cannot write home. I miss my old students. I miss Terra. I do not know what to do with myself.

What I want to do is find the truth. Why would anyone react as Concordia did? I understand that she did not say no, she might even have said yes, but why does she want me to see "the truth"? Why does she think I do not see the truth? What is the truth that she wants me to see? What is the truth as she sees it? If her truth is that there is no Havo, I will never see that. If her truth is that the Church is false . . .

My mind returns to the images of the Prism and the apostates on the ground, particularly the one in the middle, in which he is shooting them. I simply cannot accept that a Prism would do such a thing. I decide it must be apostate propaganda, featuring apostates in costumes acting out the whole scene to prejudice children against the Church. But a part of me cannot remove a nagging doubt. It looked real. It looked old.

A knock comes softly at the cabin door. Surprised, I answer it. Concordia pushes her way in. "Shut the door," she says.

"Is not this your work shift?"

"I left early. I finished my work, and Brutus will cover for me."

"What are you doing here?"

"Telling you the plan," she says.

"Do not you think Lucretia saw you?"

"She left. I followed her, then came back. She's gone for the night."

"Do not you think you owe me an apology?"

"Sorry," she says in a businesslike manner. "Listen." She sits on one of the cabin's two chairs. "I have been thinking about your proposal."

"Yes?"

"You know you cannot just go back home and live your life as it was before, right?"

"Yes." I sigh.

"I have also been thinking about your very noble idea to enlighten the entire World to the truth." She sounds sarcastic. I do not say anything. "We cannot take a small ship, even if there is one parked in this station somewhere," Concordia says at length. "As I said before, it would get shot down, burned up, whatever."

"So . . . what can we do?"

"Take the Station."

"Take the Station?" I am so loud I suddenly remember myself and become very quiet. I sit down, afraid. "Take the Station?" I whisper.

"Yes. We can do it. You and I aren't the only ones thinking about going back. If we all do what we need to do at the right time, we can gain control of this station and take it back home—whether Gabrielus likes it or not."

I look at Concordia in horror. I shake my head. "No . . . no." I stand up again. "No. I will not participate in an unnecessary coup. We must ask Gabrielus."

"He'll never agree." Concordia leans back. "He'll say, 'We're safe here, why risk everything, the Church will destroy the Station and kill us, and we will lose it all for nothing. Why go back?' He will say we only have one life: 'When we die, that is it! That is why we have to be careful with our lives. Anything else is suicidal.' And I have to say, until I spoke with you, I agreed with that position. I was happy! Why did you have to ruin it?"

"You are unhappy because you live apart from Havo," I say, "but I do not believe that he will say those things. And what truth do you want me to see?"

"The truth about your church." I feel a pang of pain. I do not know to what truth she refers, but I feel a dread of what might be behind her words. The Church has been my extended family my whole life. I do not want to lose it.

"Perhaps it is you who needs to see the truth. Perhaps if we take this station to Terra—with Gabrielus' blessing—, the Church will feel nothing but joy at its—our—return. Perhaps you are wrong about everything."

"The Church sentenced me to death! On Terra, my family was hated for being different. The Church could tell our professions of belief were not sincere, so we were targeted. The local Prisms decided to make an example of us. They took everything we owned and sent my brothers to one of their work camps. I decided to strike their library and was caught. My parents begged and groveled, but the Prisms wanted to teach my family—and everyone else—a lesson even more severe. Here I am."

I cannot bear it. "Surely there is some misunderstanding." I am pleading.

"There is—in you. You misunderstand the nature of the beast. You think it is not the Church. It is. It is the evil of human beings who wish to use the system to oppress other human beings. This has nothing to do with Havo! And whenever someone gets in their way, poof. And you want to go back there, Sister Naïve." I am still sitting on my chair, and Concordia leans in close to my face. "That is why I am not going there without this station. We need the strength—in numbers and equipment. This station was modified for warfare. It will be much harder for them to knock out than a small ship. It is the obvious—the only—choice. And we need to do it whether Gabrielus likes it or not."

We both hear a knock on the cabin door. I open it a crack to find Paula standing there alone in her new dark green jumpsuit. "May I come in?" she asks after I stare at her a moment too long.

"It is almost my sleep shift," I say. "What is the matter, Paula?"

"Well, I do not really think you want me discussing what you are planning in this corridor, do you?"

I freeze, then look at her searchingly. "What?"

"Please let me in," Paula urges.

I let her in, shut the door, and ask, "What do you mean, 'what we are planning'?"

Paula comes into the room, nods at Concordia, and says, "It is obvious to anyone looking that you are planning something. Fortunately for you, no one else is looking—not even those who are supposed to be."

"I came here to apologize for blowing up at Cassiopeia for trying to convert me," Concordia says.

"That might be your story, but I do not buy it. Cassie's not the missionary type." How does she know that? Cassie?

"What do you want here?" I ask her without admitting anything.

"I want to help you. I assume you are planning to return to Terra, since that is the only logical thing you could be planning—or trying to deny planning."

"Yes," I say. "We are."

Concordia stands up and says, "How dare you! You do not know where her loyalties lie! She could be interested in handing us over to the Holy Havian Empire—or turning us in to Gabrielus!"

"Would I be here in this manner if it were either?" Paula asks. "Let's just think logically for a moment. If I wanted to 'hand you over' to either the Church or to Gabrielus, I would not reveal my awareness of your plot to *you*. I would bide my time until the right moment to expose you. I would either lead Gabrielus to you at an incriminating moment or sabotage you in reach of the Church, in Terra's orbit. Again, revealing my knowledge to you removes both options."

I cannot argue with her. She is right.

"What do you want?" Concordia asks.

"The Church abused all of us, clearly—in different ways. I assume you want to bring the truth back home."

"That is right," Concordia says. "What does that have to do with you?"

"I want the same thing."

Her answer is simple and clear, and yet I do not trust her.

"What do you propose?" I ask.

"Well, I assume you are planning to take the whole station, since one small ship will just get you killed immediately."

Concordia and I give Paula worried looks, confirming her hypothesis.

"So, we are all involved," she says. "We are all affected. I think that gives me a say over some things, do not you? This is my future too we are talking about here."

The look on Concordia's face tells me I may have to make sure she doesn't murder Paula at an opportune moment.

"Forget your future, for a moment," Concordia says. "I want to know more about your past. What's your story? We do not know anything about you, except that you were on that ship. You claim to believe in Havo, but you could be a church agent entrapping us. What else? What is your history, Paula?"

"My family is in the law," Paula says. "I worked in the Provincia ____ Court as a clerk. I had one sister . . . " She pauses. "Now deceased. I was chosen at random like the rest, and here I am."

"The rest were not chosen at random," Concordia says.

"I was," I say, then I remember Arcturus.

"Were you?" Concordia asks.

"No," I say. "I remember my Prism saying he suggested me."

"I wonder why," Concordia says.

I have no answer for her.

"How did your sister die?" Concordia asks Paula.

"Train accident," Paula says with clinical detachment. "She was at the station when she slipped and fell onto the tracks. The train couldn't stop in time." After speaking she stares off.

"Terrible," I say. She nods. Concordia seems to be sniffing the air, as if she does not know whether to trust her or not, but what choice do we have? As she said, she could have turned us in already. Why would she come to us unless she was sincere? I have no real basis for suspicion, and I wish to demonstrate Havian fairness. Concordia is giving Paula the toughest of times.

"I do not see that we have much choice but to accept your offer of help," Concordia says, "but know this: I will be watching you. At the first sign of treachery, I am going to kill you. Do you understand me?"

"Perfectly," she says. "I would expect nothing less, and I will not disappoint you."

Concordia gets up to leave. I stand as well. Paula, following our cue, turns to leave. Concordia and she walk out. I stand at the cabin door and bid them good night.

Turning back into the cabin after shutting the door, I cannot help but feel trepidation, though I was ready to fly into the Sun mere days ago.

I find it hard to concentrate in the hydroponics bay and greenhouse, yet the thought of seeing my father again is the one thing drawing me farther into my plan. I jump at the slightest sound, while trying not to arouse Cymus's suspicion. I am not used to living in secrecy or fear, and Lucretia comes at the end of my shift to escort me. Is this what apostates experience back home? This has nothing to do with Havo, she said.

Lucretia and I go to supper in the cafeteria. Near the end of our meal, Mattheus comes to us holding a statue of Havo slaying Scar, usually represented by a black hole, the Light Defeating the Dark, one of the most prominent images in the Church.

"I thought Cassiopeia might like to see this," Mattheus explains.

"Where did you find this?" I ask without greeting him.

"There are many relics here from the time before the Day of Havo," he says. "Gabrielus thought you might like something like this and let us dig through the relics for you."

I take and cradle the statue as I would an infant. The Light and Dark, the familiar human figures of each in front, bring me great comfort. Havo is of course a man, mighty, his arm raised to throw more rays of light at the cowering Scar.

"Thank you," I say.

"Here's this too." Under his arm is a folded cloth, which he reveals is a Havian banner from before the Day, silver with spectra trim. He opens it up enough for me to see that it is emblazoned with the Triangle, the symbol of the Prism. Though it is worn and faded, I gasp, unable to believe the sight of such an object.

"I know they're not much," he says.

"They're beautiful," I say. "Thank you."

He nods and leaves the banner on the table, next to the statue.

We finish supper and Lucretia escorts me to my cabin. I thank Mattheus silently as I walk.

"That was very kind of him," Lucretia says.

"Yes, it was," I say. "Gabrielus and the others have been very kind to me." And I ask: "Any idea when they'll be kind enough to trust me on my own?"

"It is clear to me you are trustworthy, Cassiopeia Ovatio, and I have told Gabrielus this. I apologize for the necessity of our standard operating procedure. In the past we had the occasional problem when we did not do this. I expect you will be cleared for solitary citizenship soon, based on how well you are adjusting."

I nod. "Thank you," I say.

I bring the statue and banner into my cabin. I hang the banner on the wall over my bed. I place the sculpture on the small table inside the cabin door, at the foot of our bunk. It will bring me peaceful dreams.

I am sitting on the edge of my bed regarding the statue when something wells up inside me and I begin crying. I am sitting on a small, unremarkable bed in a small, plain room with rivets, pipes, and painted numerals on the walls. I live in an old tiny box. I used to roam the countryside. Now, to Terra and my father, I am dead.

I wipe my eyes and face, feeling the enormity of what has happened. I have been taken away from my father to meet Havo . . . and I have not met Havo. I have been kidnapped by these . . . apostates still fighting the War without the courage to fight it. They hide on the other side of the Sun year round and call this courage. They have shown me things I can hardly believe and people . . . people I thought were dead. Why am I here? Why am I sitting in this room, looking at this silent statue? What am I supposed to do?

I pray again, but Havo does not answer me.

The statue, too, is worn and scratched. I notice the figure of Havo is missing a finger.

How could Havo allow this to happen?

I sleep.

The next few days I see no sign of Concordia.

I continue to dine in the cafeteria with Lucretia, before and after my work shift. I decide to wear my grey flight suit. I will need something else when the flight suit needs laundering. Lucretia offers to get me a dark green jumpsuit.

I accept, feeling more and more defeated. When it is clean, I wear the flight suit.

After one of my work shifts, I visit the Paraxials in an effort to cheer myself. Klarcia is pleased to see me. I find the sight and sound of smiling, playing, learning children cheers me again. I see Livia, the daughter of Mattheus and Iulia. Then the sadness seeps back. I feel like sobbing when I hear Livia ask, "What if Havo reached out from the Sun and grabbed the Station and pulled us all into the Sun?"

"Havo isn't real," another girl says to her.

"Oh, yeah?" Livia asks. "Ask her—she believes in Him." I realize Livia is pointing at me.

The two girls come over to me.

"Salve, girls," I say. "How are you today?"

"Maria says Havo isn't real," Livia says.

"Well, what do you think?" I ask.

"I do not know," she says.

"There is no Havo, and people who believe in him are stupid," Maria says. "That is what my dad says."

"Well, I believe in Him. Am I stupid?"

The girl Maria listens and thinks.

"Maybe people can disagree on it and still be smart," I say.

"You are stupid," Maria says and leaves.

"I am sorry," I say to Livia. I hold out my arms to embrace her, and she lets me. I draw strength from her as she does from me.

"Have you heard anyone say that before?" I ask.

"Yes, but it is not nice."

"No," I say. "It is not."

After a few minutes, Lucretia and I leave. On the walk back, I see Gabrielus approaching in the corridor. "There you are," he says. "How's everything going?"

"All right," I say.

"Good," Gabrielus says. "Would you have supper with me tonight? Just wait in your room, and I'll come by to escort you." Lucretia nods.

"Very well," I say. We part, and Lucretia escorts me back to my room, where I rest and try to decide how I feel. I realize I have started to trust Gabrielus. This man prevented Havo from receiving His Offerings, I remind myself. This man may have perpetuated the infertility back home.

I have very little to do before supper. I shower and groom myself. I will not face my captor looking any more like a prisoner than necessary.

I wait, in my prison. Gabrielus comes. I open the door. He smiles and gestures for me to come with him, so I do.

As we walk, I do not look at him. I note the faces of those we pass, looking at and speaking to Gabrielus with respect. He seems to have charmed his crew, at least.

Gabrielus leads me to the greenhouse above the hydroponics bay, where a table and chairs have been placed at the far end and two crew members wait to serve us. Lucretia is not here. The Sun burns and flares brightly despite the darkened windows, flickering constantly across everything in the greenhouse, including us.

"Why did you do this?" I ask skeptically.

"You work here. This place is familiar to you, and, hopefully, comfortable."

I do feel more peaceful here than in any other place on the Station.

"Yes," I say and take the seat offered to me.

"Excellent," Gabrielus says and sits. "Dinner tonight was made by . . . you," he says, because Cymus, a few others, and I grow all our fruit and vegetables. The Station does have eggs and chicken, but these are raised in a hangar on the Ring.

The two others, I suspect cafeteria workers, serve us food and drink. Gabrielus then asks them to leave us. After they close the hatch and descend the ladder, he goes over to lift the hatch and make sure they have gone. Satisfied, he comes back.

"So," Gabrielus says. "How are you doing?"

"Not well," I say. "I often think I should have left on the *Messenger*. I feel like a traitor to Havo. A part of me hates you for this."

"Oh," Gabrielus says, nodding. "I see." He nods. "That was a very hard and momentous decision you made." He takes a sip of water. "But I thought you decided I was merely an agent of Havo?"

"My church decreed that I was to meet Havo, and I was eager to do so. But you are right that the decision was mine. Now, every minute I am here is a heresy of my own, and I do not know what to do. For the first time ever, I am uncertain of Havo's will. For the first time ever, I am *questioning my church*," I say with emphasis, in the hope of making him understand not only how difficult it was but exactly *how* momentous. "Your very existence, let alone your actions, contradicts everything I have been taught—about not only this station and the war but my church's fidelity to truth and justice. You threw me into such profound doubt that I went against my church that I could resolve my doubt before facing my god. That is how I am doing."

"Questioning is a good thing," Gabrielus says, putting down his water and looking at me. "But you could have just as easily reboarded the *Messenger* and allowed Havo to answer your questions."

"Because I cannot fathom why Havo would permit what you do. Because I cannot give myself freely to a god I cannot understand. You made me doubt my god!" I hold my head in grief.

"Perhaps, as you say, we are agents of Havo's will. That leaves only the Church. I guess we get back to that age-old question: who are you going to believe, me or your own eyes?" He chuckles in that self-satisfied way I have already come to find highly annoying.

I say nothing.

"It is terrible, I agree," he says. "The Church has done this to every group of Offerings we have saved. But if you are wondering why I wanted to dine with you, it was to talk with you about our future."

"To what do you refer?" I ask. "It is my intention to make a new life here."

"Concordia tried to raise a group to hijack this station," Gabrielus says. "And at first I was stunned. I asked myself, 'Why would a strong antitheist such as Concordia try to raise interest in a mutiny to bring the

Station back to Terra?' But then I thought, 'I'll bet she's not alone. I'll bet she's acting with someone else.' I wondered who on this station could arrange and command such a stunning display of ingratitude." He pauses to watch me. He can see that I am uncomfortable. "So you go from piety to theft, kidnapping, and threats of murder and force? Could it be that you doubt your worthiness of Havo now?"

Once again, I am unable to speak.

"Do not feel a need to speak, to explain or to defend yourself. I understand as well as anyone that a person moved by religion—or any other strong cause, such as survival or a desire to share the truth—will do anything in the name of that cause. Really, I was foolish to expect anything else, except that you had me more concerned for your life than for your plotting to take my station away from me. As you can imagine, we deal with this sort of thing every year. I'll give you credit, though: this was the first time an antitheist got involved. She must really like you." He chuckles again, then pauses to take some food. "You have not touched your kale."

The Sun's red and orange light continues to flicker over everything: the food, the table, the walls, and Gabrielus' expression. I do not think of eating or speaking. I just watch him, helpless. It occurs to me that, at least as of now, he does not want anyone else to know. He is protecting me, at least for the moment, by interviewing me privately.

"The only question remaining is: what were you trying to do?" He takes another bite of his salad, then gestures at me with his fork. "Did you want to take this station into the Sun? Because if so, I will personally throw you out an airlock."

I shake my head no.

"Then what?"

"While I would enjoy being at home again with my father," I say, "I know that such a life is no longer possible for me. The Church would not allow such a heresy." Gabrielus nods. "I want more than that now, regardless: I want everyone to know the truth. Truth conquers all, and I want the World to know the Church has been lying." I express this last looking at him and with more anger in my voice than I had intended. Gabrielus regards me carefully.

"There is hope for you yet, Sister. I had thought there might be more to you than the pious country bumpkin. Of course you realize the dangers."

"I have already faced what I believed to be a certain death," I say. He nods again. "Now it is time to do what is right."

"It is a funny thing about belief," Gabrielus says. "It is not always informed by facts. Please, eat your dinner."

"What are you going to do with me?"

Gabrielus regards me with amusement. "Why, I am going to return to Terra with you."

I am really not certain of what I think I may have just heard. "I am sorry?" I ask.

"We are all going to Terra. On this station," Gabrielus says, continuing to eat. "Concordia and you have persuaded me."

"May I ask why?"

"As you can also probably imagine, some of the antitheists here have long wanted to return. They want to take the Church head on—with force and violence. Some of them would even like to do the believers on this station harm." He pauses. "Yes, protecting you is part of my job." He takes another bite of food.

"So why go back?"

I wait for him to finish chewing before he speaks again.

"Well, some of us have wanted to go back for a long time, as I said. Many apostates are eager for justice—not all, but many. The believers who have chosen to be here tend to be content to remain in Space, simply counting their blessings. But you . . . " He looks at me intently. "You are the first *believer* who wanted to try to change things without violence by showing everyone the truth. And if a believer wants to change things, that tells me it is time, after all these years and generations."

Emboldened, I ask, "Where is Concordia?"

"Oh, coming off her shift in engineering about now, I would assume."

"You did not arrest her?"

"I *agree* with her." He smiles. "Of course I arrested the ones in past years, but again, now there's you."

"What did you do with them after arresting them?"

"Well, it is kind of hard out here." He indicates Space out the window. "In the past it was all believers, and their goal was to destroy this station for Havo, so I would say to them they had a choice: either take the next ship to the Sun or drop the mutiny idea." He pauses to move the food on his plate about.

"And?"

"Oh, some took one, and some took the other. Nobody reneged."

"And if they had?"

Gabrielus looks at me. "Then I would have put them out into Space rather than waste resources keeping them alive until the next ship. Fortunately, we have not had to do that. Your friend, however, made things more interesting. Rather, you did. Leave it to a believer to bridge the gap." He takes another bite of his salad.

We talk of our lives. He is from Pax Orientalium, Provincia Sinis. He was a business owner before. "We sold equipment to farms." Modest but important work.

"You do not get to do such business anymore."

"No, but I get to use my managing skills."

"Who knows? You might get to run a business again."

He seems wistful. "That would be my dream come true, but doubtful."

I do not eat much. We finish eating, and he escorts me back to my cabin.

"Dining with the Station leader? You are favored," Arista says after the door is closed.

"One person's favor is another person's punishment," I say.

"You are lucky," Dea says. "Some of us have liked him for years."

"There is no such thing as luck, only Havo's will."

They stop speaking.

I am desperate to talk with Concordia but do not wish to be seen with her again right now. I pray and silently thank Havo for this clear sign of His will, Gabriel's decision.

Havo be praised!

We are going back, or at least Gabrielus is going to try to make it happen. I understand he may fail. Many here, apostates and Havians, are comfortable, despite concerns relating to the Church's increasing technology and reach. My heart soars at even the possibility of being reunited with my father. I cannot fathom Havo's plan, but everything seems to be happening by His design. I feel a larger force at work, and I cannot help but think that, no matter what happens, my questions will be answered if we return home. I have always felt a thirst for knowledge, a thirst I know that Havo gave to help me in this life. How could it be otherwise? He wants us not only to survive but thrive, despite the Original Crime, because He is a loving god—the source of all love.

My soul soars for the first time in a long time. I wake and feel joy. I can barely concentrate on the smallest things, such as eating breakfast with Lucretia.

I try to contain myself but Lucretia can see I am happy. "I hear you had supper with Gabrielus last night," she says.

I say nothing.

"Others will likely envy you."

I say nothing.

"He is still young. Knowing him has obvious benefits."

"Gabrielus is beneficial to everyone on this station," I say.

"Of course." She smiles. "Those who underestimate you do so at their peril."

"I do not understand your meaning."

"Don't get me wrong—I'm happy for you. Gabrielus hasn't had anyone in his life for a while. But beware of jealousy and distrust. Some people will think you're corrupting him."

"Corrupting him!" I cannot help my response. "He is the apostate, not me!"

"I didn't say you were. But there are some who will think you are, who will always think badly of a Havian—rightly or wrongly. Not everyone gets along here. The Havians and non-Havians tend not to interact, which makes your . . . which makes you so special."

"I am not special. But speaking of trust, how much longer do you think it will be before I am trusted to walk down a corridor?"

"Oh, it seems to me you already are." Remembering herself, she says, more professionally, "I'll check with him today."

She takes me to the hydroponics bay. When Cymus sends me up the ladder to the greenhouse, I do my work there then stare out the windows, looking . . . for what? For my own joy reflected, I suppose. No one knows of Gabrielus' decision yet.

I have been avoiding Octavius, not wishing to endanger him, but I decide to seek him out after my work shift. I miss him.

Shortly after my shift begins, however, I hear Mattheus's voice over the loudspeakers saying, "Good day, everyone! Gabrielus is calling a special meeting in the cafeteria at thirteen-hundred hours, immediately following the twelve-hundred meal. All nonessential personnel are requested to attend. This means you! Except, of course, unless it doesn't."

He's going to tell everyone. I feel both joy and trepidation. I continue, distracted, until the work with Cymus takes my attention back. Eventually Lucretia comes and collects me. The three of us go to the cafeteria in the Ring.

"On one hand," she says quietly to me in the corridor, "Gabrielus says you can walk alone now. On the other hand, after this meeting you probably *shouldn't* walk alone—for your own safety."

The irony hits me, but I not only understand and appreciate his concern, I agree with him.

The shift meal: chicken with broccoli. "Hello again," I say to the broccoli. I wonder what my father is eating.

Lucretia bids me joy in what we both expect to be temporary freedom and leaves me to my own devices. I sit with Mattheus and Iulia again. Their daughter Livia sits off at a distance at the same table. Klarcia sits with other believers. I remain the only one wearing a grey flight suit in the Station, but I believe everyone else has become accustomed to this. Everyone is at least silent about it.

"So, how's everything in the . . . *hydroponics bay*?" Mattheus asks in a melodramatic voice. His playful expression startles me.

"Growing," I jest in joy and nervous excitement. I am eager for everyone to know what I can barely contain.

"Did you just—did she just make a joke?" Mattheus asks Iulia in mock shock. I smile. "I can hardly believe it. I'm glad I'm sitting down. Pinch me." He offers his arm across the table to his daughter, who pinches him. "Ow! It must be true."

We eat. We make more small talk. Despite my jest, they can see that I am nervous. Toward the end of our meal, Gabrielus appears at the end of the room away from the serving line. "Can everyone hear me, or do I need to ask Mattheus for a microphone?" he asks.

"Hey, I'm eating!" Mattheus calls out.

The assembled say they can hear him.

"Okay, good. You can keep eating, Mattheus." He smiles. "Now, you all know that no one here has any special love for the Church." Gabrielus looks at me. "Except, of course, for those who do." He chuckles, but no one else laughs. "As you know, every year the best news reports we get of Terra are those given to us by the Offerings we rescue— or who agree to stay with us. Well, it has come to my attention that things on Terra are changing." Some persons fidget. "Not only do we know it is only a matter of time before the Church detects us, but the character of Havians is changing. For years I have been waiting for signs of change on Terra, and I think, finally, the time is right . . . for us to take this station back to Terra, before the Church comes to us on terms we will not like at all."

The room erupts in voices—some demanding explanation, some protesting in absolute opposition.

"Friends, friends," Gabrielus says, trying to restore calm. "I know this comes as a shock. It came as a big but welcome surprise to me. But I seek and request your agreement, which is why I called this meeting. I will not take us there without a majority vote of support for the decision."

"No!" Iulia says to Gabrielus. "The Church will kill all of us. It is that simple."

I am a Havian. Does she think that I would kill her?

"They might do it first," Mattheus jokes, indicating the angry apostates in the cafeteria with a jerk of his thumb.

"I will not let the Church *or anyone else* harm anyone on this station," Gabrielus says pointedly over the din. "Let us vote. The majority decides."

I feel smaller and smaller, like a particle of dust.

"Now listen to me, everyone," Gabrielus says. "Have I ever led you astray? No, I have not. Have I ever betrayed your trust in me? No, I have not. Cassiopeia here—" Did he say my name? I feel I am in a dream. "Cassiopeia here, without even trying, persuaded me last night that now is the time. She did not even know that I had been considering this for some time. She is a believer, but *she* has begun to realize the Church is not all it claims to be. It lies, cheats, steals, tortures, rapes, and murders. Yes, I know you all know this, but when she came here, she was prepared to die and even kill for Havo."

"She still is! Look at her!" someone shouts.

"No," Gabrielus says. "No." He raises his hands for order. "In the span of just a few short weeks since we intercepted the Offering ship, thanks to living with us, Cassiopeia Ovatio has come to realize that not everything is as she had thought it to be. She has seen the archive of atrocities. She now knows what you have all always known. Is she still learning? Yes. But she has taken the most important first step on her journey."

I do not hear him. I hear an angry mob. I imagine hiding under the table.

"Gabrielus," a man says. I look to see who it is: an older man I do not know. "Gabrielus, you have not led us astray up to now. You are the reason we all still live, and we would all do well to remember this." The man looks about and shames some of the hotter-headed. "But I do not think you have thought this through. We do not know what advances the Church has made in technology since we left. We do know the Church will do everything in its power to destroy us in such a way that the populace on Terra will never learn our existence. For all we know, they have already learned of us despite our hiding and sent this young woman who seems to have caught your ear to deceive you." The man indicates me. "I think of you as a son, but have you considered that it might be a trap?"

"I assure you, Alaric, that I have both considered the possibility and rejected it, for the best of reasons."

"And what are those best of reasons?"

"Cassiopeia here is open to the truth. That means that others are ready too, enough others that the time is right."

More voices grumble. I hear someone murmur, "It is a trap."

Someone else calls out, "She would lead us to our deaths, at long last!"

"That is not the case, I assure you," Gabrielus says.

"She's corrupted you!" another shouts.

"He's a traitor!"

Some stand, and Gabrielus tries unsuccessfully to calm them. They rush him. He holds his ground until he is overwhelmed by numbers.

Someone comes at me. I stand, ready to defend myself.

"You labor under a delusion," I state.

"That's rich coming from you, *lupa!*"

"Throw her out the airlock!" someone yells.

Mattheus and Iulia try to protect me, but they are surrounded and prevented by others. "You are not the problem," someone tells them.

A couple men grab me, pick me up, and carry me to the front of the room, despite my efforts to fight them and free myself. The apostates argue about what to do with us.

I recite Havo's Prayer to myself, but I cry out when I see another man strike Gabrielus across the face.

"No!" I hear someone call out. "Take them to the brig!"

They take us to the station brig and lock us in separate cells. I slump on the small cot in the cell and cry, then wipe my face with my hands and pull myself together.

Gabrielus was wrong. Gabrielus was wrong. He overestimated the tolerance—or underestimated the intolerance—of his people.

The door and walls of the cell are less scratched and dented than those in my quarters. The apostates must not have had much use for holding cells over the years, I think. It amazes me to think these walls are older than I am.

I stand and look through the barred window of the door into the corridor outside the cell. I see two more such doors and windows across from me, very close, the spacing of which doors suggest there are cells opposite them, on either side of mine. I feel pinched by the narrowness of the corridor as well as by my confinement.

"Gabrielus?" I ask.

He appears in one of the door windows opposite. I feel a small degree of relief to have someone with whom to converse.

"What are they going to do with us?" I ask.

Gabrielus shakes his head. "I do not know," he says. "This has never happened before. But I think it is clear they're not taking us back to Terra."

"Will they kill us?"

"No," he says firmly, then hesitates. "At least I think not. Right now they're probably debating it. I am still popular. I might be demoted but not killed."

He does not make predictions regarding me.

"Thanks for trying," I say.

"I should have gone about it a different way," he says. "Involved some of the others first, gained their support."

"Or resistance. I don't see how you could have done it differently. Rumors would have caused more problems. Direct honesty was the best course of action. You involved everyone in a decision affecting everyone."

Gabrielus nods. "Yes, I did. And they are involved, all right."

Loud clanks and unlocking sounds herald someone's approach. Gabrielus and I cease speaking but remain standing and watching. A young man I do not know comes down the hall.

"Pallium," says Gabrielus.

"Gabrielus," the man says. He opens Gabrielus' door then waits for him to come out. Gabrielus walks out in front of the young man, leaving me alone with my thoughts.

I kneel and pray without my mother's prism to hold, which is yet another injustice I shall not forget.

My Sun, I do not question your wisdom. I ask you for strength and guidance as I endure what you have asked me to endure. I am weak. I have come to know, to respect, and even to admire some of these . . . apostates . . . against my own will but in accordance with what I take to be Yours. How can I do otherwise, when it is clear to me you have brought me here for purposes of Your own I cannot divine. Is it true you wish me to lead this station back to Terra? They will be in danger, I am coming to see now. Is it true the Church has done these things? What about the Prism in the photograph? How can this be? Please help me to find the truth. Amen.

I open my eyes, feeling greater resolve than before. It is amazing the peace that prayer can bring. I remember with sadness the memory of praying with my father before I left Terra. I felt much happier, more confident then. Now . . . I do not know what to think.

What will these apostates do? Whence do they derive their justice, their morality? A part of them must still feel Havo's love and justice, even if they deny it. There is no morality outside of Havo. He is the Heat, the Light, and the Life.

Where is Concordia?

Eventually someone comes to bring me a meal. "What is happening?" I ask the young man as he slides a tray of food through a slot in the door.

He does not answer, shuts the door slot, and leaves. I eat the simple food gratefully. I do not feel any ill will toward them or wish them any harm. I just want to do Havo's will. I also find myself thinking of Octavius again. What must he think of me? Does he too think I have "corrupted" Gabrielus?

I lie on the cot. I can do nothing. I can only think of what has happened and what it means. I remember being told that apostates, in the past, were vicious and cruel, savages without the morality and wisdom bestowed by Havo. I had always wondered why Havo would create such savages. "Free will" was the answer, but why would anyone choose to live a life without morality?

"We are better than that now," the Prisms had said at church. "We do not behave as savages."

"What happened to them?" I had the temerity to ask once when I was small.

"They were defeated," Mother said, sighing sadly. "Those who saw the Light of Havo were welcomed as brothers and sisters. The rest chose death."

Chose death? This had stunned me as a girl. "Why would anyone choose death? To meet Havo?"

"No," Mother said. "The apostates chose eternal darkness."

There was no greater punishment than separation from the Light, and there was no reason anyone would choose eternal darkness. It made no sense to me then, and it makes no sense to me now. I suppose that is the answer: a lack of sense causes nonsensical choices.

Another thing that has always troubled me is why the sermons sometimes warned us to be "ever vigilant" against blasphemy, heresy, and apostasy. How could these be threats now, when everyone believes? Against what are we to be ever vigilant? "Scar will try to tempt you," they would say. But how could He succeed, assuming everyone on Terra to be a true Havian? I remember now: not everyone's faith is genuine. But how could anyone reject Havo, Havia, and their love surrounding us? This has troubled me, but I have never had the courage to ask about it. I was older when that question struck me, therefore more afraid of censure, afraid of being thought to doubt my own faith. Outwardly, I left the subtle doctrinal mysteries to the theologians and limited myself to teaching practice. I learned how to make language, science, mathematics, and physical activity entertaining for youngsters and kept my thoughts to myself. I was no threat to the Church. I didn't even speak my doctrinal criticisms outside our home. I did find myself thinking the Prisms could have used some lessons on making their messages more engaging to Rays, and Arcturus adopted some of my suggestions.

Was I a heretic, even then? Did Havo find me unworthy of uniting with Him? Is this station Barathrum?

But the existence of these apostates is a shock I must address, even if only in my thoughts. How can everything I have experienced since waking in the *Messenger* be true? Concordia and the rest claim to be apostates sentenced to death—she said she had been sentenced to death for attempting to burn the library in Eboracum Novum. How can this be explained? The Church does not sentence anyone to death. We have prisons but no punishments, only rehabilitation and guidance for those who are lost. Spiritual guidance for lost souls above all.

Why would Concordia lie about this? To save herself? No, we were already on the Station . . . the Station that saved us . . . or harmed us by taking us from Havo. Why? There are clearly apostates alive and well. They do not seem to be suffering harm, but how can *this* be? If the Church lied about them, about what else might it not be lying? What is true? I do not know. I am starting to feel that these apostates, these enemies, might not be my enemies after all. Will they let me show them? I wanted to shine Havo's Light on them. Now I think they might not be all wrong. They still need Havo, but they might be right about . . . the Church . . . in some small way.

The media had not said anything about an attack on the library. The news were always good. It had brought me great comfort to know the World was a happy place filled with Havians who loved each other. Concordia's mere existence, true or false, disproves that. She is a walking disproof.

I notice my hair, disheveled when someone grabbed me, and attempt to fix it without a mirror.

I lose track of time.

Eventually, I hear the clanking again. My door opens. Octavius steps in.

"What are you doing here?" I ask.

"Is it true, what they say?" he asks.

"Is what true?"

"That you seduced and corrupted him?"

"No, of course not. Why are you here?"

"To escort you. They let me be the one."

He motions for me to go out of the cell. The guard, Pallium, waits outside. I walk ahead of them both to the end of the hall, which opens out onto a room with a counter. The guard goes to the door opposite and opens it, then motions for us to follow. I go through the door, Octavius follows, and Pallium comes behind us. We leave the brig and enter the Ring. For the first time in my life I am glad not to be wearing my Havian robes. They would only inflame passions here.

I have done nothing wrong, and yet the faces of passersby make me feel as if I have. Some stop and stare, some walk faster past us.

Octavius leads me down one of the Struts to the command center, then to a room I have not visited before. I see a long table from the side, one chair on the nearer side, in the middle, apparently for me.

"Please sit," Pallium says, so I do.

Pallium stands in a corner. Octavius goes around the table and sits at the seat farthest from me to my right. A door in the corner behind the table to my left opens. Alaric, Gabrielus, and two others I do not know come in, followed by Concordia. I gasp at the sight of her. Concordia acts as if she does not know or care that I exist. I can barely concentrate on anything else as they all take seats, Concordia next to Octavius, then Gabrielus, then Alaric directly in front of me, then the two older women.

After a few uncomfortable moments, Alaric looks at me and asks, "Cassiopeia Ovatio of Pax Cascadia, what is your mission here?" I am surprised, but not shocked, in light of what has happened.

"My mission?"

"Why were you sent here?"

"I was sent to meet Havo."

"You see? I told you," the woman at the end on my left murmurs.

"You intercepted me yourselves. You know this to be true."

Alaric gazes at me intently.

"You might have known we would do so, if the Church knew and told you," he says.

"If it knows, it did not tell me."

"But when the others on your ship chose to meet Havo, you chose to stay here. Why?"

I look down. My voice becomes small. "I am ashamed to admit that I am not sure. Havo's will . . . is not always easy to determine."

"Havo's will? Your church told you Havo's will, did not it?"

"My church . . . " I say. "I am even more ashamed to admit I am no longer sure it is my church."

"Why?" asks the woman I do not know.

"I saw things . . . in your museum. Lucretia showed me things that made me question the Church."

"Was it Havo's—or your church's—will that you find and destroy us?" she asks.

"Destroy you? I did not want to come here. You chose to intervene. You did this! You took away my meeting with Havo. I could be with my mother now." My voice trails off into a sob. I do not know what I am saying.

"How did we do that?"

"I told you! You made me doubt the Church. That picture . . . "

"Picture?"

"Of the Prism shooting apostates. Why would a Prism do that?"

I see strange looks on some of their faces.

"I told you," Concordia says. "She doesn't know."

"Is it Havo's will that you bring us back to Terra?" Alaric asks.

"I do not know," I say.

That causes a murmur through the table.

"I think we should discuss this privately," Gabrielus says.

"What are you going to do with me?" I ask. "Why aren't you interrogating Paula? She chose to stay too."

"Paula has gone to meet Havo," Gabrielus says.

"What?" I ask. "What has happened?"

Pallium approaches me. I stand and look to the others. "What has happened?" But they do not respond.

Pallium escorts me from the room to a narrow corridor. Behind the closed door, I hear their voices again. I cannot imagine what they're going to do with me. *Paula is dead.*

"How did she meet Havo?" I ask. Pallium says nothing. Dazed, I ask, "Is Alaric the leader of the station now?"

"He is."

"How did Paula meet Havo?"

"She went into an airlock and opened it."

How would she know how to open it? I do not ask.

"I see your face, but we have it on video," Pallium says.

My immediate concern is Havo's will, my own fate, and apostate justice. They think my motives evil. How can I convince them otherwise? The action, going back to Terra, would be the same, though the outcome would not show treachery on my part. To them, a return to Terra must seem as death. They will surely kill me. Will Octavius or Concordia argue on my behalf? I am not certain of them either. How is Concordia free? Did she trick them? Did Gabrielus keep her secret? Did she say she was spying on me, playing along with me to help them?

I kneel and pray to make my peace with Havo before they send me to Him. I ignore all else. *Our Sun, who art in the sky, hallowed be thy name.* I bear no one any ill will. I wish to bring only peace, light, and compassion.

The corridor door opens, and Pallium brings me back inside the room, where I sit at the table again. Alaric looks about him at the others. "We are in agreement," he says.

I expect death.

"We have a mission for you. We have long suspected that the Inopia was caused by the Church, intentionally, to sow fear and obedience in the face of waning belief. We want you to find the proof."

I am dumbfounded.

"We will take the station back to Terra," Alaric continues. I see his lips moving, but I can barely hear him. "You will likely be treated as a heroine for 'capturing' the Station. If not, our existence will at least discredit the Church in the eyes of Terra. Either way, the sincerity of *your* belief will not be doubted. We will take the blame for your continued existence. You will be treated as a heroine or a martyr, and you will be trusted completely. To the extent you are not, you will need to be willing to break some rules and find what is hidden—and guarded. This should appeal to someone whose stated goal is to seek and reveal the truth to all. We will support you materially. What do you say?"

"I do not know what to say . . . except Havo be praised."

"I told you," Concordia says. "She's a true believer."

"We leave as soon as possible," Alaric says.

"But I do not know anything about the Inopia," I say. "I am an elementary-school teacher! I do not know where such secrets would be kept."

"That is why it is a hard job," Alaric says. "But what is hard for you would be impossible for us. You will be trusted, at least more than we will be. If they ask why you did not go back aboard the *Messenger* or steal another small craft, you can say we prevented you, tortured you—anything."

I realize he is right. And if what he says is true about the Inopia . . . but how could it be? I must learn the truth for myself. It is now that I realize I have found Havo's purpose for me.

The Station Michael engines, already holding us stationary relative to the Sun, roar to greater life, and our journey home begins.

Everything changes now. I wish even more than before not to provoke violence, so I still wear my grey jumpsuit, despite my shame that it represents neither the Station nor Havo. I still draw second glances from adults and stares from children, but the quality of their gaze has changed from one of fear to fascination. Some adults nod or greet me to the extent of our acquaintance. The ones who had issued expressions of hatred are now subdued. I am the same person on the inside; all that has changed is the perception of me. It is hard not to wonder at Havo's mysterious ways.

I do not go back to work in the hydroponics bay. We have a return to Terra to plan, and they tell me I am now too important to jeopardize on unnecessary walks through the Station. Lucretia says they miss me there. I am more limited in my movements and contacts, and Pallium is my bodyguard now, though I am not sure where his loyalties lie and would rather not find out. I miss the tranquility of my solitary work. Now I spend hours poring over maps and documents, information on Terra and the Church. I read reports, intercepted communications, secret documents from inside the Church hierarchy, all of which if true would indicate corruption and lies of almost unimaginable scale. When I say this to Gabrielus, he nods and answers, "The Church is the Cancer afflicting us all." I say nothing.

I want to question the Father of All of Us, Lux Aduro.

The facts and figures on battles and deaths, even the descriptions of torture and murder, become meaningless. As I read, I become numb. I still resist the idea that the church I know and love could do these things. If it is possible, then surely it happened long ago and we know better now, no? In the midst of it all, a personal account written by someone captured by the Church stands out to me. His name is lost to Time, but he wrote in part:

> *What is sensible and logical does not change even if a society abandons sense and logic. I am surrounded by Havians, and yet their errors do not matter as long as I know what is right and true. They may think as they wish. They may torture, even murder me, but they will never change what I think. They cannot take away my mind, my heart, or my soul.*

I have moved beyond shock. I have arrived at the question why.

Why were apostates, blasphemers, and heretics suppressed with violence? Was this truly necessary to protect the Church? If so, what does that say about the Church? Now that I know there are outsiders . . . I find I can no longer use the term "apostates" . . . it seems too pejorative . . . I must know why the Church does not allow outsiders to do as they wish, to live and let live. Can it truly be as simple as that the Church cannot allow questioning and disagreement because these will threaten the Church? Can the Church truly be threatened by questioning and inquiry? I have never thought so before. I have seen the Church as the champion of discovery of Havo's truth in all its kaleidoscopic facets. And if the Church is suppressing freedom of thought and action, why does Havo permit it? "Havo is freedom," I have been taught my whole life. The Church represents love, light, compassion, and warmth, which is why all Havians are now free and at peace . . . aren't they?

I ask Gabrielus about this manuscript.

"Vergilius," he says. "One of our greatest heroes from the period before the Fall of Reason—what you call the Day. You were reading from his prison journal."

"Prison?"

"Well, of course. The Church runs many prisons all over the World. They routinely imprison apostates, blasphemers, heretics—and worse. Sometimes they take whoever a Prism takes a liking to, so he can do what he wishes to them. And no one is ever the wiser. Sometimes they just say, 'Havo must have taken him to Haven,' or 'She's in a better place.'"

"This must not be true," I whisper.

Gabrielus grabs me by the shoulders. I prepare for the worst.

"It is true, Cassiopeia, and when we get back, you will see it for yourself. Have you never known anyone to disappear or die suddenly? Think, Cassiopeia."

I do not need to think very far. I do not know what happened to my mother. I only know what the Church said, and it has never made sense to me.

"Use your mind. Hasn't there ever been a time when the Church's words rang false to you?" I feel him release my shoulders.

My silent tears answer him.

"I am sorry," Gabrielus says. "It is painful to learn the truth. But it is more painful to live a lie."

"Why is this man Vergilius your hero?" I manage to ask.

"He was the leader who brought us closest to victory before he was betrayed. The history of Terra would have gone quite differently had not a Havian spy deceived him. You were feared to be attempting the same with me. After his capture, he wrote *Against Havia*, a tract smuggled out by his guards and so masterfully written the Church could not stop its spread."

"Against Havia, the Mother of Us All?"

"No, the word also means 'Havo's Realm'. The Church was then in the process of renaming Mary."

"I have not heard of it."

"You will forgive me, but that means little. We owe him our thanks. I hope someday you come to appreciate what he has done for all of us. He is why you are alive right now."

Gabrielus walks away, leaving me shaken in a corridor.

By the beginning of October, I begin to feel secure on Station Michael. I forget the suspicion, the fear, and the anger that the idea of our return to Terra engendered and relish the fact that our return is now the official plan. Pallium stays with me. I am not allowed private visitors, but Octavius and I have meals together whenever we can. I miss Jinx.

In the Ring corridor, Pallium and I see Gaiseric, Huneric, Totila, and two other men waiting, looking secretive yet impatient. When they see us approach, Gaiseric smiles menacingly and comes toward me.

I greet them. "May Havo light your way, Gaiseric."

"First you tried to kill us one way, and now you are trying to kill us another way."

Pallium steps between us. "All right. It's time to move along."

"I am not trying to kill anyone, Gaiseric," I say.

"You think you have tricked us all, but you have not."

The other men surround us. Pallium places me behind him as he looks around.

I begin to speak again, but Gaiseric steps past Pallium and slaps me so hard I fall to the corridor floor. Pallium and he begin to wrestle. I start to rise, but another man—I see it is Totila—grabs me and throws me down again. I try to roll away.

"You are not going anywhere, you theist bitch!" Totila says, grabbing and punching me across the face with the heel of his hand. I raise my arms instinctively and hear voices say "hitting a woman" and "just wanted to scare her".

Pallium knocks Gaiseric out and grabs Totila. Huneric and two others I do not know attack Pallium.

"She wants to kill us all!" Huneric says.

I spit blood, but I do not scream. I cannot help but be reminded of Concordia in the *Messenger*, accusing me of trying to kill them all. They forget I gave myself to save Terra, back when my faith was pure.

One of the four remaining attackers hits me so hard I lose consciousness.

"Gaiseric," I say.

"They got him and the others. They're in the brig, awaiting trial. Pallium is all right."

I drift in and out of consciousness.

I wake in the Station infirmary, Octavius and Lucretia by my bedside. "What are you doing here?" I move my lips into saying with difficulty. My jaw and face are bandaged and taped tightly.

"Gabrielus just left," Lucretia says. "Many of us have been coming and going. It is true we still need to work, but we care about you."

"Why wouldn't we be here?" Octavius asks.

"What . . . happened?" I ask, gripping the railing of my infirmary bed tightly with my right hand, trying to rise and failing.

"I thought you'd tell us," Lucretia says.

"I mean . . . this," I say, waving my left hand at my face.

"Oh, well, the doctor says your jaw is broken," Octavius says, "but it should heal."

"And my eye?"

Octavius and Lucretia look at each other, apparently confused.

"My eye," I say, indicating my left eye. "I cannot feel anything on it, but there must be something, yes?"

Lucretia shakes her head no.

"Why?" Octavius asks.

"Well, I cannot see out of it, so there must be some bandage on it, yes?"

The looks on their faces tell me there isn't.

The doctors examine me and say I have suffered a concussion, the swelling from which has applied pressure to my left optic nerve, blinding me. They do not know if this will be permanent. "You need to stay in the infirmary for observation in case," one of them says.

"No," I say. "I must show that I am strong, even if I am not."

The doctors look at each other and at my companions.

"Your physical health is more important than politics, right now," one of them says.

"My physical health depends on politics, Doctor," I say. "Do I have the right to refuse treatment or not?"

Their response shows me I have the right.

"We cannot be held responsible if you do not follow our advice," another one says.

"You are not Havo. You are not responsible for anyone else's life or death," I say. "You can give advice and make recommendations, but I am responsible for my health whether I follow your advice or not."

"Please stay here and let them monitor you," Octavius urges. "I will stay with you night and day."

"You can do that?"

"I will obtain permission."

"You will ask."

"I will obtain permission."

I consent to stay in the infirmary.

Now everything I see with my left eye is blurry. It does not hurt, though I do feel a dull ache in the left side of my head, a dull ache which blends into the sharp agony of my cracked jaw. At times I cry from the pain. The doctor gives me pain medicine, which does not help completely but does make me feel ill.

"Gaiseric and the others are going to be punished," Lucretia tells me.

"I forgive him," I say.

"Cassie, how can you say that after what they did?"

"I am starting to think their rage is understandable," I say. "We do not know what the Church did to them back home. They see me as the embodiment of everything they hate, everything that has hurt them. That doesn't excuse what they did . . . but it does explain it. And if it is understandable . . . I understand it."

I look down and fidget with my blanket.

"We must overcome it," I say. "We must reform the Church. It cannot be allowed to continue such abuses as would prompt a grown man to attack a defenseless woman because he is blind with rage. It cannot."

"We are still going back," Lucretia says. "It will take months, even at the Station's top speed, but we are going back. They still want you to lead the diplomacy."

"I cannot even talk," I mumble.

"Cassie," Octavius says when we are alone, "I am sorry I was hard on you."

"Were you?" I ask.

"Yes, I was."

"I do not think you were, but I forgive you." This seems to help him.

My eye looks normal, thankfully. I find it hard to concentrate on anything with it open. I find myself covering it with my hand constantly just to see with the other eye. Gabrielus appears in my room holding something behind his back.

"What is it?" I ask.

"Close your eyes," he says, then immediately regrets his words.

"It is all right," I say and close both eyes.

"All right—open your good one," he says. I open it to see him holding something silver toward me.

"What is that?" I ask.

"An eye patch," he says, coming closer. He begins to fit it to my head. "This will enable your eye to rest, so you can work with your other one." It is a Sunsend. I start to cry for joy, but he misunderstands, startled.

"No, no," I say, holding my hand to my chin. "It is lovely. Thank you. A very thoughtful gift. How is it silver?"

"It came from a statue in storage," Gabrielus says, intriguing me. "It belonged to a nefarious Prism."

"A nefarious Prism?" I raise my eyebrows.

"You will give it a better use, I feel certain."

I adjust the small silver cloth and string device to rest comfortably over my eye. "May I have a mirror?" I ask.

Gabrielus obtains one and hands it to me. I look in the mirror for the first time in a long time. My hair is still light brown, my face is still mine, but now I have this patch on my left eye. I look like some Havo's Eve character. A nefarious Prism.

The doctors say I can go back to my cabin. They can do nothing but monitor my concussion and healing closely. I will come back to the infirmary every day for several days until they tell me the swelling has gone down. Pallium and his fellows will guard me more closely. Gabrielus, who has been given the rank of second in command of the station, Octavius, and Concordia walk me back to my cabin. Concordia wants the others to see her supporting me. I tell her that is not necessary.

"But it is," she says. "We are bridging the gap of distrust. If I do not do this, someone else will be attacked—or you might be again. They need to see believers and nonbelievers working together. They need to know their opportunity for sowing division has passed."

"This is quite a change, coming from you."

"I was not the one who tried to kill us all. I was the one who tried to save us all from the beginning."

I know she is right, and I cannot express the gratitude I feel toward her in this moment, this woman who hated me . . . this woman I . . . did I hate her? I did not want to believe it true, but I suppose in my way I did hate her. I did not understand her, that much is true. I feared her. I pitied her. Now I feel differently.

They change my cabin again. I am alone until I demand at least one roommate. They give me Jillian, a young woman of twenty. Pallium stands guard outside our cabin two of every three shifts, Octavius the third, each with other men. Jillian and I agree we feel like prisoners. She works in the cafeteria and brings my meals to me. When I am not in the cabin, I am in Gabrielus' office, a small cubbyhole next to the command bridge, working with Alaric, Gabrielus, and the others. There are his desk, a table of maps and materials, and my chair on the other side.

I feel a need to speak with Gaiseric, though he may not wish to speak with me.

Jillian does not comment on my eye patch, but I notice in those I pass that the looks of fascination change to looks of fear. Adults and children murmur and turn away as I remind them of this . . . notorious Prism? I must learn more. I have just begun to feel comfortable on the station, and now I withdraw farther into myself than before, sad and alone. If I take the patch off, I may harm my eyesight. I instruct Pallium only to allow a few to visit me, and only Gabrielus and Concordia do until one night Octavius comes.

I place my papers to one side and answer the door.

"I . . . wanted to see you," he says when he sees me.

"You see me now," I say. "You have not come before."

"I . . . was nervous."

"About me?"

He looks down. I draw him in and close the door.

"You . . . are going to lead us," he says.

"That is what they tell me," I say. "I think I am just going to be a diplomat. I am not a leader."

"You were a teacher," he says. "Teachers are leaders."

In a moment of boldness, he comes closer to me. I look up at his beautiful face. He leans his head down to kiss me. I am nervous, but I close my eyes and tilt my face up toward his.

After we kiss, I turn away so he will not see my struggle. *The Book of Havo* clearly requires no intimacy before marriage, and yet . . .

"No," I say.

"Cassiopeia, I . . . "

"Please leave," I say without turning to face him. I hear his arm fall to his side, then his departure.

I weep, alone in my bed.

Forgive me, Octavius!

"It is going to take us months to get back," I say to Gabrielus in his office. He leans back in an office chair behind his small desk, which is also covered with papers.

"Our station is faster than your ship, but you are right. It will take about four months, Ray Ovatio."

"Are we all going to hibernate in cryogenic sleep?"

"No. Though we can operate on a skeleton crew while the rest hibernate, we do not possess cryogenic sleep beds."

"Then we are going to stay awake."

"Yes."

"That is going to make for a long voyage."

"You will learn more about us. You might even make new friends. Do you have other plans?" He smiles.

"No," I blush and look down. "I meant no disrespect or complaint. I merely comment on the logistical difficulty."

"Oh, you do not even know what the logistical difficulty is."

I look back up at him.

"What is . . . the logistical difficulty?"

"Fuel. Yes, we have enough for the return trip to Terra, but that is all. We are not coming back here, whatever the outcome. We have kept ourselves parked near the Sun since our escape from *your* church—from *the* Church. And now . . . is the end, one way or another. The intention was always to return home when it was safe, when the time was right—when we would be free on Terra, not hated and hunted. But we were going to decide that based on scout reports from the occasional supply mission. Many are telling Alaric that it is still not the time." Gabrielus looks at me intently, with a curious mixture of pain and hope. "But I had faith in you. I *have* faith in you. Something about you changed my mind—and his. He will not reverse himself."

"That is quite ironic, coming from a faithless man."

"Isn't it?" Gabrielus sits forward, letting his chair come to rest on the floor. "But I am convinced that now *is* the time and you are the woman to make it happen."

"To make what happen?"

"Change."

"Hmm."

"There is something about you." He raises his finger toward me. I gaze at him steadily. "Concordia sees it too. Do not be deceived by her."

"Deceived? She hates me."

"No. She does not. She may prove to be your greatest ally. She will protect you. Perhaps even when no one else will."

I am secretly pleased to hear this. I do not know why, but I admire her.

A cloud passes over Gabrielus. "I have said too much," he says. "Yes, we have the return trip ahead. We've prepared for it all our lives, though none of us thought we would actually see it. We are all a little excited, a little on edge—and some of us would rather kill you than go back. Remember that also."

"Oh, I do."

"Stay with Pallium. He will protect you."

"Havo will protect me. Pallium and his men are strong, but Havo is stronger."

Gabrielus nods in an absent manner. I can sense that our relationship has changed permanently due to my costing him his position. I cannot relieve his loss. I can only try to prove worthy of having caused it. "I thank you for your advice and all you have done for me. I will try to prove worthy."

He nods again. I leave him for now. As I walk away from his office, I hear his words again in my mind: *We are not coming back here, whatever the outcome.*

As a part of my reading on the Church, I discover a document written one thousand three hundred years before, a document written by the Father of Us All at that time, Innocentius IV, in which the torture of heretics is allowed. The torture of heretics was allowed over *thirteen hundred* years before, which means that during all this time, heretics have been tortured.

They are telling the truth.

The restrictions on torture listed in the document matter not; I know human nature all too well. I can see easily how individual Fathers and Prisms could and would do as they pleased. I am not so blind that I do not see that.

This is a Havican document; there is no forgery of such a document. As painful as it is for me to realize, I realize that everything I have been told is true.

It is clear to me now that those who attacked me had every right to be angry, even to see me as the symbol of their oppression. I can never make amends to them for all the Church has done, though I can try to earn their trust by working to right the wrongs, at least to do as much good as I can.

I confess, Havo, that I too am beginning to feel anger. The Church deceived everyone on Terra including me. I must remember to temper my anger with prudence and justice. I must never allow it to reduce me to the level of a savage, or I will be little better than those who would attack an innocent.

The lives of everyone on the Station depend on my success, but I do not even know what I am supposed to do, how I am supposed to succeed. My adversary, my opponent, is now my beloved church. How can I fight, even trick, those I love and until recently trusted more than myself?

Time looms ahead long yet short, a dreadful respite before a dreadful return. I am an Offering who disobeyed her church. Until now the Church did not need to know or care about Offerings who chose not to die. Now the Church will learn. How will it respond?

I do not know how I will survive the next four months, let alone fit in. Alaric, Concordia, Gabrielus, Justina, Octavius, and Tiberius form an unofficial governing council. They tell me that when we arrive back at Terra I will do the talking. I have not seen Octavius in the halls; he has avoided me. But we must attend these meetings.

"We will assume orbit around Terra," I say, seated at the planning table with them, "and I will announce what I have found to the Church only, to demonstrate respect and promote goodwill. The laity will remain unaware of Station Michael until the Church hierarchy agrees."

Concordia says, "The Church will not agree to anything exposing its lies."

"After the Church agrees to the announcement of the existence of the Station," I continue, "we will prepare for our return to our homes and our lives. There should be no reason for disharmony or conflict, once I explain what has happened."

"Are you out of your mind?" Octavius demands, looking me in the eyes for the first time since I asked him to leave my room several nights before. I wonder how much of his outrage is on behalf of the Station and how much against me personally. "The Church sentenced all of us to death! We are all heretics and apostates to the Church. The Havians will do everything in their power to shoot us down." He looks around for validation.

"I am a Havian," I say, "and I would not."

"These are not Havians," Concordia says. "These are . . . monsters."

"Whatever we call them," Alaric says, "what Octavius says is true. We must be on guard. On that we all agree."

"Surely their science is on the verge of detecting us," Gabrielus says. "We must do something before it is too late."

"We already had that debate," Alaric says. "And we agreed with you."

Gabrielus becomes quiet.

"We need a back-up plan," Justina says.

"What do we do if they fire on us?" Octavius asks.

"*When* they fire on us," Concordia says. "What is the weaponry of this station?"

I stand to depart. "I will not discuss firing on anyone—Havian or apostate," I say.

"It is just a contingency," Alaric says.

"Discuss it without me," I say.

Alaric thinks it over, then nods to indicate I may go.

I turn and leave. Pallium, standing outside, assumes his regular distance from me and follows. I think of him as my shadow. I hear the door to the briefing room open again and someone, Octavius, pursue me. I stop and turn to face him.

Coming upon me, he suddenly doubts himself and his purpose.

"Yes, Octavius?"

"Why have you been avoiding me?"

"I have not been," I say.

"I have not seen you."

"Yes, I got the impression you were avoiding me."

"I was not!" he insists, then laughs. "All right, I suppose I was."

"Yes, you were. Why?"

"You know why."

"You know why I said what I said."

"Yes, I do."

We begin walking together.

"Have supper with me tonight," I suggest.

"I will. Thank you," Octavius says.

"It hurt me, you know," I say as we walk toward the cafeteria, "that you avoided me. I . . . " We stop at the doors, and he looks at me intently. "I did not want to turn you away."

"Well, I understand why you did. You were protecting me."

"Us all." I caress his cheek.

"I don't care who sees us," he says and opens the cafeteria door. We walk in to the stares of dozens, silence punctuated by intrigued murmurs. We walk to the line and pick up trays.

The cooks speak with nervous courtesy. I speak in a flat, polite voice so as not to spark controversy. We move to find a table. Even now I feel wrong in my flight suit and long for my Havian robes. I may never grow accustomed to their absence. I may ask to make my own.

"Cassiopeia! Octavius!"

I look to see Mattheus waving us to join his family and him at a table. I look at Octavius questioningly. He seems not to mind, so we join them.

"You can all go back to eating and drinking now," Mattheus says to the room. "We'll take it from here." He laughs. "Wow. You've been here a month, and already you have stirred up enough controversy to last a lifetime." I stare at him. "Well, you have caused quite a ruckus."

"I have done nothing of the sort," I say. "I am merely the passive instrument of Havo's will."

"Of course," Mattheus says, turning to Octavius. "And how about you? I know you two knew each other before, yes? Well, has Cassiopeia changed? Have you? And do you find you have changed since you last knew each other?" Octavius and I cannot help but make eye contact.

"Oh, I see," Mattheus says before anyone can respond. "Well, good luck with that."

"When Octavius was chosen, I was glad for Havo," I say. "He would receive the best we had to offer."

"Cassie is the same as ever," Octavius manages to say. "And I love her."

"Well!" Mattheus says. "This is getting interesting."

I blush.

"Mattheus," Iulia, sitting on the other side of Mattheus, says, "shut up."

"Shutting up."

"Octavius and I are old friends," I say. "When he left he was a boy. Now I find he is becoming a man. A man I like."

"Well, that is good enough for me," Mattheus says. "Oh, that's right—I'm shutting up. God, I miss beer. That alone will make returning worth it. Excuse me." He gets up to get something.

"You must excuse my husband," Iulia says. "He is nervous about the decision to return to Terra. We all are."

This is my fault, I think. I nod.

"I think we will all feel better when it is all over," she says.

"I hope so," I say. After thinking a moment, I add, "Your husband doesn't seem nervous."

"He hides it behind being the life of the party."

"Well, he is that," I say.

"Speaking of hiding, though," Iulia says, "I would definitely advise the two of you to keep your relationship . . . maybe not a secret but quiet. Not loud."

"Octavius and I have known each other for years. We are both Offerings. We have both suffered much here. I do not engage in relationships to provoke anger, nor do I limit my relationships to prevent it."

"I understand, but these apostates have every reason to feel anger," Iulia says. "It's not just that you are Havian. They have accepted the former Offerings here—even Octavius—up to now because we have left each other alone. You, on the other hand . . . well, you have stirred up a bunch of stuff."

"Stercus," Octavius says.

"I am building bridges," I say, "between Havian and non-Havian alike."

"Be careful how you build," Iulia says. "And look both before and behind you with your remaining eye." Her point is made. "There are many on *both* sides who oppose this."

The days pass through October to Sol's victory games and Havo's Eve. I wonder about my students' costumes and start to cry again.

Octavius becomes my greatest comfort. However, after our return to Terra is planned, I find myself frustrated at not having purposeful work to do, so I ask to return to the hydroponics bay. This is granted, and now there are three of us: Cymus, Phaedra, and I. Phaedra has been working in the bay for a few days already, but I am still able to teach her some things.

Pallium checks the bay before each one of my shifts and stands guard outside for its entirety. Lucretia, too, is glad to see me back there, though she does not work in the bay. The time passes more swiftly when one is absorbed in a project, and once again I feel the joy I felt working in the garden with my father. He would feel proud of my work here. I think of seeing him again and, overcome with the extremes I have experienced since leaving Terra, I begin to cry. Thankfully I am alone in the greenhouse, half in shadow. I master myself, finish my shift, and go out to the corridor and Pallium. He escorts me to the cafeteria, where I continue to ignore the stares and condemning looks. I do not sit with Octavius again. In public, we pretend to be distant. I no longer remember my eye patch, though the occasional child reminds me of it. The adults, however used to it they are, do not act as if they notice it.

"Marry me," Octavius says one night in November on an observation deck, Pallium standing far enough away not to hear, and seems immediately to regret having said it. "We are going to die. Let us at least be married before we do."

"Octavius," I say, then struggle for words. "I remember before you questioned Havo, but you accepted Offering to show your duty and your love despite your doubts. You were the bravest man I had ever known. Before we marry, I must know: do you believe in Havo?"

"I do not. I am sorry."

The words sting me like blows. "You always believed before," I say quietly.

"No, I had doubts, but I knew I could not share them with you."

"I wish I'd known."

"For what it's worth, I wanted to tell you. But I couldn't."

"Why not?"

"I knew you cared for me, but I could not risk it. I could not know how you would react."

"I would only have tried to help you see Havo's love."

"I am sorry."

"I forgive you because I love you. I will always love you."

"And I you. But now I am free to declare my disbelief openly, here on this station, and, like many others here, I fear the Church's reaction to our return."

"I fear staying in Space forever not knowing."

A silence comes over us, though we are holding hands.

"I have had three years to consider everything you have faced in the past month, and my time here has removed my doubts," Octavius says. "I no longer doubt my disbelief."

"You think me deluded."

"I think you cannot prove your god any more than I can disprove him, so we are even. I love you. I loved you before, and I barely knew you then compared to now. Now that I am here with you, I know and love you more deeply than ever before. But I know that everything is . . . uncertain."

"It is uncertain. We may die. But that might be the best reason." I reach out for his hand and clasp it. "I will confess there have been times recently when I have . . . not known Havo's purpose for me." I put my head down, then chuckle and look back up. "This does not strike me as the most romantic way to say yes, or the most romantic set of circumstances, but . . . since I may not ask my father's opinion, I think that I agree with you. If we are going to die, at least let it be as husband and wife. Besides, we are already officially dead." I smile, the first real smile I have smiled in days.

Octavius's eyes, face, and entire being glow as if illuminated from the inside. We embrace. I close my eyes and lose myself in the moment as we kiss. When we separate, Octavius looks older, wiser, more mature. I love him.

"You will not regret this."

"I know I will not."

"I will take care of you."

"We will take care of each other."

"Yes." He nods.

Octavius takes my hand to his lips.

"I love you," he says and kisses my hand.

"I love you too," I say. "I always did, but this is more. We are no longer children."

"Yes."

"Good night," Octavius says.

"Good night," I say. "May Havo's light shine on you tonight," I add, repeating something my mother used to say to me at night when I was young.

He smiles and steps away. Pallium approaches, and we walk back to my cabin.

"Good night, Pallium, and I thank you for your attentions," I say outside the door.

Pallium says, "They will add more guards starting tomorrow. Do not worry: the others are as good as I am."

"I am not worried, Pallium. Thank you."

Octavius and I agree on December 1 as the date of our wedding. Alaric does not want to announce our wedding. Gabrielus again takes my side. The council votes without Octavius and me. Alaric and Tiberius vote no. Justina surprises me by voting yes. Gabrielus votes yes. Concordia votes yes.

"We will hold it," Alaric says without further comment. "Security will be my responsibility."

"Why did you vote yes?" I ask Concordia in private.

"You have taught me the value of building bridges, not just blowing them up."

The wedding announcement changes the dynamic in the Station further. The union of Octavius, who has lived on the Station for three years known to all, with me renders me more legitimate in many eyes, though I am sure there are some who view this as just another manipulation or trick on my part, as if I am just scheming to ingratiate myself and gain power. It is odd how nonbelievers are so suspicious. Are they capable of trusting or believing anything or anyone?

Lucretia realizes her mistake and blesses our union. "He's much better suited to you," she says.

The ceremony will be held in the solarium nearest the cafeteria. Though not as large as the cafeteria, the solarium features a glass outer wall and a relatively large open space in which chairs can be placed and an audience can assemble. I do not wish to be married in a cafeteria.

The ceremony for all Havians is the same, but I do not know Octavius's desire. My groom is no longer Havian. When I raise the issue with him, he says the Havian ceremony is fine with him. This puts my mind at ease. I thank him.

At my request, Gabrielus will officiate.

The Havians congratulate me, the majority of the nonHavians nod when they see me, the minority of nonHavians continue to ignore me or betray fear in their reactions. I do not wish them to fear me, but I cannot control what they think, feel, or do. I rely on Havo's will.

The night before the ceremony, full Havian robes in my size appear on my bed. I have not seen such robes anyplace on the Station. I run my hands across the fabric, then lift up the robes to press them against myself.

I smell the silver cloth with visions of home and pain at missing my father and mother. The triangular hat sits under the robes.

Where could these robes have come from? I will have to ask Lucretia. She must know.

I decide to keep the secret a little longer, until the next day. After trying them on to make sure everything is in order, I gently fold and place the robes in the locker next to my bed. My grey jumpsuit is frayed and patched but still serviceable. I only wear the green when the grey is being laundered.

The Station residents will be even more surprised by my robe than I was to find it.

Pallium and Jillian plead ignorance and seem sincere. Someone must have done it while we were all at supper, someone with access to my locked cabin. I will hope to learn at or after the ceremony. I can only assume that whoever did it is my friend.

I cannot banish thoughts of murder and torture *committed by the Church* from my mind. I cannot stop questioning. My mind works over and over what I have seen and read until I can take it no more and tell Octavius what I have seen and read.

"Yes," he says. "It is all true."

"But how? How can it be that our church would do these things?"

"The Church is led by human beings, Cassiopeia, and when human beings gain power, their worst traits emerge."

"But these are Havians."

"They are humans above all."

"They are *not* Havians."

"Be that as it may, they dress in Havian clothes and speak the Havian words."

"Surely the Father of Us All cannot know of these things. But how can he not?"

"He knows, he participates, he directs. He lets his minions do as they please as long as they also do his bidding. And what they are all best at is keeping secrets. They are dangerous, and we cannot trust them."

"You don't really think of the Church and its Prisms that way, do you?"

"I do."

"But all our lives we are told how disordered the World was before, how the Church had struggled for over two thousand years to bring order and finally succeeded."

"We are told this by the Church."

"All around us we see—at home, we saw—peace and order. There was no violence. How could these stories of abuses be true? I just want to understand. It seems impossible to me. The Church is good and loving. It takes care of our every earthly need as we all serve Havo. The Church has been kind to me."

"There are good persons even in evil organizations, people who perform good deeds when their leaders are not looking. Good deeds are allowed as long as they do not go against the Church's goals. The Church has every interest in maintaining a good public image—that is what keeps it in power. Cassiopeia, I understand it is hard to accept. It took me a while too. I am sorry."

He kisses me.

"Forgive me for my . . . ignorance," I say. "This is all new to me."

"Ignorance is no crime, and we are all indoctrinated from birth—by our parents, by our society. In my time here, I—like everyone else here—have learned about the abuses of the Church. Yes, they sentence nonbelievers to death. Yes, they kidnap and torture. Oftentimes they let their victims return to society under threat. The victims never speak of their suffering. They know they could be killed for doing so. They would not even be believed. They live with their knowledge, powerless to do anything about it—and those are the lucky ones. Sometimes they are the most outspoken supporters of the Church, just to prevent being punished again. The unlucky ones disappear forever."

I feel a shudder.

"If you and I are to be married," Octavius continues, "our marriage must be based on honesty and trust. Do you agree?"

"Yes."

"You may believe what you wish about Havo, of course, but I must inform you that I view the Church as a Worldwide crime syndicate, a fraudulent organization peddling lies for the sole purpose of maintaining power and controlling its populace."

"Does no one in the Church believe in Havo?" I plead.

"Oh, I'm sure many of them do, even those who do harm, but they think they must do harm to do good. You know the old phrase: the end justifies the means. Being rewarded for what they do confirms them in their belief they are doing Havo's will. The vast majority of Havians, however, do not know what is being done in their name, or at least behind their backs."

"No true Havian would condone, let along commit, the abuses you imply."

"That is true. That is why they are kept secret. Torture, rape, murder . . . always hidden, always disguised, always gotten away with, never admitted, let alone punished."

"The Father and Mother of All would never permit such a system."

"The Father and Mother of All are the chief criminals."

"No," I say in shock and horror.

"Yes."

"But . . . we all know them! We all know their kindness, their acts of charity the World over!"

"And they do those things to keep up appearances, but even those acts are false, underneath."

"How could they be?"

"The falsehood is that the Church is necessary. The Church works to address effects before causes, to make sure there are always problems it is indispensable to 'solve'. The Church, above all, must maintain its own necessity. We cannot cure every ill, otherwise the Church would no longer be needed."

"Do you know what you are saying?

"Yes. I agree with Alaric: the Church created the Inopia."

"How can you think that?"

"Cure the Church, cure the Inopia."

"No. I do not believe that. I cannot believe it."

"On the other side of the coin, the truth is that kindness and goodness will always exist. We do not need a church or even the belief in Havo to create goodness and morality in us, though the Church would have us believe we do. We do not need a god to make us moral."

I raise my wet eyes to him. "Whence comes morality, then, Octavius?"

"My morality comes from me, not from Havo or any other god."

"How can *that* be possible? There must be something more. Do not you feel that there is something more, inside you?"

"No, I do not."

My heart is conflicted. How can I marry someone whose views are so different from, even opposed to my own?

"Morality is a random genetic mutation. Haven't you ever wondered why some human beings are less moral? Do you really think morality is a free choice given to all equally? Do you think it is more of a choice than sexuality? Think of homosexuality. We all agree nowadays this is determined before birth, genetically, and Havo smiles on all His creations, yes?"

"Yes," I answer.

"They say that sexuality is the most personal and individual part of us, so it stands to reason that if sexuality is genetic, morality is too, no?"

"But all of this is created by Havo."

"My morality is mine. I make my choices, with my free will. I do so freely, without fear of punishment or hope of reward. I do the right thing because it is the right thing, not because of what Havo or anyone else will think or whether or not someone will like me."

"I credit Havo for making you good."

"I cannot stop you from doing so, but I would thank you for crediting me for what I think, feel, say, and do. I cannot attribute to a deity I have not met credit for *my* actions."

"I can."

"That strikes me as . . . illogical, Cassie."

"But about the Church, Octavius. If the Church does these things, as you claim, then why? Why does it do them?"

"Because it can. Human beings love power, and they love being able to get away with things. Given power they abuse it. There is an old saying in a book the Church failed to purge: 'Absolute power corrupts absolutely.' Who enjoys absolute power on Terra?"

"The Church. The Father and Mother of All Things."

"Therefore, who is absolutely corrupted on Terra?"

"The Church. The Father and Mother of All Things."

"They can get away with anything, and they do, because they can."

"Why were my family and I spared?"

"Were you?"

I am confused. I do not understand his question. I search his face until a realization dawns on me. "My mother?"

He nods.

"What do you know?"

"Very little. I *suspect* she was murdered for questioning the Church."

"Octavius, you do not know that."

"That is true, I do not."

"Never speak of that to me again."

"All right, I will not."

It doesn't seem like the right moment, but I produce my gown. Octavius's eyes widen.

"Where did you get this?" he asks before I say anything.

"I do not know," I say. "Someone left it here."

"Amazing."

"Yes, but also troubling."

"Troubling?"

"Despite our separation, I feel I know you. And now that we are . . . here, I sense that others respect you. You are on the rise to become a leader." Octavius demurs. "You sat on the committee to judge me."

"They had me there because I knew you before. That is all."

I am not convinced.

"My question is: will they accept our marriage? Will this gown upset them? My understanding was this station is a place where Havians and . . . non-Havians live and work together."

"It is. So what troubles you?"

"Those who might see our marriage as the Church taking over."

Octavius chuckles softly. "Do you see it that way?"

"No. I see it as building bridges, showing that the two sides can work together, even love each other." I look at him with hope.

"As do I. And those who misinterpret things . . . " Octavius makes a helpless gesture. "They do not matter."

"They may not matter to us, but they have the capacity to cause harm." I am once again conscious of my eye patch, and I take it off. I do not want to wear it any more.

"Cassie," Octavius says. "Can you see?"

"Not with this eye, no," I say sadly. "Does it look strange?"

"It looks exactly like the other one. You look fine."

"Well, that is good," I say, then remember the subject at hand. "Obviously, there are those who cannot be trusted to honor their own stated morality, those in positions of trust who cannot be trusted." I lower my face.

"If you know that," Octavius says, kissing me on the top of my head, "then I think you have come a long way."

"Surely this is true of apostates as well as Havians."

"Yes, it is."

"Then how do we know we are safe?"

"One of the hard facts of Life to learn is that we are not. Safety is an illusion. We can only do our best and hope."

"Why would Havo allow such things?"

"I have no answer for you. It could be a test."

"Do you know what you are saying? If what you are saying were true, that would mean that almost everything we know of the Church is a lie!"

"Yes."

"That would be the biggest test on Terra—in human history!"

"Yes."

"To what end? And what if my mother's death was not an accident?"

I waver, then break down in his arms.

"I'm sure it was."

"Don't you go lying now too. Honesty, remember?"

"All right. I don't know."

I recover and look at the gown again. "Do you like it?" I ask.

"It is beautiful," he says.

"You do not really feel that way. You abhor the sight of it, of what it represents."

"It represents *you*, and you are beautiful to me . . . so yes, I do find it beautiful."

"Thank you."

We kiss, then he departs my room for the night.

After he has gone, I try on the robes and hat. Jillian and I only very a small facial mirror on our wall, but I can lean in close to see the rest of my body. Though I wear the ordinary robes of any Havian on Terra, I am overwhelmed by their beauty and splendor. No matter what happens and who does not approve, I will represent Havo proudly and joyously at my own wedding. My fiancé loves me and understands. That is all that matters, as he said.

I might be alone otherwise, but I have Havo and Octavius.

I eat, I sleep, I work in the hydroponics bay and greenhouse, I pass my leisure and sleep time with my husband and our friends Iulia, Mattheus, and Livia. I feel increasing excitement as our wedding day approaches.

Not everyone at the Station is invited to the ceremony, as some persons cannot be spared from Station operations. Some persons are opposed to the wedding and decline invitations. Some persons—very few—are simply not invited. I want to invite Gaiseric and his friends, to build bridges, but Gabrielus and Octavius explain to me that they could and would likely attempt to disrupt the proceedings. "They do not wish to build bridges," Gabrielus says. A protective isolation box cannot be built in time to accommodate them, so we leave them in the brig. I send them a note expressing my thoughts of them and my regret they cannot not attend. Everyone around me thinks me crazy, but I am becoming accustomed to that.

I ask the person on the Station to whom I feel closest, Concordia, to stand with me during the ceremony. She will be by my side. I have not seen her for several days.

The day of the ceremony, all is excitement. I dress in a small room just off the Ring. The guests, Havian and not, are seated intermingled, all in Station green, in the cafeteria, which remains the largest meeting space. Concordia is with me in the dressing room. She wears an old dress found in the archive—black, but better than dark green. I had wanted Gabrielus to marry us, but he explains to me it would be better if Alaric performs the ceremony.

"I never thought I would see the day," Concordia laughs.

"The day that two persons love each other?" I ask.

"The day that a theocrat and a freedom fighter find love."

Her words sting me. "I support the Church, if that is what you mean."

"That is what I mean."

"Miracles do happen," I say, putting on my robes and hat. "Well?"

"Gorgeous."

I have come to learn that for her, a compliment dripping with acid is indeed a compliment.

"Thank you. And thank you for agreeing to do this."

"I pity you your delusion. It is the least I can do to help you connect with some sense."

"It is the least you can do to be kind."

"What you continually fail to understand is that is the *most* I could do."

Octavius comes to the door. I brighten at the sight of him. "It is time," he says, then disappears.

Concordia, stiff in her dress, opens the door for me. Only Pallium, in the hallway, is there to see me before we open the cafeteria doors. He stands aside, watching the corridor. I take a deep breath.

"Ready?" Concordia asks, suggesting to me that some part of her understands what it is like to be a woman.

I nod, and she opens the doors. I see heads turn and hear gasps as I walk in toward Alaric and Octavius, down the central aisle past the staring guests. Octavius and I are smiling at each other, and that is all that matters. I take my place, and Alaric examines both halves of the audience to see that it quiets itself before reading the ceremony. This takes several moments. After much speaking, Octavius and I both say, "I do," and we are married.

"I now pronounce you husband and wife," Alaric declares. A part of me thinks the Church will not recognize this marriage, but a part of me feels no concern for this. A thrill of rebellion ripples through my soul, a thrill I do not even understand. What is wrong with me? How can I consider myself above the Church? Does that mean I consider myself above Havo? Absolutely not. Never. But I start to realize that my heart lies, for the first time, outside the Church's dominion.

All married couples on the Station have their own rooms, so Octavius and I are given our own, new to both of us. To relieve crowding in another cabin, Jillian will gain a new roommate. Octavius, too, had roommates, so the change is bigger for him. We enter our new home with curiosity and gratitude. Though small, the room is ours, with one large bed, one desk, one lamp, and two lockers. What a joy to be able to stretch out on an actual bed, albeit connected to the wall, not to be cramped in a bunk! We enjoy bliss after bliss for the next several weeks, making the return trip to Terra one of the happiest times of my life.

"They can see us by now," Gabrielus remarks over supper one night.

"How soon until they can shoot us down?" Mattheus asks, then chuckles. Iulia glares at him.

"They can send ships to fire on us any time," Gabrielus says.

"More importantly, Mattheus, when will they be able to communicate with us?" Iulia asks.

"Another few weeks," Mattheus says, becoming more serious. That produces silence at the table.

The agitation and excitement I feel cannot be described, only imagined. I cannot decide if I am more joyous or afraid. I feel a strange mixture of both, or every emotion combined, knowing what I now know of the Church. Yes, a part of what I feel is righteous anger, and yes, a part of me still hopes the Church can explain and disprove the allegations I have heard here. Anti-Church propaganda could explain this. There must be a good explanation. The sooner we arrive back on Terra, the sooner we—I— can determine the truth.

A part of me also fears disapproval from the church that sent me to meet Havo. It is my hope that my bringing Station Michael to light will earn me understanding, perhaps even forgiveness. It is my hope the Church will agree I was touched by Havo. It is my hope the fertility here will help the Havian scientists on Terra discover a cure. If worse comes to worst and I am not forgiven for my transgression, I am prepared to take the next Offering ship back to the Sun and will offer to do so if need be or let the Church sanction me as it sees fit.

I will do whatever I believe to be right, always.

The days pass without incident but with increasing tension. Octavius and I are given a few days off to celebrate our wedding. There are not many places we can go to celebrate. He shows me a small solarium on the outer edge of the Ring, on the other side of the Spine from the cafeteria. We declare it ours and pass hours there. We watch the Sun, already smaller in our perception than it was, grow more distant each day, through the dark glass.

"I had to get over you," he says.

"As I had to get over you," I say. "I am sorry we did not express our feelings before now."

"The time was never right. The circumstances did not allow it."

"Strange that now that we have been Offered to Havo, we are free to do so."

"Or not strange."

"Are you praising Havo?"

"I am praising freedom from the Church."

I go silent.

"I am sorry," Octavius says. "I know this has been particularly hard on you."

"I love you," I say, "and you owe me no apology. If what everyone here says is true, it is the Church who should be begging forgiveness."

"And abdicating power."

"And abdicating power."

"You know, I heard that once, there was a time when the temporal and the spiritual authorities were separate—closely entwined but separate, and everyone could worship as he or she pleased. There were different religions, and even people who did not believe in any god, living side by side in peace."

"I do not believe it. Different religions? How? Why?"

"It's just something I heard."

"It cannot be true. And life under the Church of Havo was very good for me. I did not see any of the atrocities of which I have been informed on this station."

"No, you wouldn't. You weren't meant to."

I am told that I will speak for the Station, when we arrive at Terra. We will communicate directly with the Havican, so as to protect privacy. We will not announce ourselves to Terra. We will do everything properly and diplomatically. I agree with this, as I still wish to give my church the benefit of the doubt. I have only heard the apostate side for months.

I will speak the truth, the Church will understand Havo's will, and all will be well.

"Life is about to change for us forever," Octavius says.

"It already did that," I say.

The Havians aboard Station Michael celebrate the birth of Havo on December 25. I have little to give, but I reserve small sections of soil not being used for other purposes and grow two small seedlings, one for Octavius and one for our friends. This use of soil might be begrudged, or even against the rules, but I consider the voice of the Station important enough to justify it. Cymus, who knows every leaf in the bay and greenhouse, says nothing.

The new year begins. I feel a sense of inertia and eagerness combined.

The first of February comes and goes, and we are still a few days away from Terra. I am in the office behind the command bridge. I hear Mattheus say through my open door, "Well, hello. This is it." I come to the door to observe. He looks over to Alaric.

Alaric, in the pilot's chair, asks, "What is it?"

"Oh, it is Terra—the Church. They want us to identify ourselves."

"Identify us."

"Who else could we be?"

"Identify us."

"I think they're already playing with us, but okay."

Mattheus flips a switch and speaks. "Greetings, Terra. This is the free Station Michael, returning to Terra after an extended mission. How are you today?"

Alaric watches Mattheus, who says, "They ended the communication."

"That is not very sporting," Alaric says. "They'll be seeing us soon enough. I predict they will call back—or perhaps not." Alaric thinks for a few moments. "Viatrix, change our course from a straight line to an 's' pattern. Wobble us all the way in. You can decide how wide each arc is."

"Aye, sir," a woman I have not met before says.

Alaric turns and sees me. "We are big and fast," he says, "but we are not maneuverable, and if they want to hit us it will be easy, but that doesn't mean I need to make it easy for them before they blast us into Space dust."

"I trust the Church will not attack us," I say.

"Well, Cassie, they already cut off communication," Mattheus says. "They are not exactly being friendly."

"For all you know it could have been an interruption in the communication," I say.

"Yes, that is true," Mattheus says.

The word of the contact spreads quickly through the Station. No one says much. We do not know what is going to happen next, and we are afraid to find out. Assuming it was *not* a technical difficulty, ceasing communication is not the most positive sign, and we have not heard from them again.

"What did we expect?" Mattheus asks over supper.

"I expected them to welcome us."

"That's what I love about you, Cassiopeia: you always give everyone the benefit of the doubt."

"I did not give apostates the benefit of any doubts."

I remember how I was when I first arrived . . . almost four months ago. I look about me at Octavius, Mattheus, Iulia, their daughter, and everyone else in the cafeteria. This station was alien to me when I arrived. I even felt as if it were a prison. Now . . . I feel a camaraderie. I feel almost at home, excepting that I am not at home.

"Are you satisfied?" I hear a voice I do not recognize behind me.

"Hey, easy," Mattheus says, then he and Octavius stand. Pallium, who is almost always standing by, comes closer.

"You've destroyed us all!" I turn to see a man I do not know looking down at me.

"Have faith," I say to him. He lunges at me but Pallium intervenes. Mattheus comes over the table, knocking food and drink aside, to assist. Octavius and Mattheus protect me as Pallium takes the man away.

"I am sorry for that," Octavius says.

"He will see," I say.

The last few days are hellish. I eat, sleep, and work distracted. I am tired and irritable. This is the most agitated I think I have ever been. The less said of this time the better. I even snap at Octavius, then immediately apologize. He understands.

We achieve orbit when we are in our cabin. Alaric sends word says he wants me on the command bridge. I dress in my robes and tricornered hat with flowing sidepieces. I have been taught where to stand to be seen by the camera. I stand just off camera, to Alaric's right. The camera points at him. I await usefulness.

"Well, they know we are here," Mattheus says. "If they wanted to talk with us, they would."

"They must not know *what* they want to do," Alaric says.

"They've had days to plan, so whatever they do, it *is* what they want to do," Mattheus said. "If they shot us down, the world would see it —and find pieces."

"Perhaps they wish to ignore us," Alaric said. "That will not work. Begin preparations for a worldwide broadcast."

"Worldwide broadcast?" I ask.

"Yes, Mattheus has been breaking into their communications network. It should be relatively simple to broadcast from here, yes?'

"Yes," Mattheus says. "We can use their satellites just as they can. Oh, look, there goes one now," he jests, pointing at the screen in front of us.

"So, if they will not speak with us directly—"

"They're talking," Mattheus says. "They want visual communication."

"Provide it," Alaric says. "Do not go worldwide unless I say."

After some technical crackling and static, the Father of All of Us, Lux Aduro, appears on the forward screen. I feel a joyous surge of faith and love. Our father will welcome us home, I am certain.

"Unidentified space vessel," Our Father says. "I am Lux Aduro, the spiritual and organizational leader of this planet. We have been monitoring your approach for days. Am I right in thinking this is the station named after our archangel Michael, taken from us one hundred and thirty-eight years ago?"

"Greetings, Lux Aduro," Alaric says. "I am Alaric Vorenus, leader of Station Michael. You are correct. This station was taken during the time of conflict on Earth that led to what is now known to you as the Day of Havo."

"Station Michael, please state your intentions. We do not wish hostilities with you, but we will defend ourselves if necessary."

"We are on a peaceful mission of friendship and hope."

The Father of Us All listens and considers this. "This is most welcome news," he says. "We rejoice at your return to us, Alaric Vorenus of Station Michael, and welcome you with the open arms of brother- and sisterhood. We assumed the Station destroyed many years ago. Your survival is a blessing from Havo. What an amazing story you must have to tell."

"I thank you, Lux Aduro. I can honestly say that we did not expect such a welcome."

"No? The war is over, and none of us was alive to fight it. There is no reason we should continue ancient hostility, whether you are believers or not. You may come home to live in peace among us or apart from us, as you choose, or even stay where you are. Your right to self-determination is absolute, the same as it is for those on Terra, and we will not impose on you in any way. Come and be welcomed as friends, or not, as you choose."

"I am impressed," Alaric says. "You will also be interested to know that we do have Havians aboard."

"Then there is even greater cause for rejoicing!" Lux Aduro says. "We are eager to welcome them home."

After a pause, Alaric adds, "Lux Aduro, one of the Havians here wishes to speak with you."

"Oh? By all means, our souls are full of joy! This transmission is being seen by the Sacred College of Cardinals. We have had a few days to prepare, you see, and I lost no time in summoning the College to discuss the weighty import of your arrival and what it might indicate of Havo's will."

Mattheus adjusts the camera onto me and nods to indicate I may speak and be heard on Terra.

"This is my doing, Father," I say.

Our Father squints and focuses on me, but I do not yet see recognition in his eyes.

"Cassiopeia Ovatio, Father," I say. "I was one of the Offerings this year. I have brought you this station in the name of Havo."

He listens, and I see recognition.

"I am astounded. How did you do this?"

"Every year the Station crew intercepts the Offering ship and invites Offerings to stay with them. Most do not, but some do. On the Station are many Offerings from years past. They chose to live on the Station, content with Havo's will but remaining apart from Terra. I felt it was Havo's will to bring the Station back home."

"And you persuaded the entire Station, or at least its leaders, to do so?"

I nod.

"You are truly a gift from Havo, my daughter. You have done well. "

"Lux Aduro," Alaric interjects, "Cassiopeia's desire is to share the existence of our station with the World."

"Well, of course! The whole World will be overjoyed. Terra and the Church welcome home its sons and daughters—Havian and non-Havian alike. Please come down to the surface as you wish, where you wish, when you wish. I will immediately begin preparations for a Worldwide celebration in your honor. I do invite you all to attend in Roma, shall we say in three days' time?"

"Oh, Father, that is not necessary—"

"But it is! A discovery, and a return, of this magnitude must be celebrated. And to the non-Havians aboard the Station, I wish to say: if you have been taught that the Church is your enemy, you have been misled. We will never harm Havo's creatures. We are delighted you have come home, and we hope to embrace you in person soon. Please come to us. The old war is over."

I look over to Alaric and Gabrielus as if to say, "See?" Their expressions, however, are less trusting.

"Cassiopeia Ovatio, I would like to address you personally."

"Yes, Father?"

"Every year our faith is tested by the Offering. Every year, I confess, in my heart of hearts, I hope and pray will be the year that our father Havo's mercy will end the need for our sacrifices. I further confess that your return has brought me the greatest joy I have felt in my life—Havo's will has included the return of Offerings and our long-lost brethren of Station Michael at last, unlooked for but more welcome than I could express.

"Our hearts grieve every year at having to send Offerings to Havo. It is clear that Havo works in mysterious ways, and it is equally clear that Havo did not wish you and those with you to be Offered, though He did welcome others to his bosom. He had a different purpose for you, my child. We are as surprised as can be expected that this should be the case, but we do not question His wisdom. We accept and celebrate it gratefully, as we do all his other blessings. Havo be praised!"

"Havo be praised!" I say and begin to cry.

"We will do anything in our power to assist," Our Father adds. "I will have our space agency coordinate with you, Alaric Vorenus."

"Thank you, sir," Alaric says.

"You are most welcome."

"We will communicate with you again soon."

"Very good. May Havo's light shine upon you, Cassiopeia Ovatio."

"May Havo's light shine upon you," I say.

Alaric nods.

The screen goes dark.

Space agency? I think. *I did not know the Church has a space agency.*

Someone claps. "Woo hoo! We made it home!"

My church did not disappoint me, but I still have questions. Now is not the time. Soon.

From that moment, the air in the Station is one of cautious optimism. Even the hardest opponents of the church hold their tongues, if only because they know they are outnumbered, and because we are receiving a much different welcome from the one they expected and feared. I am proud of my church and hold my head high as I walk through the corridors, Alaric's son Pallium or one of his subordinates close at hand at all times just in case. I feel our time of trial is at an end. I feel Father's wisdom will usher in a new age of harmonious relations, a new era of peace and light on Terra. This is the sign we have all sought of Havo's renewed love. Any apostates remaining on Terra will now feel safer, more loved, and I hope they will feel moved to share their views, that understanding might be promoted across the Globe. I hope they will come out of the shadows.

The time I have passed on this station has been short in the scheme of things, but it also feels long and eventful. A part of me can hardly believe I am coming home. I expected never to see Terra again. I remember Jinx and wish she were here with me, but all paths to Havo are different, and each of us must walk her or his own path alone. I hope she did not suffer long before the merciful heat put her to sleep. I am eager to see my father again. I hope he has been told already. He must have been. The whole World must have been.

The entire station bustles with activity. In the small office behind the command bridge, Alaric and Gabrielus try to anticipate every possible contingency. Then Alaric startles me.

"Cassiopeia, I want you to understand it is most likely a trap."

"A trap!"

"Yes, a trap. You can't possibly expect them to be glad to see us."

He can see in my face that I do.

"Cassiopeia, the Church ordered you to die. The Church sentenced nonbelievers to death for crimes against the Church. You have already confessed to them that you disobeyed and thwarted those orders. Your blind faith almost got you killed once, and we rescued you. This time it endangers us—and we may not be able to save you a second time."

"It was your decision to take us here."

"And I stand by that decision. But I will not fail to take precautions. Unlike you, I know all too well what the Church is and does."

"You wanted me to learn about the Inopia if possible," I say. "Your plan all along was to deceive the Havican and Our Father—and I agreed with it! And now you are worried about a trap? What if it *is* a trap? What are you going to do differently?"

"Send only Havians—for now."

"Will Octavius be allowed to come with me?"

"If he wishes. He is your husband."

"Don't you think those sent into Space against their wills would like to return?"

"I'm not sure, actually. Regardless, I will protect their safety above all. For now, non-Havians stay aboard while you conduct your mission of peace."

"And that is your choice, as Father has said. You are under no obligation to come down. You can stay up here and rot in Space as you have been doing for years. I fail to see how you are being trapped."

"Gabrielus believes you can unite us. I see you're off to a good start. You can continue your work on the planet below tomorrow."

"How will we go down?"

"We do have a few shuttles," Gabrielus says, "but Your Father, Lux, has graciously offered—no pun intended—a transport vessel, which will arrive here tomorrow." His use of "Your" pains me, but at least the two groups are interacting without bloodshed.

"From the space agency," I say.

"Apparently. It will be large enough to accommodate all Havians aboard—almost a third of us. It will be a little lonely around here, I admit."

"Will you go back to Terra?" I ask Gabrielus.

"I am not sure. It is far from safe."

I am sorry I asked.

At dinner, Mattheus says, "So! You bring us back to Terra, you get to talk with Our Father—I think next they'll make you a saint. Maybe the Saint of Bringing Back Space Stations."

I look at him with what my father called a dead face.

"Aw, come on. You've done what no one else has done before."

"I think the Church was on the verge of finding the Station without my help—I have been told this here. All I have done is speed things along. Our Father and Alaric have wisely decided to avert conflict, and I am grateful to them."

"Spoken like a true diplomat. You should go into government."

"I just want to go back to Soul River and be left alone."

"Good luck with that," Mattheus says, but I see no reason for his jest. "At the very least, you will be famous."

"I suppose there will be an undue amount of attention, for a time, but that will subside."

"Do not listen to him," Iulia says. "He's just jealous of your new status. He wants to be the center of attention."

"I am nothing more than a servant of Havo."

"Uh huh," Mattheus says. "You know how to be in the right place at the right time. I wish I had that talent."

"Mattheus, stop," Iulia says, tapping his arm.

In an attempt to change the subject, I ask, "Will you be joining us in the hangar tomorrow, to welcome the Church delegation?"

"Yes, we are," Iulia says.

"We are going back down too," Mattheus says.

I nod, pleased.

"Will you resettle where you were before?" I ask.

"Yes, we will go back to our family, or try to find what is left of it," Mattheus says. "It is been a while since we've been gone. They do not even know about her." He indicates Livia. "Plus, I am excited to see the city again."

I know he means Roma, the Heart of Havo. Having never been there, I am intimidated by it. Always I felt unworthy.

"Will you return with me?"

"Am I your husband?" He smiles. "Where you go, I go. Am I afraid of the Church? Yes. But I have a very powerful ally in you."

I smile. "Not so powerful."

"Yes."

"I will miss this place."

"You will be glad to be back home again."

"You were here three years before I came. You are tired of it."

"I am. It is old, cold, and smelly."

"But to me it is still new, and it is where I found love—again."

"Soon enough you would have been ready for a change."

"Of scenery, or of love?'

"Both." He laughs and embraces me.

"I am just happy to be with you," I say.

"As I am with you--even if that means staying on the Station forever."

"At least the Station brought us together again."

"That it did," he says, then kisses me.

"Or maybe that was the Church."

"Havo works in mysterious ways."

We kiss more passionately.

The Station council and I stand in a hangar observation deck, enclosed in glass. The hangar doors are open, and we await the arrival of the Church transport ship, which the Church has told us will be large enough to take down as many as a hundred residents of the Station—all Havians aboard. I cannot help thinking of my arrival in this hangar almost five months before. I stand patiently in my Havian robes. I notice that though the other council members are not Havian, they have dressed more formally for the occasion, wearing dark blue dress uniforms that must not have been worn for generations. I wonder if the uniforms came from the museum.

"Station Michael, this is Terra One on our approach."

"Roger, Terra One," Alaric says into a microphone. "You are clear."

The vessel comes into view through the large opening created by the absence of the hangar doors, a vessel looking like nothing more than a large dolphin or porpoise. It moves slowly but gracefully, and I begin to wonder if it will fit through the doors until it glides through perfectly. I notice myself holding my breath and look to see others doing the same. I smile slightly to myself.

The ship, modern in its design and appearance, comes to rest on the hangar floor, large hydraulic metal legs supporting it in the Station gravity. The hangar doors close slowly behind the ship, the sight of which enables me better to understand our excruciating wait five months ago.

"And now, to welcome our visitors," Alaric says to us all when the doors have shut and air begins to fill the hangar. We come out of the observation deck, down three short steps onto the flight deck, where we approach the transport vessel and line up. A door on the vessel's exterior begins to open, and we watch as young crewmembers come into view, lower a ladder, and disembark.

"Welcome to Station Michael," Alaric says, extending his hand to the first young man down the ladder. "I am Alaric Vorenus."

"Thank you," the young man says. "Bertramus Minicius, Captain of Terra One. We are honored to be here." He looks about him. "They teach in school this station was destroyed."

"It was lost to Terra," Alaric says, "but we are all very much alive, I assure you." Alaric smiles and indicates our party. "This is our leadership council. How much time do you have before you are due back?"

"Our orders are to pick up as many as wish to return to Terra with us on this trip," Bertramus Minicius says, "but I have not been given a deadline for our return. We are at your service." It is clear to me this young man is fascinated by the Station. "I could pass days exploring this station."

"I am sure that is true, but we do not wish to delay you. We have many residents who wish to visit Terra, most of them for the first time."

Despite his history textbooks, Bertramus Minicius seems surprised.

"Most of us were born and raised on this station and have only heard of Terra in stories," Alaric adds.

"I see."

"I will give the word for them to commence boarding."

"Very good. We will assist as needed." Bertramus turns and instructs his crew to facilitate boarding. They begin opening external compartments to store possessions.

"I would very much enjoy a tour of your station," Bertramus tells Alaric."

"Perhaps on your next visit," Alaric says.

"And this is Cassiopeia Ovatio?" the young captain stops and turns to me.

"It is," Alaric says.

"How do you do?" I ask.

"I do well," Bertramus says. "Will you be joining us back to Terra?"

"Yes, of course," I say.

"Our Father asked me to make certain," Bertramus says. "You are to be the Havican's most honored guest."

"Honor Havo," I say.

"We honor Havo by honoring his instrument."

"We are all instruments of Havo, whether we know it or not."

Alaric gives me a look to remind me of my duty.

"I am sorry; forgive me, Bertramus Marcinius. I am not used to such attentions."

Bertramus Marcinius laughs. "I suggest that you steel yourself. The whole World speaks of nothing but you. Above all, your father was overjoyed to learn of your survival. He awaits you below."

"I am eager to see him again, Havo be praised. I understand we are also in time for Paternalia."

"Yes," he says. "Why?"

"I must honor my mother."

"Ah."

I miss both my mother and my father. I want to go home, with Octavius, to start our new life together. Most of all, I wish everything could be as it was before, with Octavius added. I know my fanciful dreams are impossible and chide myself for even making wishes.

The Havians come, with their belongings packed, and everything is loaded aboard. I bid the council a temporary farewell.

"Thank you, Alaric," I say.

He nods. I can see that he remains deeply skeptical.

"I hope to see nonHavians on Terra soon," say.

He says nothing.

I turn to Pallium. "Thank you for watching over me," I say. "I think I will be safe now."

"I asked to go down with you," he says. "Alaric said no."

"Why would you ask that?"

"I think you will be in greater danger than before." I do not understand this.

"I will be among Havians."

He says nothing.

I do not relate to Pallium as a person, but I will miss him. His presence has been one of the few constants in my life on the Station.

Sixty-eight residents of the Station have elected to return to Terra in Terra One. Octavius and I climb the short ladder. I am struck by the difference between this ship and the *Messenger*. Where the *Messenger* was tiny and cramped, this vessel is large and spacious. We wait as everyone boards and luggage is stowed, but we are content.

"I never thought I'd see Terra again," Octavius says. "You really have changed everything."

"I have changed nothing," I say. "Havo changes everything."

The ship reminds me of the airplane in which I rode as a little girl, with rows of seats and windows. I cannot help but wonder at its purpose. Is the Church planning to colonize the Moon and offer vacations?

Octavius sits to my left, I sit next to a window. We wait for the launch, and I consider my joy at returning home to my father and my world. Soon the ship's engines come to life and lift it off the hangar floor. Most passengers carry on quiet conversations with their immediate neighbors. I hold Octavius' hand and look out my window.

When our vessel emerges from the Station, the sight of Terra fills my heart with awe and joy. There are no words to describe the sight or sensations we experience. We soon land outside Roma, on a giant platform, where a large group of Havians receives us. We leave the ship and walk to some small buildings near the landing pad. I notice Octavius and I are given unspoken deference.

When we reach the first small building, a small woman, stooped with age and surrounded by assistants, greets us at the first door. "Welcome home, welcome. I am Lavinia, secretary to His Holiness." I bow my head. "Welcome, Cassiopeia Ovatio," she says. I look up at her. "I will show you all to your new lodging, as you rest and prepare for the rest of your journey."

She leads us to a silver tram, which we board for a short ride to the Havican. Lavinia joins Octavius and me in the same tram car. "We could not be more delighted—the whole World is in a tizzy, my dear," she says.

"I did not mean to cause any of this," I say.

"In some sense, you did not cause it. In another, you did. Praise Havo."

"Praise Havo," I say.

The ride is short, and we disembark underneath the Havican.

I feel lighter and lighter, filled with joy. Havo has brought Station Michael and me home to serve an unexpected purpose. I am eager and happy to serve His will in any way He sees fit, and we are to meet Lux Aduro, Our Father. I confess I feel some awe at this. Our Father is Our Sun's primary representative on Terra. We are all His Rays, but Our Father has always been the Ray first in prominence in my heart—in the hearts of all Havians.

We leave the train, go up stairs into the ground floor, and follow our guides to luxurious suites, where we are bathed, clothed in new robes, given time to rest, then taken to a magnificent dining hall for supper. One long table sits on a dais. Several others sit below perpendicular to the dais and its table.

"Please, here," an attendant says to Octavius and me. She leads us to the center of the dais table, overlooking the rest. "Right here." Octavius sits to my right. Everyone else sits below.

Our Father arrives, attended by Lavinia and other servants. All the Havians already seated stand without a thought, but Our Father raises his hands to quiet us. "My children, please remain seated. We will not stand on ceremony for such distinguished guests. Our hearts are too full of joy to require formality." He sits, to my astonishment, to my left! Other Church leaders fill the rest of our table, all facing the large audience. I spot Mattheus, Iulia, and Livia at one nearby table, Klarcia at another.

"Friends," Our Father says and everyone else falls silent. "Tonight might be the greatest occasion of our lives. An ancient prophet said there is no providence in the fall of a sparrow, but there is, and there is even greater providence in the return of our beloved Offerings via the station we all thought lost. Havo has heard our prayers and answered us in a way we could never have dreamed!

"In this return, of our Offerings and our long-lost Station Michael, I see a sign that Havo will soon be ending the punishment we have long endured, the punishment of the lack of children's laughter and voices across our world.

"In the coming days, I will be praying and reflecting with our Offerings, and their families who might never have set foot on Terra before, on their experiences. I will seek guidance above all from Havo on our best course forward. In the mean time, I welcome you all and bid you dine well. You are home, and you are loved.

"Before we dine, a short prayer. I have thought these past days over what prayer would be most appropriate to welcome you back. I have thought healing and joy, of course, but it seemed to me the most primal and basic feeling is one of love. Let us express our love for Havo, for our world that Havia and He have given us, and for each other here tonight, thankful as we are beyond hope or measure that you have all returned to us per His wisdom. Let us pray." Our Father bows his head.

"O, My Sun, I love you above all things, with my whole heart and soul, because you are all-good and worthy of all love. I love my neighbor as myself for the love of you. I forgive all who have injured me and ask pardon of all whom I have injured. Amen."

"Amen," we all say. This is the church I have loved with all my heart. This is the love I expect from my church. I am filled with love, joy, and hope for our mutual future.

Our Father sits and comments to me, "As we give thanks to Havo, we must also give thanks to Him for making you His instrument. The whole World is delighted."

I nod.

"But most especially your father, of course. He is waiting without. I wanted our first welcome to be for those who returned only. Afterward family will join us all."

"Of course," I say, appreciating the solemnity of the occasion and his desire to honor Havo directly, privately, first.

However, I am bursting to mention Concordia and the others sentenced to death. Instead I decide I I will wait until we may speak freely. I decide to discuss the apostates on the Station.

"Father," I say, "before I left Terra I had heard stories of apostates— the same old stories we all hear in school—, but I did not believe any existed. I must confess myself surprised and amazed to have met them."

"And to live among them!" Our Father says. "How was this experience for you—not too challenging, I hope? I note they honored Havo's will and yours by bringing you home to us."

"I came to see them as children of Havo who simply have not found His light yet."

"Well put!" Our Father says. "Cassiopeia Ovatio, you have expressed Havo's love perfectly. It is clear that Havo has a purpose for all His children. He spared them and you for a reason, and we can only rejoice to honor His will—and to express our gratitude that even they were touched by it. Such is the power of Havo. That said, I too must confess to having felt great surprise when you all appeared on our instruments." Our Father chuckled. "We will divine His larger will together, you and I."

"I, Father?"

"It is equally clear to me that you were Our Sun's most powerful and significant instrument in this time of change. I would be remiss in my duties if I did not acknowledge that to the extent of relying on your counsel as I plan my next acts as Father of Us All."

I find it hard to eat my supper. I am in shock. It is clear I will be given the opportunity to speak privately with Our Father soon.

Part Two:

Globus Ignis

[EDITED TO HERE as of September 28, 2016.]

"Two hundred years ago, before this church was even created, scientists discovered that our species was reduced to as few as seventy members millennia ago before rebounding. This explains much of our genetic makeup, why we suffer diseases and deformities, why some of us resemble each other more than one would expect from a species of a billion members. There is only a certain number of combinations. We are limited."

I wonder why she is telling me this.

"This itself, as a scientific curiosity, is a shame. We are fated to be limited and flawed, and that would have been the end of the matter, other than medicine trying to cure our ailments—cancer and so forth. But then, as a matter of control . . . "

I catch her eye.

"Someone realized that with so few combinations, and with our genome mapped, we could activate—or suppress—the genes and processes required for conception and childbirth."

I feel a creeping horror at the edge of my consciousness.

"The Church learned how to switch off childbearing.   We can decide when a woman will conceive a child and carry it to term."

"You mean . . . ?"

"There is no Worldwide infertility problem," the woman says.   "No Inopia.   There is the Church ruling with science and fear."

Deleted Scenes

At first I had Cassiopeia, vulnerable from her ordeals, welcome Octavius into her bed at the first opportunity. Then I decided that was not what she would do. Here is the scene as originally written:

"We should not have done that," I say.

"Why?" he asks.

"It is against the will of Havo."

"How do you know what is against the will of Havo?"

I am shocked by this question. I look at him, upset.

"We all know the will of Havo!" I say.

"Do we?"

"Havo says no intimacy before marriage."

Octavius steps toward me, flushed and eager.

"Has He said that to you personally?" he demands.

I do not answer at first. Then I say, "We all know *The Book of Havo.*"

"I do not believe the *The Book of Havo*," Octavius says.

Can it be that Octavius has become an apostate?

"What have they done to you?" I ask.

"Nothing," he says. "I am sorry I troubled you." He turns to go.

"No," I say. "I want you here."

He stops and turns back toward me.

I place my arms around his neck and kiss him, this time more passionately.

The rest is for Octavius and me alone.

At first I had Our Father reject the Station from the outset. Here is the scene and beyond as originally written:

"I am told this is the commandeered station Michael taken from us one hundred and thirty-seven, one hundred and thirty-eight years ago," Our Father says.

"Greetings," Alaric says. "That is correct."

"Why are you here?"

"We are here—"

I interrupt Alaric.

"It is my doing, Father," I say. Our Father squints and focuses on me. "Cassiopeia Ovatio, Father. I was on the *Messenger* this past summer."

Our Father's eyes widen.

"You are supposed to be with Havo!"

"The men and women on this station intervened," I say.

"And you did not resist them?"

"Every year they detain the Offering ship," I say. "Every year they offer the Offerings a choice."

"And you chose to stay with them?"

I struggle to respond.

"I did. I thought Terra would want to see and know the truth of this station."

Our Father sits silently, fuming in a way I have not seen before.

"I am disappointed," Father says. "Of all last year's Offerings, you struck me as the most devout. I can see now that even I am not infallible. Tertia Cassiopeia Ovatio Noli, I hereby excommunicate you from the life and love of Havo and His Church for apostasy, and I sentence you all to death for crimes against Terra, against Havo, and against His Holy Church."

I faint.

I wake in the small conference room near the bridge, alone. I rise and find my way out the door to the corridor. Pallium, surprised, rushes to me.

"Where are you going?" he asks.

"To assist."

"There is nothing we can do."

"Out of my way."

He stands aside, and I open the bridge door to a scene of silence.

"What is happening?" I ask.

"Cassiopeia," Alaric says. "Come here." I go to him. "Stand here and get ready." He nods to Mattheus.

"Get ready for what?"

"To address Terra. Mattheus's found a way to tap into the Worldwide media network."

"With your buddy Concordia's help," Mattheus jests. When I glare at him, he adds, "Hey, her cell had the most recent information on the system infrastructure."

I do not have time to think anything except I am glad I no longer wear the eye patch and Octavius said I look fine without it. The people of Terra will not know I can only see out my right eye if I pretend.

"Okay, you are on," Mattheus says. "No pressure." He smiles his usual rakish smile.

I do not see anything on the screen. I look at Mattheus, who fusses with some buttons. "There," he says. The Planet Terra comes on the screen.

"People of Terra," I say. "I am Tertia Cassiopeia Ovatio Noli." I think of my father, who must be watching this along with everyone else, and my dead mother. I hope she would be proud of me now. I clear my throat and continue: "I was sent to meet Havo last summer. Instead I met these persons around me now, the persons of Station Michael. We were told this station was lost, destroyed, in the war that led to the Day. That was not true. We were told that apostates no longer existed. That was not true. What is true is they not only exist but are routinely sentenced to death on our world. Four of the Offerings on my ship were apostates sentenced to death. Were they meant to greet Havo? No, they were meant to die. Our church does not practice the love that it preaches. We have always been told that all Offerings were willing. That too was a lie. I myself, just a short time ago, was excommunicated and sentenced to death by Our Father. All for telling the truth and bringing it to you. Right now, as I speak to you, the Church is attempting to destroy us all, to commit murder, by shooting us out of the Sky. Is this the way Havians react to the truth? Is our faith so weak we cannot tolerate Havo's truth? Remember, that which is true is Havo's truth. That which is false is . . . the work of Scar. On this station, I have seen evidence to suggest that the Church's version of the War of Day is not accurate, and if the Church lies about one thing, such as this station, about what else might not it be lying? We need the truth for the good of all, so I call upon all Havians of good will to work for the truth and reconciliation. Question the church; demand the truth; and please help us to return home to our families and friends that we may examine the record with you. We do not wish to die for lies, or to preserve the power of liars. Our Father does not practice the love and forgiveness that he preaches, and I am proof of this. Havo be praised, and peace be with you." I bow my head.

"Okay, you are off," Mattheus says. The bridge falls silent again.

"Thank you, Cassiopeia," Alaric says. "We do not know how they will respond. Right now I would like to make sure you are safe. Pallium, please take her to the bottom of the Ball." I do not know what this means.

"Havo will protect me," I say. Those nearest to us look up. I cannot tell if they think me courageous or foolhardy.

"It is times like this that I question the sanity of Havians," Alaric says. "Besides, Havo's main guy just kicked you out of Havo's house. Aren't you with Scar now?"

"I am a follower of Havo," I say, but I can see this will not persuade him to let me stay.

"Regardless, we all just heard Our Father sentence you to death, which means that finally, fully, and firmly you are on our side, and I will make sure that everyone on this station hears it."

"Our Father is fallible."

"Fallible or not, no one will doubt you any longer."

"I appreciate that, but I would prefer that each person judge me on my own merits." I do not consider myself to be on any "side" but that of Havo and truth, but I understand what he means. I may be safer now among the apostates than I am among the vast majority of Terra.

"Your words and deeds have consequences. Those consequences help define you. Now please find safety. Pallium?"

"I do not want to hide when I might be useful."

"I respect that, and if we need you, we will send for you. You have already served well, Cassiopeia Ovatio, and I want you alive in case you are needed again." I appreciate this and nod my assent. I understand that he is right. Our Father sentenced us all to death, which means that none of us is safe, and an attack could come at any time. I also understand my value to the Station residents and their—my—allies on Terra.

"What are you going to do?" I ask.

"Well, we hope they will invite us for tea, but if they do not, I need to defend this station, and things could become dangerous."

"We cannot fire upon Havians," I say. "Promise me you will not."

"Cassiopeia, if we are fired upon, we will have to defend ourselves," Alaric says. "And if we are fired upon, we will only return fire to the installations attacking us, not civilians."

I suppose I do not have the right to tell them everything they may do. I acquiesce and step back. The crew of the entire Station is working to keep us alive. I feel useless.

"Father, why have they taken no action?" Pallium asks. The bridge is quiet with tension.

"I do not know, but it worries me, and that is why I want you away from here. The bridge would be their first target. Now go, my son."

We withdraw quickly to the corridor.

"What is the bottom of the Ball?" I ask him as we turn to hurry.

"The most secret part of the Station, the one part you have not seen."

"That is true."

"Most of us here have not seen it."

I suppose they refer to the central ball of Command and Engineering, where we are. Pallium takes me from the "top" of the ball, Command, through Engineering, to the "bottom", the other side. Along the way I insist on finding Octavius, who works in Engineering.

"You heard Alaric," Pallium says.

"Now hear me," I say. "I will not go further until I see my husband. And what is at the bottom of the Ball, anyway?"

"A shuttle."

"A shuttle?" Alaric is trying to keep me safe in case anything happens to the Station. That means he is at least allowing for the possibility that the Station might be destroyed. "How large is this shuttle?" I ask.

"It can seat four."

We pass down through Engineering. Men and women are busy working at consoles. I spot Octavius and run to him, my robes attracting attention.

"What are you doing here?" Octavius asks.

"They're sending me to a secret shuttle in case we lose the Station."

He gulps.

"I want you to come with me."

He looks at Pallium.

"Cassie, my orders and my place are here. I can do the most good here. What if my presence means the difference between success and failure?"

"I do not think it will. Come with me. I cannot bear to lose you . . . again."

Octavius is torn, but he nods. "I must notify my superior."

"There is no time," Pallium says. "We have already delayed too long."

I spy Concordia at the other end of the area. She does not see me. I approach her. "Concordia." She looks up from a schematic diagram in puzzlement and dismay.

"What are you doing here?"

"Come with us. Alaric' order."

"All . . . right."

I lead her back to Pallium and Octavius. I give Pallium a look that says, "Do not object."

"Are we ready?" Pallium asks.

"Yes."

He leads us out of the work area to a corridor and an unmarked door. He produces a key and unlocks it with a rusty grind. The door has evidently not been opened for a long time.

"This has not been used . . . before," Pallium says.

"What hasn't?" Concordia asks.

"Follow us," Pallium says.

The door opens to stairs downward, with dim lights in metal cages every three meters or so. Some of the lights are not working, making the staircase gloomier than it was intended to be. I note the silence of the staircase after Octavius closes the door behind us all. I hear only our steps and my own breaths as we go down.

I feel grateful to Pallium for telling me the nature of the safe place. If he had not, I would feel alone and torn now.

We reach a door at the bottom of the stairs, and Pallium opens it. We emerge to see a small shuttle parked at a small dock, with doors that open upward, doors that also serve as additional windows, next to the two front windows across the nose. The rest of the craft is rounded and resembles an insect, a ladybug.

"What is this?" Concordia asks.

"It looks like a ladybug," Octavius says.

"This is us being safe," I say.

Pallium opens the near door and waits for us to board. I look around the hangar. Bare girders, old lights, and a desk built into the wall covered with papers. I wonder what the papers contain, but Pallium calls for me to enter, so I do. He comes in behind us and assumes the pilot's seat. Concordia, I notice, has assumed the co-pilot's seat. This is probably the best choice.

"So Alaric wants to protect our excommunicated ambassador?" Concordia asks. Even Pallium seems surprised by this question.

"How did you know about that?" I ask.

"Mattheus piped your exchange through the whole station, as he told me he would," Concordia says.

I look at Octavius for confirmation, and he nods grimly. At least Alaric will not have much notifying to do.

"So were just supposed to sit here?" Concordia asks.

Pallium nods. "In case."

"In case we need to run away from our friends and loved ones? And why did Alaric want *me* to come along?"

"He . . . must have thought we could use your technical expertise, your connections on the surface," I say. Concordia sees through my lie.

"You! You lied to me! Why did you lie?"

"I am sorry," I say. "You do not have to come. I just . . . "

"You just what?"

"I consider you a friend."

"A friend who does not share your belief in Havo?"

"My father used to say he did not trust anyone until that person disagreed with him."

Concordia sits back in a feeling I cannot read.

"You trust me?"

"I do."

"Let me guess: you think Havo put me in your life for a reason?"

"I think everything happens in accord with Havo's will."

"Of course you do."

"But you know this. Why ask again?"

"Because I can hardly believe it."

"So when you doubt something you ask the same question again?"

"When I find something hard to believe I poke and prod it to find out if it is real and true."

"It is," I say with resolve.

We sit in the shuttle silent for a time. I wonder when we will know it is safe to return to the bridge. I also wonder when we would know if it were not. I also wonder if Pallium knows how to launch the shuttle from the Station, let alone fly it.

Until now I have seen the Church as my warmth, my light, my comfort. Now I feel an emptiness as I have not felt an emptiness before. Thankfully, I still feel Havo's love and warmth inside me, but this only tells me that something is wrong. Our church has lost its way. I have not left the Church—the Church has left me, and a part of me cannot even believe what I have seen with my own eyes and heard with my own ears, as it makes less sense than something out of a child's nightmare.

Before, the church was my communion. Now the church has turned against me. I can hear my father saying, "Be your own communion." But in my heart, I know that Havo does not disagree with me. In my heart, I know that Our Father is . . . wrong. In my heart, I feel renewed strength and uplifted. I feel Havo's love, my father's, and Octavius's.

And though I am still not afraid to die, I do not believe Havo wishes me to die for seeking or promoting the truth. It is that inescapable feeling that has motivated me from the moment Station Michael intervened in our fate. It became obvious in that moment, I realize now, that Havo has a plan for me that is larger than I know, as He has a plan for everyone. It is my duty, nothing more, to learn what that plan may be, to the best of my limited ability, to act upon that plan, and to prove worthy of it.

I am here, my Sun, to do your will.

Up on the bridge, Alaric, Gabrielus, Mattheus, and the others sit, watch, and wait. "They cannot let us alone for long, having sentenced us all to death," Alaric says. "They also cannot let the world know any more f what is happening. They'll probably try to pretend Cassiopeia's broadcast did not exist."

"That is what they're doing," Mattheus says, listening to an ear piece. "It is all the usual about the winter weather and the coming spring festival. 'Havo returns', as He returns every year."

"I thought you were a believer," Alaric says.

"I am a believer, but some of that stuff is ridiculous," Mattheus says.

"They cannot have anything they could shoot at us this high, could they?" Alaric asked aloud.

"Missiles," Gabrielus says. "But they could have had those ready days ago."

It is then that the men and women of the bridge crew begin to notice small shapes in the Terran atmosphere. "Picking something up," one of the young men on the bridge says.

"Yes," Alaric says.

"Ships."

We sit in the shuttle for what seems an interminable amount of time. We buckle our seat belts in case. Pallium seems to know how to start and fly the shuttle Concordia cannot help examining its instruments and admiring its technology. I cannot help smiling. Octavius and I hold hands.

We do not hear anything. We see only the inside of the hangar.

"We might be able to contact the bridge," Pallium says, "but we will have to turn it on first." He looks at the rest of us. "Do we want to do that?"

Octavius and I nod. Concordia seems not to care.

Pallium begins flicking switches. The interior and console lights come on. "All right. We do not need to fire the engines. Hello, bridge? Come in bridge."

"Pallium!" We hear Alaric' voice. He sounds anguished. "We are under attack! Stay where you are!"

Just then we lose communication, as we lose the hangar doors below us and find ourselves being thrown out into Space in a spray of metal, debris, and papers from the desk.

"Ah!" I cry. I hear a loud noise on the hull of the ship.

"Engines!" Pallium cries, manipulating controls. Concordia tries to help. We are spinning out of control, Terra filling the windows and not at different moments. The engines come on. The lack of gravity in the shuttle has prevented me from feeling dizzy, but I am grateful for the stabilization of the shuttle.

"Where do we go? How do we get back?" I cry.

"Terra," Concordia says.

"Terra?"

"And that is if we make it: look."

We all see small shuttle craft firing on the Station and being fired upon in turn from the Station. We see holes in numerous places and debris floating, including bodies. I gasp.

"We cannot go back to the hangar," Pallium says. "Even if we could dock, it no longer contains air."

I realize he is right.

"There is the main hangar bay," I suddenly remember.

"They wouldn't open it during a battle," Octavius says. "Besides, the whole point was to get you off the Station."

I realize he is right.

"Terra," I say.

Pallium and Concordia begin to pilot us down to the Planet.

"Where on Terra?" I ask.

"First let's get past these fighters," Pallium says. "Right now I think they have not noticed us. They might think we are debris. But we do not have weapons. We need to get out of here."

We begin our course straight away from the Station. "We are being followed," Concordia reports. On a small screen in front of her, a line goes around in a circle. Each time the line goes around, it strikes a small dot near the center. "That is a ship following us—and gaining," Concordia says.

"How do you know we do not have weapons?" Octavius asks.

"This ship was built in secret," Pallium says. "The weapons department was not involved. The idea was to keep the secret. On the bright side, it is lighter and faster than most ships out there—and we know our opponents have weapons systems that will slow them down. Unless, of course, their engines are more powerful." He pauses. "Sorry I cannot be more helpful than that."

I grip Octavius's hand more tightly.

A laser blast goes past our windows.

"A laser!" I exclaim. "They abuse Havo's powers!"

"What else is new?" Concordia asks under her breath.

"Light is the province of Havo! We may burn candles and electric lights! The Church disavows lasers!"

"The Church lies," Octavius says.

"The Church doesn't . . . " I say, then stop. The Church lies. Those are lasers. The Church is attempting to kill every man, woman, and child on Station Michael. For the briefest of moments, I consider the possibility this is all an elaborate trick, that the ships are not Havian, but this defies all logic. Pallium changes the ship's course frequently to avoid laser fire, but I fear we will be hit soon.

"How can they do this?" I ask no one in particular.

"It is what they do," Concordia says from in front of me. "You've been living in a bubble, dear."

Her words sting me, and yet I seem to like it, her words stinging me, I seek it out enough. She tells the truth as she sees it, and I find this strangely refreshing. As much as her words pain me, I find they strengthen me too.

"We have to get away from them," I say.

"Obvious, but the first sensible thing you have said in a while," Concordia cracks.

I look at Octavius. "I love you," I say.

"I love you," he says.

"This is not at all what I envisioned for my life—or death," I say.

"They'll get us down," Octavius says.

I note the laser fire seems to be missing more and more. "Why is that?" I ask.

"We are getting farther away," Pallium explains. "We are faster."

I relax slightly, but my thoughts return to the profanity of abusing Havo's light. *They cannot do this.*

"I do not suppose anyone's thought of this, but was this craft designed for entering an atmosphere?" Concordia asks.

Pallium looks up. "I do not know," he says.

"We certainly do not know," I say, looking to Octavius for confirmation.

"Well, we have two choices: turn around and go back to the Station, or test the friction tolerance on this thing."

"Clearly, the wise thing to do is turn around," I say. "We can outrun the enemy ships and make it into the hangar."

"If they open it," Concordia says.

"If we ask them to do so."

"Station Michael," Pallium says over the radio. "Come in, Station Michael."

"Pallium?" we hear Alaric say. "Where are you?"

"We got blown out of the Station. We are all right. Permission to come back aboard in the main hangar."

"No! Stay away. It is not safe. I am sending out Michael One as a precaution."

"Michael One? A precaution? It is not safe out here! Can that thing even fly?"

"Rom, trust your father."

"Father, this is madness! Do not send it out. But keep the hangar doors open. Were coming back."

Pallium waits for an answer but receives none. He looks to us.

"Turn us around," I say to Pallium. Octavius nods.

Concordia grudgingly nods as well.

Pallium turns our ladybug shuttle about.

"What is this Michael One?" Concordia asks.

"The second Offering ship, the first one saved. We've kept as a museum and educational tool. It hasn't flown as long as I have been alive. I cannot even believe he would do that. Why—?"

We see explosions across the Station, then its rupture into two halves. The Ball falls free, its struts cracking and tearing. Human beings blow out into Space from the Ring and the struts, human beings we cannot save. Debris fills our field of vision, debris and Church ships still firing. The large pieces of the Station begin drifting in orbit. There is no doubt in my mind there are living persons trapped on those large sections. My mind and heart are filled with overwhelming pain, anguish, and horror. I think of the children. I think of the Church that did this. No one speaks for several moments, after which I remember what we had discussed moments before.

"What about the ship Alaric mentioned?" I ask desperately.

"Pray for it," Concordia snaps.

Pallium grabs his little hand-held microphone.

"Michael One, this is Pallium. Michael One, this is Pallium. Come in. Michael One, are you outside the Station?"

No answer.

"It looks as if they did not make it," Concordia says. "Still think coming back was a good idea?"

She is right. These deaths are on my conscience. These good men, women, and children—yes, good, all of them—died for me. And for an idea. The idea of justice. I must give it to them.

I let go of Octavius's hand for a moment and order Pallium in a shaky voice, "Take us down to Terra. This is a shuttle, and it looks fancier than anything else in the Station. I am guessing it was made by the Church to take the heat of re-entry. Let's find out."

"Are you crazy?" Concordia asks.

"Have a little faith," I say. "Besides, what choice do we have?"

Silence.

I think of Havo testing us.

"Michael One," Pallium says slowly, "this is Pallium. If you can hear us, we are going down to Terra. If you can, follow us."

I was going to ask about the photograph I saw, but I have just seen the Church murder a thousand souls, Havian and non-Havian alike. I suffer no doubt; I have seen this with my own eyes. Our Father on Terra ordered this, intending to kill me as well. If he finds me, he will kill me. Realizing the idea will not be easy.

He must not find me.

"Concordia, when we get down there . . . " I begin.

"Let's worry about burning up first," Concordia says. "Pallium here is a skilled pilot. He's going to try to bring us down slowly and gradually. If we get down, then you can ask your question."

I press Octavius's hand, sad it is all I can do.

"Crossing Kármán line," Pallium says to Concordia. "We should be feeling some turbulence soon."

No sooner has he said this than we begin to bounce in our seats, pressing hard against our straps and belts. I do not know how Pallium and Concordia can focus their eyes on the controls, everything is so blurry from jarring back and forth, up and down.

"Slower," Concordia says.

Pallium does not respond with words but slows the speed of the craft. I study the ceiling, the walls. They seem strong yet light. Truth be told, the design does not seem that of the Church. "Does any of you know anything about the history of this ship?" I ask.

"Again?" Concordia demands. "What is it with you and ships? Isn't it enough that we are going to die? Why do you have to know everything?"

"That is rich, coming from you," I say and turn my attention out my window. Below I see the tranquil white clouds, blue seas, and green earth of Terra.

I do not feel I am going to die. I feel that Havo will protect us. I feel that I will bring justice to Terra.

The ship rocks so violently no one can speak. I see Pallium and Concordia fighting to maintain control of the ship and squeeze Octavius's hand tightly. Just when I think the ship cannot become warmer or vibrate more without coming apart, it ceases to shake and its temperature cools. We are now moving much faster than I would like, but we are within the upper atmosphere, on a slowly descending course toward the Eastern horizon.

I am struck by the horizon's gradient from dark blue to light blue coming down to the white clouds, the Sun bathing everything in a golden glow, all testament to the genius and beauty of Havo's omnipresent, omniscient, and immortal soul. At this height, the clouds blend together to form a blanket around Terra, a blanket we can never touch. Gradually, land comes into view below us, but I cannot tell which Continent it is.

"Where are we going to land?" I ask.

"I'll just drop you in Saint Peter's Square," Concordia says. "I am sure Your Father would love to see you."

"I am sure Concordia has friends we could visit," Octavius points out.

"I do, but do not you think the Church is watching us right now? Monitoring our communications? I honestly do not know what to do."

"You seemed to think you could just slip back to Earth a few months ago."

"That was before you brought the Station back to Terra and let the Church kill everyone."

It is at this moment that I crack. Concordia's words hit me, and all the strength and courage I have been trying to project collapse under the weight of the horror and sadness of what we have seen. I begin crying, then sobbing and leaning into Octavius for support, moaning with grief until I can moan no more. No one speaks.

"I do not know what to do, but I am open to suggestions," Concordia says, acting as if I did not lose control of myself.

"It is possible they did not see us," Pallium says.

"It is equally possible they are tracking us in the hope we will lead them to our friends," Concordia says. "But as I am sure you have figured out, there is a worldwide underground network of blasphemers, heretics, and apostates. It almost doesn't matter where we go. Someone will help us."

"All right, but I would like to see my father."

"Do not you think that would be their first thought?" Pallium asks. "I mean no disrespect, Cassiopeia Ovatio, but the Church probably has him in custody and your home surrounded by now."

"Not if they think I am dead up there."

"Well, that brings us back to not knowing if they saw us or not. They could just be following us right now."

I look to Octavius for his opinion. He doesn't seem to have a perfect plan. I look at Pallium then Concordia, both of whom are looking at me as we fly level eastward over the Atlantic Ocean.

"All right," I say, "Can we prevent our communications from being heard?"

"I . . . think so," Concordia says.

"You think so?"

"We obtained the network's codes last year. We commandeered the network today, as you know." Concordia eyes me sharply. "We might be able to do so again . . . on a more limited scale . . . or cloak our communications if we masquerade as a Church signal." Her mind racing, Concordia begins to manipulate communications controls. "The problem is this shuttle is limited."

"Can we exchange messages with the underground?" I ask.

"I . . . think so," Concordia says. "But our range is limited."

"How limited?"

"A hundred kilometers at most. And our message would look like a Church message—unless the resistance is expecting it, they will not listen to us."

Pallium explains to me, "The call sign would be official—Church— but if they accept the message they would hear our voices." I nod.

They all think on this for a moment, then Octavius says, "You know, we could just slip into a port at night. Sink the ship in the water, swim to shore, blend into the city, find the resistance on foot and in person."

"That is a good plan," Pallium says. "It would be hard for them to track and find us. We could easily connect with your associates," he says to Concordia.

"What port?" Concordia asks.

"Which one do you have the best connections at?"

"San Francisco."

I think a moment.

"No," I say. "You said there are members of the underground all over the World, yes?"

Concordia nods.

"Where would they least expect us to go?" I ask.

Concordia in front of me, Pallium to her right, and Octavius to my right look at me without conceiving my idea.

"Rome," I say.

The three of them look at me as if I have lost my mind. Octavius looks to Pallium for his thoughts, finds none, then says, "Uh, Cassie . . . "

"I know what I am doing, Octavius. We are already dead, remember?"

"This is where I came in!" Concordia says. "You are going to take a ship I am on to certain death again?"

"It is not certain death," I say.

"How do you propose we reach Rome unopposed and undiscovered?"

"I am sure Cassie has a plan," Octavius says. They all wait to hear it.

"You said yourself there is underground there.," I say to Concordia. "No one would expect us there—that is the element of surprise, isn't it?" Pallium nods. "That alone would make us less likely to be spotted or questioned. We just sail in—surely this ship has a navigation computer, no?"

"Yes," Pallium says, "though I do not know if it has Terran maps."

"All right. We can use radar and our eyes. We sail in, park our ship, get out—the three of you will need Havian robes—and go about our business like any good Havians."

They look dismayed, but they do not argue. I see them straining to come with a better plan. Finally Octavius says, "All right. I cannot deny it. I am scared to death, but I agree with you."

"You've got comfortable on the Station," I tease him. "It is time for a change of pace."

Concordia gives me a look suggesting she thinks I have lost my mind, but Octavius takes my jest the way I intended it.

"My duty is to keep you safe," Pallium says, "not to tell you where you may go. If you decide that is where you must go, I will protect you."

"Thank you," I say and place my hand on his shoulder.

"Well, I think it is nuts," Concordia says, "but it is not the first thing you have said or done I thought was nuts."

"And yet here you are," I say. I cannot help smiling.

"How are you going to obtain these robes?" Pallium asks.

"I'll go ashore and buy some, then come back," I say.

"With what money?" Concordia demands. She is right: I do not have any.

"I do not know, but I'll think of something. Havo will provide." I smile. Concordia purses her lips in frustration.

"Well, you have got time to think," Concordia says. We are over one of the Oceans now, but I know in a few minutes we will no longer be. I am not worried about how things will go. I trust in Havo.

"Land," Pallium says at length.

"The Sea of Havo?" Octavius hopes quietly.

"Scar's Teeth, right there," Concordia says. Pallium steers toward the main entrance to the Sea of Havo. As he does so, I notice other ships for the first time, coming and going.

We pass through Scar's Teeth into the Sea of Havo, other ships near but not reacting to us. The design of our shuttle is odd, but it is not so odd as to cause undue attention. It could be from a different part of the World.

We fly eastward over the Sea of Havo toward Rome, Havo's Heart, each of us silent. Though not worried, I feel excited, in a state of elevated awareness and attention. I am conscious of the dangers ahead, the support I expect to receive, and the certainty of Havo's ultimate triumph. There can be no doubt of that.

We sight the coasts, islands. We pass more ships. We see, on the horizon, the shape of Havia's Boot jutting out into the Sea, then the urban center of Rome as a collection of light shapes and boxes growing larger.

"Now," Pallium says. "Do we need a permit?" Octavius and Concordia chuckle, as space shuttles do not usually land in nautical ports.

"Unidentified vessel," a voice suddenly says through our speakers. "What is your registry, destination, and purpose?"

Affecting a local accent, Pallium says, "Our registry is ____. Our destination is the office of the ____ vineyard. We are here on vineyard business to serve Our Father."

After a pause, the voice came back on to say, "I do not have a record of that registry. Please assume a holding pattern outside the City and await further instructions."

"Will do," Pallium says, ending the communication link, then looks at me, I do not know why.

After a moment, Pallium asks me, "What would you like me to do, Cassiopeia?"

I am surprised back into remembering our current situation. My lifelong comfort with the Church had taken me over. "Oh! Um, what do you think?"

"Run right into town and ditch the shuttle," Concordia says. "Hide as fast as we can."

I look to Octavius, who nods.

"Let's do that then," I say to Pallium.

Pallium changes course from his holding pattern to head straight into the Port of Rome.

"They're trying to hail us again," Pallium says.

"Disregard them," I say. "Bring us into port."

Pallium pilots us into the port of the city, over ships, boats, and other small water craft. Havians walking on the pier notice us, point, and stare. Pallium aims us straight into the heart of the port and the City, bringing us gently to rest on the water next to the pier. I detach my harness and say, "Perhaps you'd better come with me. They might come to our ship. We can always say you are some kind of laborers."

"There is no doubt they are already on their way," Pallium says.

The crowd greets us at the top of the pier, but I keep my hand over the left side of my face to hinder recognition. I cannot see more than blurry lights through my left eye regardless. We quickly extricate ourselves and walk away into the crowds of Havians, some of whom, I note, are not wearing robes. The Station jumpsuits might not need to be replaced, at least not right away. I am surprised, as Rome has the reputation of being more formal than the rest of Terra.

We walk among Havians—Havians on Terra!—for the first time, for Concordia and me, in months. For Octavius it has been three years. For Pallium it is his first time, as he was born on the Station. I keep my hand to my face, and I am careful to avoid eye contact with anyone, as I do not wish to be recognized.

As we walk both hurriedly and leisurely, attempting to find and strike the right balance without attracting attention, I notice a screen across and above the street ahead, on our side. Crowds walk to and fro beneath it, stopping to wait to cross the street. My vision, even with one eye, is not so poor that I cannot recognize my own face. On the screen, frozen in time, is a photograph of me taken from my broadcast to Terra. The Station bridge behind me has been removed; only I have been taken out and superimposed onto a silver background (I notice the color spectrum lining the rectangular image at its edges), words next to my image reading:

TERTIA CASSIOPEIA OVATIO NOLI
BORN 24/5/113
HAIR: BROWN
EYES: BLUE
SERVANT OF SCAR
DETAIN AND DESTROY

These words glow gold on the silver field. I stop walking to stare at the screen.

"Cassie, come on!" Octavius urges softly, grabbing my hand and pulling me along. I did not realize I had stopped, blocking others who merely flowed around me on both sides as does water around a rock in a river.

"I am sorry," I say haltingly. "I . . . "

"I know. Let's go. Keep your face down as much as you can."

I will. I do. I do not know if it will work, but I do not wish to be destroyed. Would these Havians all about me destroy me? Havo said, "Thou shalt not kill." How could any Havian follow such a decree? I steal furtive glances at the faces. Do they question? Do they see the contradiction? Havo is peace, not war or violence. This is the least Havian decree I have seen from the Havican in my life, and it is directed at me, to bring about my destruction. I do not even know how to feel about this. It is absurd.

The four of us walk as swiftly as we dare through the crowds, with no plan but to leave the shuttle as far behind as possible, when, a few city blocks from the pier, I cannot escape the feeling we are being followed. "This way," I say, leading us to the shade of a column under a stone building. We wait in the shadow of the building, watching passersby in each direction. Suddenly a little man with a reddish beard approaches us, not at all puzzled or confused. He gives the air of having followed us, of being glad to catch up with us.

"Thank you," he says. "My legs are not as long as yours." Pallium steps between this little man and me to protect me, but the little man waves him away. "We do not have time for this. We must get away from here immediately."

"And you are?" I ask, stepping out from behind Pallium.

"I am Hostus," the little man says, "and I am an ally. I would like to take you someplace safe."

We look at each other. I look at the passersby. A woman catches my glance. Her expression changes from casual interest to recognition to shock. She cries out: "It is her! It is her! Here, in Havo's heart!" Then she faints, and a crowd of pedestrians stops to help the fallen woman.

"Run!" Hostus says. "This way." As we all start out and pass him, he says to Pallium. "Carry me!" Hostus leads us down ancient narrow cobble-stoned alleys.

"I think we lost them," Hostus says after a while. "That was close."

"Where are we?" Octavius asks.

"Here," the little man says. "Just a little farther. Over there."

I see nothing more than more ordinary shops and buildings, busy streets as far as the eye can see in three directions. A fountain occupies the intersection of three streets. Beyond and two our right our guide leads us, into a store selling carpets. As we reach the counter area, the little man walks past the counter without looking back. We follow him into a back room, where he stops before a small, wooden, cracking and peeling door. "Go in," he says. "I am the proprietor of this establishment, and I must attend to my duties. I thank you for your patronage, and I am sorry I could not find what you were looking for." He leaves us and goes back to the front, where we hear him greeting a customer.

Once again we look at each other. What could be the meaning of this? I regard the nondescript, fading door that might once have been white and decide to be the boldest in the group. I reach out for the knob, turn it, and open the door to reveal a staircase downward. I look at the others and raise my eyebrows.

Pallium immediately volunteers to go first, and I find myself more grateful than ever before that he is with us. Octavius goes next, then I do, then Concordia does. She shuts the door behind her. "This is the least secure escape ever," she grumbles.

"We do not even know where we are going, or who that man is," I point out. "It could not even be an escape."

She glares at me. "That is right. So why we are here I have no idea, but once again my situation is our fault."

"I promise to make it up to you, Concordia," I say with exaggerated sweetness, turning my attention forward again. The stairs are dark, wooden, and creaky. I cannot imagine Our Father himself cannot hear us, they creak so loudly. At the bottom of one flight of stairs we find another small wooden door. Pallium opens it to reveal a stone passage, as small as the door it covered, declining gradually into the earth. We look at each other again. I nod. We go in the same order again, Pallium leading. Concordia shuts the door, leaving us in darkness.

"I suppose he did not have time to give us a candle," Octavius whispers back to me.

It occurs to me to wonder why I trusted the man calling himself Hostus, but there was something in his manner that told me he was trustworthy. I cannot explain it further. He seemed good and kind. I know this may sound absurd, but I trusted him from the moment I first saw him, due to his look and his manner. I understand that going on intuition alone might not be the best way to make decisions, but sometimes that is all we have. Life and death might hinge upon nothing more or less. We needed a friend; we were looking for the underground; and it stood to reason he represented it. I realize I forgot to ask how he came to find or notice us. I also neglected to ask if he was a member of the resistance, but I felt sure that he was.

The corridor suddenly turns upward again, and in the distance we see a pinprick of light, light that begins to burn a mark in my one good retina. Well, my eyes are both good, but my left optic nerve has not decided to resume working fully yet. My left eye sees only blurry shapes, soft images, and in darkness like this it is useless. My right eye, at least, can make out the tiny sliver of light ahead.

As we approach the light, none of us speaking, I imagine we will come upon a giant underground cavern, the worldwide headquarters of the entire underground resistance movement. I imagine a large gathering of thousands, moved by speakers at a podium denouncing the Church and calling for violent overthrow. A part of me cannot blame them, but I feel violence is not the answer. We cannot harm Havians who do not know better, Havians who are still as I was. I was like the woman on the street who shrieked at the sight of me. I believed Our Father was as close to Havo as a son to his father. I believed apostates, if they existed at all, were evil sons of Scar.

We come to the small opening, still the size of the small door, and emerge into a room to find two men seated at a table. The walls of this entire place are a dark orange/yellow. The table is a light blond wood, with six chairs of the same wood. The four of us come out and stand to our full heights again, grateful for the relief to our backs that doing so provides. "Ah," some of us sigh.

"Yes, I do not know why that corridor is so small," one of the men says. "It is as if Hostus cut it out of the rock himself."

"Except that he's too lazy," the other man, apparently younger, jokes.

"Now, who are you?" the first man asks. "Well, not you," he said to me. "Everyone knows who you are." He stands. "We are honored by your visit, Cassiopeia Ovatio, and we stand ready to assist you."

"What is this place?" Concordia asks.

"This is our most secret meeting place, directly below the Havican."

"What?"

"As you can imagine, every member of the underground is a good Havian by day. Good Havians unsuspected have a way of being able to make things happen without arousing suspicion."

This only makes sense, and yet it had not occurred to me.

"We have members in every walk and station of life and society. We go through the motions. We do not betray our thoughts and feelings. We hide the truth." He gestures toward the four of us. "You are the truth."

"And what do we do next?" I ask.

"I was going to ask you that," he says. "You are the face of Station Michael, the lost Station lost again, destroyed in orbit today for all to see. Right now the Church is going through its greatest crisis. Our Father is defending his orders. The deaths are causing great shock throughout the World."

"As they should," I say.

"Yes, well, there's also the matter that the deaths are of apostates. Do apostate lives matter as much as do the lives of Havians? And what of the existence of the apostates and Station Michael to begin with? Did the Church lie to us? To what end? These are questions the Church was not planning to answer or even wrestle with today. The Church was not prepared. So, from my point of view, you have won the first engagement. You have employed the advantage of surprise. The next move must be to exploit the advantage further, in my opinion, to disorient and confuse the enemy more."

"Allow me to explain something to you," I say, sounding more annoyed than I intend. "No Havian is the enemy. I understand that you have felt or even been oppressed. I am sorry for that. But that does not give you the right to commit violence." I glance over at Concordia.

"Then this will be a very short revolution."

"If your way worked, you would have succeeded by now," I say. "I am not here to foment, lead, or encourage revolution. I am here to enlighten the people to the truth of the matter. The truth of the matter is that there has been some confusion regarding one space station. Once this is cleared up, I expect to be able to go back home to my father's house and live peacefully."

The man laughs. "You really are naive!" He sits back down. "This is an . . . opponent . . . who will torture you to death. If he hasn't already, Our Father will sentence you to death. Then he will have his way with you. And I would not put anything past him." The man eyes Concordia and me particularly. "I was going to ask your next move, but I see now you do not know how things are. Stay with us and we will show you."

"Thank you," I say. "We accept your hospitality. We have noplace else to go."

"Well, at least you realize that," the man says. "Rest assured, you will be safe here. Come with us." He stands again. "I am _____, this is

____. We are leaders here. We are respected. And we will work with you to accomplish the greatest good with the least number of lives lost, I promise you." He pauses. "But there will be lives lost, I promise you that as well."

"I can see we came to the right place," I say.

"You did," ____ says.

They rise and lead us out another door into a corridor with many doors on either side.

I remember my mission. I decide I need to find a leader of this organization to share it with, but something tells me these two men are not the leaders I seek. As if reading my mind, Concordia says, "I hope this is all worth it." I know she means the deaths, the loss of the Station, and everything else we have been through. I notice my body aches. I am tired. I am hungry. I tend not to think of these things. At least my robes are dry, as are the jumpsuits of the others.

"Now, in here are private quarters for special occasions and visitors," the more talkative man says. "It is not dinner time yet, but pick a room, settle down. You will be here for several days, I am sure. If you need anything else, there will always be someone here to help you."

"I would like to speak with whoever is in charge of the entire organization," I say.

The two men wear expressions of surprise and dismay.

"We are leaders," __ says.

"I understand that you are high in the organization," I say, "and I mean no disrespect, but my mission is for the ears of the supreme leader only."

They react slowly, but they nod.

"I will relay your message," Spurius says.

"I thank you," I say.

They leave us. We choose rooms, each of which is well appointed, with a bed, a lamp, and subtle artwork on the walls. Octavius and I find a room with a bed large enough for the two of us. Pallium takes a room next to us, and Concordia the room on the other side of him. We return to the room with the table afterward.

"I do not like it," Concordia says.

"These are your comrades," Octavius says.

"My comrades are over in Provincia Cascadia. I have never dealt with these men or anyone like them."

"They seem to want violence," I say. "I thought you would approve."

For the first time, Concordia looks hurt.

"You advocate armed overthrow, do not you?" I ask.

"I advocate . . . whatever is best for Terra," Concordia says quietly.

"We do need to know more," Pallium says. "We cannot be completely at their mercy. We do not even know who they are."

"The man calling himself Hostus saved us," Octavius points out. "These men might not be very bright, but they do seem to be on the right side of things. We just need to talk with them about strategy and tactics."

"No," I say, contradicting my husband in front of others for the first time. "I need to speak with their leader. Their leader will speak with them." I realize I do not consider myself one of them. I identify with those on the Station, not these men on the ground, yet.

Time passes slowly. We sit and wait. Eventually we hear someone come. The door at the other end of the hall opens, and a small old woman comes through carrying a tray of food. She walks slowly dow the hall, then down the short corridor into the table room.

"Good evening," she says to us all, "and welcome."

We thank her for the food. She remains. I study her.

"You wanted to see me, I believe," the old woman says to me.

"Yes." I stand to walk with this wise-eyed old woman as the others react with surprise.

"You are the worldwide leader?" Concordia demands. "You are Lavina?" Apparently, though these are not her comrades, Concordia has heard the worldwide leader's code name.

The old woman turns back. "A leader may not carry food?" This silences Concordia and establishes Lavina's authority with us. Lavina and I leave the others at the table and walk to the other end of the corridor, far enough to ensure private conversation but still within sight of the others, through the single door connecting the table room with the corridor.

"Now, my child," Lavina says with the manner of a Prism, "I saw your broadcast, as did we all. I applaud your courage, and, like you, I lament the loss of the Station after all this time. I too had hoped for its safe return. But how can I help you?"

"I do not know what to call you," I say.

"Lavina is my code name."

"That does not seem appropriate."

"What do you wish to call me?"

"Mother."

"You may, if you like."

"Mother, we came back not only to show the World the truth of the Station." The old woman raises an eyebrow and smiles, with amused curiosity.

"Hmm?"

"The leaders of the Station suspect the Church may be behind the Inopia. They wanted me to investigate, that the results might be shared with the World, that the true . . . evil of the Church might be exposed."

Mother Lavina considers this. "An interesting hypothesis, and a good plan," she says. "The truth must come to light. Right now, however, you are the most hunted woman on Terra."

"Yes, things did not go according to plan."

"They never do. That is Life."

"Can you help us?"

"Of course. Most of us here are high officials in the Church, manoeuvring on more than one level. I will speak with my colleagues in the science department. In the mean time, stay here. Your shuttle has already been impounded. They know someone from the Station is here, and it will not be long before they learn it is you from the woman who cried out on the street."

"You know about her?"

"From Hostus, an old and trusted friend. But have no fear. Your location is hidden, and to obtain you the Church would have to defeat our entire organization. That will not happen. But they can make life more difficult for all of us. There is already talk of closing the City."

I feel terrible for the trouble I have caused this group of revolutionaries.

"Eat something. Sleep well. Tomorrow we continue." She smiles a warm and motherly smile. "May the light of Havo be upon you."

"Thank you, Mother," I say.

She turns to depart, then pauses and turns back.

"There is something else I have been wanting to say since your broadcast," Mother Lavina says. I wait expectantly. "I was very impressed by both your bravery and your suffering. You have been through more than most Havians ever experience in a lifetime. I admire you, though you are less than half, perhaps even a third, my age. Above all, I admire you." She reaches out and grasps my hand warmly. "Until tomorrow."

She leaves, and I cry, at the end of the hall, where my husband and friends can see me standing but not my tears. I join them after I compose myself.

I know that I am not brave. I have merely been pushed by my circumstances. I have done only what any other true Havian would do.

I feel honored both by meeting Mother Lavina and by her praises, but I feel uneasy with the two men she has chosen to serve her and us. I intend to ask her about them. I do not know where they went. I do not know how long we will be in this place.

I do not know a great deal, it seems.

I return to the table room, where my husband and companions are eating fruit and bread, drinking wine and water.

"This hits the spot," Pallium says. "How long has it been since we ate?"

"Since this morning," Octavius says.

"Now what?" Concordia asks between grapes. "I do not want to sit here for days."

"We might not have a choice," I say.

"Well, I do not know about you," Concordia says, "but I do not feel comfortable not having a choice. We do not even know who these people are. We trust them because we met a dwarf on the street? Is this is a child's fairy tale? Yes, it is. I forgot."

I do not know what to say to her, but it is apparent to me that life in Provincia Cascadia has made Concordia distrustful. She did not live far from me, only a few hundred miles. What could have happened to her?

"It can be difficult to be patient, I agree," I say. "I will not regale you with stories from the Book of Havo—"

"Havo be praised," Concordia says.

"—But I will say that I see great strength in you, Concordia . . . what is your together-name?

"Vala."

"Vala. Concordia Vala, I know you have already conquered harder adversity than this, including opposition from me when I wanted us all to meet Havo."

Concordia is silent.

"Further, I am relying on you. Your strength, your wisdom, your good humor, and your ingenuity in a crisis. In short, we need you—I need you—now, to help us prepare for whatever lies ahead."

"All right," Concordia says. "I do not trust these guys. I say we should find out what is beyond the other end of that corridor. We know what is back the way we came, and that is an option too. But they say we are under the Havican. Who's to say that is true? How do we know? For all we know this is an elaborate Church trap and we are all being recorded right now." She sighed.

"I am not one to trust. I know you are used to faith. I am not."

We all sit quietly until I say, "I have been, yes, but—thanks to you— I have come to doubt my church. I have been . . . disappointed by my church, to say the least."

I can see Octavius, Pallium, and Concordia recalling the death sentence we all share. Concordia becomes more quiet.

"I know we will get through this," I say. "We've been through worse, together." I grasp Octavius's hand, squeeze it, and look into his eyes. He smiles a slight smile of encouragement.

"Besides," Octavius offers. "They cannot hurt us without a fight."

"My father died today," Pallium says. "We all lost family or friends. We are tired, hungry, scared, and grieving. It is understandable to feel irritable. And yet the four of us have been fortunate in more than one way today."

Concordia nodded. "I would just feel better if I had my old comrades here. I know them. I trust them."

"I think we'd all feel better if things were different," Octavius says, and I cannot help but agree. "We are going to have to trust each other."

We finish dining and retire for the night. Our hosts, whoever they are, have thought of everything: a lavatory with bath sits at the far end of the hall, the end where I spoke with Mother Lavina last night. I study the walls and fixtures as I walk down the hall again. The walls are bare of art, but the wooden doors to the rooms are smooth with beautiful golden handles. The lavatory itself contains the finest porcelain, ceramics, metal, and glass. Despite Concordia's remark, I feel as if I am in a palace from a children's story. Thinking this reminds me of my father, and I cannot help but cry. Pallium, guarding in the hall outside, hears this and summons Octavius, who comes in.

"I am all right," I say.

"None of us is all right," Octavius says, helping me rise from the floor. "And we will not be all right until we can defeat the Church."

"I have no desire to defeat the Church," I say. "I wish merely to serve Havo."

"In this case, serving Havo means fighting a church that has turned its back on Havo's teachings."

I know he is right.

"I do not think I can do it, Octavius."

"What?"

"I do not think I can defeat the Church."

"If anyone can, it is you."

"I am a simple woman who lives in Soul River with her father. I sew his clothing when it tears."

"Cassie, you are much more than that. You always have been." Octavius crouches down. "You inspire me. You bring me confidence. What do you think I would be doing right now it you weren't here with us?"

"The same thing you have been doing?"

"No. I would be demanding answers from those two men and leading an expedition out the door right here."

"I was thinking of doing the same thing."

"I do not want you doing that."

"Well, husband, I do not want you doing that either. So let us agree that neither of us shall do that."

"Agreed."

We kiss.

"Now I truly need to visit the lavatory."

"All right. I'll wait outside."

"I am also going to bathe."

"I'll wait in our room." Octavius leaves Pallium guarding outside the door and returns to our room. I enjoy the bath. I wish I could wash my robes, but the water they gained in the Port of Rome will have to suffice for now, I tell myself.

In our room, Octavius covers me with kisses and I yield, returning them and more. In some ways, things are better for me, thank Havo. My husband sees me not as the Face of Station Michael but as a woman. Thank Havo.

The next morning, I open the door of the room I share with Octavius to find Pallium asleep against our door. He falls inward; I jump back; he wakes with a start before hitting his head on the floor, thank Havo.

"Rom," Octavius calls from bed. "What were you doing?"

"Guarding you," Pallium answers groggily. I offer him a hand to help him rise, and he accepts it. I am pleasantly surprised.

"Thank you," he says.

"Thank *you*," I say.

"Good morning!" we suddenly hear Spurius call out from the far doorway. "You are the talk of the town for the second day in a row," he says loudly coming down the hall pushing a small cart of food. We step out of our room, and he hands me the day's news on an electronic pad. "I wouldn't go out for a walk if I were you. City closed, now they're talking about going door to door. But do not worry—you are safe here."

"We are also ready to do more than stay safe here," Pallium says.

"Well, if you want to go get captured and killed, probably tortured first, go right ahead," Spurius says.

"What is Lavina planning?" I ask. "We would like to know what to expect."

"With all due respect, Cassiopeia Ovatio, and much to my chagrin, Lavina does not confide her every thought in us. She is considering moves and countermoves, playing chess. Her brother is doing the same."

"Her brother?" I am confused.

"Our Father."

"The Father of All of Us is the brother of the leader of the underground?"

"It is a funny world, isn't it?" Spurius asks. "I am glad I do not have to try to understand the divine plan of a supreme being." He chuckles. "Breakfast is served, with the compliments of Lavina, and of course her brother." He turns and indicates the cart, loaded with fruit, vegetables, breads, rolls, oatmeal, and even coffee. He wheels the cart to the table room and lets us enjoy it.

"How did you secure this?" Pallium asks.

"One of the kitchen staff is one of our men."

"I hope he will not be discovered."

"So do I—I like coffee."

I see the edge of Pallium' mouth curl in a semi-smile.

I notice Concordia has not yet come out of her room. I walk to her door and knock on it. No response comes. I knock again. "Concordia?"

"I know, Havo cannot live or function without me. I shall appear momentarily, Your Grace."

We sit at the rectangular table. I study the electronic pad. Our Father has announced our arrival, declared us "scandalous apostates and defilers", and called for all Havians to aid in our capture.

"That is me," Octavius says. "Scandalous."

I read about myself depicted as a criminal. It seems to be about someone else—the person described is an intolerant apostate monster, a traitor pretending to believe in Havo, an enemy of Terra. Then I remember my father would have assumed me dead after the Station's explosion. This announcement from Our Father will tell my father I survived the destruction of the Station. A part of me cannot but feel grateful to Our Father, Lavina's brother. I can hear my father urging me to stay strong and do the right thing, however painful it might be. *I will, my father.* I pass the pad to the others.

Despite Concordia's desire not to sit here for days, we pass three more nights this way. We talk, we wait, we wonder what is happening above, I pray. The next morning, Lavina comes to us again with new robes.

"No," Concordia says.

"I am sorry, my child. These are for your protection. Camouflage, nothing more. Please be ready to leave in ten minutes." We do not know where we are going or why.

"What is our plan, Mother?" I ask.

"I am attempting to smuggle you to safety," Lavina says. "Out of the City."

"Just give us the clothes and we will get ourselves out," Concordia says. I gasp at her discourtesy. "I am sorry, but we do not know you from Havia."

Lavina turns to her. "That is true, you do not. And perhaps you are right. Take Spurius and Postumus with you. They are useful. Go out Hostus' shop. If you are caught . . . I will try to help you."

"Spurius said you are his sister," Concordia says.

"Yes," Lavina says. "Prisms do have brothers and sisters. He rose through the Prismhood. I took a different path. He condemned me. Seeing the way of the World, I persuaded him I had changed my mind. He brought me here and gave me a secretarial position. I am very organized and good at organizing others. This vantage has served our efforts—the underground's—well, and I daresay his overconfident belief in my loyalty is our greatest strength."

I am impressed. Concordia is too, I observe.

"You mean to tell me that we are being helped by a Havican secretary—who is the brother of Our Father?"

"The personal secretary to Our Father, no less."

"If we kidnap you, we can blackmail our way out of this city," Concordia says. Spurius and Postumus become tense.

"That is true," Lavina says. "But I assure you I can be of greater use to you behind the scenes."

"And if we are running loose in Rome, how can you help us?" I do not think Concordia knows what she wants.

"Well, I would prefer it if you came with me. But if you wish to go it alone, I can try to slow down your pursuers, at least."

"And how can you do that?" Concordia demands.

"Oh, I have been helping the resistance here for many years, but I admit this is a new case. I do have some ideas I have been toying with." The old woman smiles. "You know, the city is cut off, with a curfew, but I do not remember ever seeing it so alive or engaged. Station Michael and its survivors in Rome are Worldwide news—all anyone can talk about. We are now on our fifth day. So I thank you for that. You have already brought the spirit of inquiry back to our society."

"In more than one way," I say.

"What *are* we going to do?" Concordia asks me. I almost do not notice she has just validated my authority.

A part of me feels each plan has an equal chance of success. A part of me feels Lavina's plan has a better chance of success. A part of me feels I should favor Concordia's plan to earn her trust. A part of me feels this is Havo's will, that friendship is more important than any other consideration, that partnership between Havians and nonHavians begins here and now in this small room below the Havican. I do not take a vote. Havo has granted me this role, and I intend to fulfill it, without injustice.

"'There comes a time in the life of every human when he or she must decide to risk life, fortune, and sacred honor on an outcome dubious,'" Spurius says. "That time for you is now," he says to me. "What's it going to be?" I find him annoying, I must admit to myself.

"Concordia," I say, "I like your plan. Mother Lavina seems to think it has a chance. I imagine her smuggling us would have about an equal chance of success—it all depends on not being recognized." Pallium nods. "And I do not wish to jeopardize her position either. If we are with her, that puts her at risk. Concordia, I say we will adopt your plan. What did you call it? 'Getting ourselves out'. Are you prepared to accept the assistance of Spurius and Postumus, these two men Lavina wishes us to take with us? That is the price."

Concordia eyes them skeptically then nods grudgingly.

"All right!" Spurius says. "Let's go."

We take the robes from Lavina and put them on. Concordia eyes hers. "I really thought I would never put these on again."

"I am sorry," I say. She looks up at me in surprise.

"No, you are not. You are excited to lead a crusade to make Havo stronger than ever."

I am stunned. "Is that how you see me?"

"You are just another religious zealot. I do not even know why I am helping you."

"We share a mutual adversary," I manage to say.

"Yes, I suppose that is true. But if—*if*—we survive this, the moment he is defeated, I am going to turn around and start opposing *you*."

"Ho, ho!" Spurius erupted. "Dissension in the ranks! And here I thought you all thought and felt the same."

Concordia and I say nothing. Pallium and Octavius speak only of preparations.

I suppose I had no right to expect anything else. When we are all ready, we follow Spurius and Postumus into the tunnel back to the shop. This time the stooping, half-crawling trip passes very quickly, making me wonder how it seemed much longer the first time. We come out into the small room in the back of the shop. "Excuse me," I hear Hostus tell someone before I see him come through the curtains into the back room. "And was everything to your liking?" he asks. "No? I am sorry. Oh, well." He leads us through the curtains into the main shop, where we see a bored woman examining knick-knacks. To her he says, "Are you sure I cannot interest you in that sculpture? It is pre-Havian." I glance at the small sculpture, of a seated man thinking, and wonder what life on Terra could have been like before the Church of Havo came to power. I only know the former church was called the Universal Roman Church. Was this small sculpture a Universal work of art? What god or gods did Universal Church believers worship?

"Thanks anyway," Spurius says to Hostus and leads us out the door. The customer glances up at us disinterestedly then returns to considering the sculpture.

"It is a real bargain," I hear Hostus say, "and one of a kind. You will not find another in the World."

We step out into the busy street. My image is still up on the nearest screen, at the next intersection. The passersby do not notice us, but we need to make a decision. I nod, and we step out into the current of pedestrians.

Where are we going to go?

Behind me I hear a Church police car, its warning siren beeping, demanding that passersby move aside. I panic. Where can we go? We cannot run and draw attention to ourselves. As we are facing away from it, it is simply not possible the car has been drawn to us; it is a coincidence. We just need to stay calm and continue walking. Our backs are to the vehicle. It will not stop us; it has no reason to stop us. We are one group of persons among many. Besides, the Church is seeking one woman, not a group of six. We continue to walk. The car pulls alongside us. I have my hand on the side of my face, but now I think it will be suspicious if I leave it there. I have no choice but to let my left hand drop, exposing my face to the car that is also to my left. I keep my eyes straight ahead. A few moments pass before I notice I am being addressed from the vehicle. I turn to look in the window of the vehicle, which is keeping pace with me. Inside I see, with perhaps the greatest relief I have ever felt, Lavina.

"Come in," she calls out. I notice Pallium is already opening the square armored vehicle's side doors.

"How . . . ?" I ask as I step up and inside.

"There are allies in every station of Life," Lavina says. "Fortunately, my position and status will remove all suspicion from the officer who allowed me the use of the vehicle, should my use come to light. No one would blame him, though he was of course the one who made this possible."

I thank this unnamed officer in my mind. Someday I hope I will be able to thank him in person.

Onlookers look on as we drive away, but we do not attract undue attention.

"Where are we going?" I ask.

"I am still planning to get you out of the City," Lavina says. "Yes, we have a network here, but we have even more allies outside the City, where we can plot our next move."

A part of me does not want to retreat. Now that I have learned that Our Father is my enemy, I want to advance even to his office. I want to attack his position—not him—and weaken it.

"We could try to blow up the Havican," Concordia says.

Lavina and the others react with surprise. "But then I would be out of a job, dear," Lavina reminds her. "I think it is better if we do not destroy buildings."

"We must also work not to harm Havians," I say, "or non-Havians. Blowing up a building would invariably hurt someone." Lavina nods.

"I am going to get you out of Rome," Lavina says. "Then we can plan our next move."

"How are you going to get us out of Rome?" Concordia asks. 'You told us yourself the city is closed."

"As the secretary to Our Father, I am above suspicion," Lavina says. "Our Father also trusts me completely, so I enjoy great latitude." We drive to a checkpoint to the east of the city, where Church soldiers in silver uniforms stand guard, preventing anyone from leaving. We drive up to the soldiers. I turn my face down and away from them. A soldier walks up to Lavina's window.

"May the light of Havo shine upon you," the soldier says.

"And also upon you," Lavina says.

"The city is closed," the soldier says. "Your party must turn about."

"I am Our Father's secretary, Lavina," Lavina says. The soldier's eyes widen.

"You may research me, of course." Lavina hands the soldier her identification papers.

"No, no—no need," the soldier says at the sight of the Havican seal on her papers. "How can we assist you, Secretary Lavina?"

"Our Father has asked me to evaluate the measures you have been taking here."

The soldier gulps with nervousness.

"Well, Secretary, as you know, this is all new to us—we've never had to do this before."

"That is no excuse for laxity. What measures have you put into effect here to keep the apostate terrorists from escaping?"

"As you see, we have a gate with guards. We tell everyone to turn about and go home."

"Do you take note of their identities, for cross-checking and future reference?"

"Uh, no. We did not think of that."

"Think of it now." She studies him closely. The young man becomes more nervous with each passing second.

"I will be making a report that this gate is not yet fully secure. I suggest you make additional efforts to improve."

"Yes, Secretary."

"And please open the gate. We have some other business outside the perimeter."

"But Secretary!"

"Yes?" Lavina's tone suggests mild annoyance at the delay.

"It is just that—it is just that my orders are not to open the gate for anyone." The soldier sounds as if he has just confessed a crime.

"I am here on official business for Our Father," Lavina reminds the soldier. "Would you like me to call Our Father for you, so he can ask you himself to clear the way for me?"

The soldier hesitates, then begins to say no too late.

"I will be glad to do so." Lavina takes out a personal communicator. Only Prisms and those of higher rank are permitted these devices, and this one is only the second I have seen, the first being Prism Arcturus' device, back in Soul River. "Could you please get your commander, that they might speak together about your refusal to assist me?"

"No!" the soldier bursts. "I mean, no, thank you, Secretary!"

"You'd like to speak with him yourself? I understand. I do not have a preference, myself." Lavina makes the call and reaches her brother. I feel myself grow more tense than before.

I see another man rise and come out of the small guard shack to ask what is going on.

"Well, sir, we have Our Father's secretary here—"

"And?"

"And she wants to go through the gate."

"Well, why aren't you letting her go through the gate?" The two soldiers then listen to Lavina:

"Yes, Lux," Lavina says. "I am checking the gates. I also have a lead, and I would like to pursue it. The soldiers will not let me out. Is it all right? Yes, I have security with me. No, no—I'll be all right. Be back in a few hours. All right? All right. Here's . . . the commander, yes?."

The commander takes the phone. The younger soldier seems paler than before.

"Havo be praised!" the commander says into the phone, then listens. "Yes, Father. Yes, Father," he says. "Yes, Father. Yes, Father. Yes." He hands the device back to Lavina, then turns to the makeshift gate and others standing there. "Open the gate!" he calls. "Let them pass, by order of Our Father himself!" He then turns back to apologize to the Secretary. "I am sorry our men have not yet learned the proper respect in performance of their duties," the commander says.

"Not at all, Commander. This young man was merely being careful," Lavina says. "You never know who might be lurking about. We happen to be following a report of terrorist activity just south of the City. If we find anything, we will come back through this gate to share our news with you." The soldiers relax visibly. Lavina adds, with a note of disappointment, "We are afraid the apostate terrorist Cassiopeia Ovatio might have slipped out of town as well. I hope not, for the sake of all soldiers on duty today." She eyes the two men pointedly.

"I hope not too," the young soldier says, forgetting himself. The commander, an older man, appears to remember the presence of the young soldier with annoyance.

"If we are fortunate and she has not, it will be up to soldiers like you to prevent it," Lavina adds. "We are counting on you." Neither soldier speaks, but the commander nods. "May Havo be with you both," Lavina says. As we drive away, I hear the commander's voice issuing angry tones at the younger soldier, the younger soldier's voice issuing pleading tones.

When the gate is open, Lavina drives through it slowly enough not to arouse suspicion but quickly enough not to arouse suspicion. After all, she is supposedly chasing a terrorist: me.

She gives a light wave to the guards as we pass through, then we drive away from Rome, the only persons permitted to do so during the curfew.

Once we are on the road again, Pallium says, "That was close."

"Too close!" Spurius agrees. "Lavina, you almost made me pee my pants."

Lavina smiles. "Sometimes it is not enough to be nonchalant. Sometimes one must be *assertively* nonchalant."

As we drive into the countryside, I look at Concordia again. She looks beautiful in the Havian robes she detests. Again I wonder how anyone could not believe in Havo. Havo is the only god. Without Havo there is nothing, and yet I realize suddenly with a shock that, of the six of us in this vehicle, I am the only believer. I have never been in this position before.

I remember hearing of other, false gods who existed before Havo, most notably the belief that a poor man who died over two thousand years ago was a god. Everyone knows the Havian Church was founded on the ashes of his church. When its last leader went back in Time and sent the man's body forward, the truth was revealed. Crisis erupted, as would be expected, with cries of "Hoax!", but the faith was destroyed. Then, one great leader, Marcellus, stepped forward to reveal the truth of Havo. "Yahweh is dead," he proclaimed. "Havo is the one true god." It all made sense: how could a man be a god when all life came from the Sun? Others in the past had known the truth, but Humanity had forgot. "I believe in Havo," Marcellus said, "as I believe that the Sun has risen: not only because I see it, but because by it I see everything else." With these and other words, he restored the faith of the shattered, the devastated, the lost. After Marcellus and the Church corrected the great error, however, some Jehovah believers refused to see the truth. They left the Church, joining with apostates, beginning the time of great trial and decades of fighting culminating in the War . . . and the Day. Everything is better now. I look at their faces as we drive. Spurius and Postumus continue to laugh and joke, and everyone else is silent. Concordia still looks beautiful but grave. Octavius is serious and purposeful. Pallium, in the front passenger seat, watches for threats. We pass the occasional Church vehicle identical to ours, carrying Church soldiers.

I wonder why Time-travel technology was lost, or if it has been. The Church has certainly not mentioned having employed it again since. A part of me wishes I could use it now.

"I just do not agree that violence is never the answer," I hear Concordia say suddenly, interrupting my reverie and bringing my attention back to the matters at hand. "We could target the Havican. It is symbolic. If we destroy or even just damage it—without hurting any Havians—it would make the most dramatic possible statement to the World. I am good with bombs. I could—"

"I agree it would make a statement," I say. "It would say that we are not above violence. It would say that we do not possess moral authority. Correct me if I am wrong, Lavina, but Our Father would use that against us."

"He certainly would," Lavina says. "We would become terrorists." I note her use of "we", despite her secure and powerful position. She truly is one of us, first and foremost, in her heart.

"This is a fight between us and them," Concordia says.

"The fact that I am riding in this car with you says we are all together. It is not a matter of us and them, only *us*, with some who see things one way and some who see things another—or more than one other —way. We must rise above the forces, and impulses, of violence and lead through moral authority," I say. This gives me an idea. "We must reach the people with the truth. Do we have the means to do so?"

"The only Worldwide system is in the Havican, though each Provincia has its own local transmitter.," Lavina says.

"Could a local transmitter broadcast to the entire network?" I ask.

"Yes, but the others would have to be willing to receive it."

I ponder this.

"Lavina," I ask. "Could your contacts in other Provinces arrange to be willing to receive a broadcast from this Provincia?"

"It is possible," she says, "though not all Provinces might go along. What I mean is the underground is stronger in some places than in others, and in some places it has less reach than others."

"I understand."

"But I will see what I can do and arrange."

"Thank you. I think we need to counterbalance Our Father and give the opposition some hope." I look to the faces of my comrades. I see surprise and thoughtful expressions considering the idea. No one argues with me; apparently they agree.

We drive to the north for more than two hours and stop at a small farm. A low fence surrounds the property; all is quiet. The house itself is very old, with no glass in its windows. Its tile roof and stone walls need repair, but the structure seems intact. Lavina drives up to the house and stops.

"The Church will never find you here," she says.

"Why is that?" Pallium asks.

"This is our childhood home," Lavina says. "Why would Our Father look for you here?"

We go inside to find a charming little country home, with enough room for the six of us to sleep if some of us sleep on the floor. Lavina invites us to partake of anything we need from the house, then bids us farewell. This distresses me.

"I have already been gone two hours, and I told my brother I would be back soon," Lavina says. "Come outside with me," she says. The two of us go back outside, near the police vehicle, for privacy. She tells me, "There is something else I have been wanting to tell you, but I have not been able to find the right words, or the right opportunity."

I listen and watch her face.

"I looked you up in the church files. As you know, every single citizen on Terra has a church file."

"Yes. And?"

"And I wanted to tell you something I found that disturbed me."

"What is that?"

Lavina struggles visibly to find the right words. I feel for her, but I do not push or rush her. I merely await her words.

"What do you know about your mother's death?"

"I know that she drowned in the creek behind my home."

Lavina becomes silent. The thoughtful look of concentration on her face causes me to realize I may have been right.

"What . . . did you find?"

"There is no easy way to say this," Lavina says. "Your mother was murdered."

My suspicions confirmed, at last. I ask, "By whom?"

"By the Church," Lavina says.

This is almost more than I can bear.

"Why?"

"She went against the Church. She questioned doctrine."

"How did she question doctrine?"

"The file said she felt the Church was unnecessary. Apparently she tried to persuade the town to rid itself of the local church."

The town would not have gone along with that, I know.

"Some townsfolk reported her. She was reprimanded. The Provincia Administrator decided to make an example of her."

"We solve problems by murdering?"

"No, of course not, Cassiopeia."

"That is what they did! This is my church!"

Lavina nods.

"I am sorry," Lavina said. "I must go. I wish I could stay and comfort you, Cassiopeia Ovatio."

I nod. Lavina opens and enters her vehicle, then nods at me again before driving away.

I walk back into the house slowly, in a daze.

"Well, you are in good with the Boss, aren't you?" Concordia asks sardonically. I do not answer. "Planning to make her your secretary when you are the next Mother of All?"

"Leave her alone," Octavius says.

"And are you going to be the Father?" Concordia laughs.

Octavius stands and comes to me. I shake my head and walk away from him, not cruelly, just indicating I wish to be alone.

I find a small bedroom in the back of the house, where I sit on the bed.

My mother was the bold speaker and questioner in our home, but to try to remove a church from a town was unheard of. I feel surprise and alarm that my mother would wish to rid our town of the church that brought me hope and comfort all these years. At the same time, a part of me is fascinated to hear these news of my mother, this side of her I had no idea existed. A part of me even feels some pride in her. In her own way, she tried to serve justice.

But how could anyone see going against Havo or the Church as justice? How could anyone disbelieve in Havo? I have long wondered this in a quiet way, but now I must know. I rise from the bed, walk back into the common room, and ask Octavius, Pallium, Concordia, Spurius, and Postumus a general question.

"I am sorry to trouble you, my friends, with this question, but I find myself troubled by it."

"What is it, Cassie?" Octavius asks.

"I believe in Havo, as you know all too well," I say. "Why do not you believe in Him? How is it possible for someone not to believe in him?" I look from face to face for an answer.

"Whoah," Spurius says. "That is kind of heavy."

"Well," says Octavius, "for me it is a lack of evidence. I see no evidence for a god named Havo, or named anything else, really."

"But the evidence is all about us," I say. "I am sorry; I will listen. Please continue."

"We are told that Havo is supernatural, and yet all the evidence presented is natural. There is no supernatural evidence, so how can we believe in the supernatural?"

I ponder this.

"Belief implies acceptance without evidence," Octavius concludes. "Ergo, I do not 'believe' in a god or gods, as I do not accept anything without proper evidence."

"The other big one is the Problem of Evil," Concordia says. "The idea of a being that is omnipotent, omniscient, and nothing but benevolent is absurd, based on the reality we know."

"What do you mean?" I ask.

"I mean if those three characteristics co-existed in one being, it would be impossible for there to be suffering of innocents. Yet it is obvious that such suffering occurs. Why? A good god would not create such conditions, and an evil god could not create anything good. Now, we could have a semi-malicious god, but why? The Universe would not make any sense at all if it were run by a semi-malicious or otherwise capricious supreme being. You do not believe in one either. It makes much more sense to say there is no divine agency running things than a malicious one. Things are exactly as they appear to be, which is randomness governed by physics."

"What about free will?" I ask. "We have free will for a reason."

"No, consciousness is a happy accident. I for one am grateful for it, but I see no reason to credit a god for my ability to murder my neighbor. What we do with our consciousness is entirely up to us. No god controls us. No god responds to our good or evil. Ultimately, it doesn't matter whether there is a god or not, because he or she does not influence us or events in any discernible way." Concordia pauses, then concludes:

"The idea that an omniscient being created us with free will has always baffled me. If Havo is truly all-knowing, then he knew what choices I would make with my 'free will' before creating me, which means that Havo is responsible for what I have done, not me. Why would Havo or anyone punish me for choosing a path he provided?"

Pallium adds, "I do not respect or believe in or admire a god that willingly allows such unspeakable tragedy that happens throughout the world every single day. Why would he allow my father and everyone else aboard Station Michael—including children—to die? He wouldn't. Even if Havo existed, I would willingly go to Scar's side instead. I do not agree with or condone senseless and unneeded tragedy on a daily basis. Scar at least is honest." I gasp. "My second reason, of course, is that I think of myself as a logical and reasonable person, and the *Book of Havo* is the exact opposite of logic and reason. It makes absolutely no sense. That is why, in a nut shell."

"I am going to tell you something I have not told anyone else," Spurius says. "My first moment of doubt was a strange one. I attempted to sell my soul to Scar when I was nine years old. It did not work, and I decided that if Scar did not want my soul, I must be pretty useless. After a few more attempts, I began to question his existence. In the end, I concluded there was no Scar, and, by extension, no Havo who created him. That was easy."

"Proof," Postumus says abruptly. "Plain and simple. I need real, verifiable proof to believe something. I have not gotten any. That is it. And arguments aren't proof."

"The 'Havo Hypothesis' doesn't really explain anything," Octavius adds.

"What?"

"Science tries to understand how things work at the smallest scale possible. It looks at the behavior of matter and how cells work together at the microscopic level. Havians just say, 'Havo did it,' which doesn't explain anything or get us closer to the answer. *How* did he do it? What mechanisms did he use? When did he do it? How did he create the Universe from nothing and fine-tune its constants? More importantly, why? A perfect being, content within itself, would have no need to create anything. The existence of anything else disproves a perfect god. Sorry, Honey."

I stand dumbfounded.

"I see Havo everywhere," I say. "I see Havo in our freedom to choose good or evil. I see Havo in the consciousness of all animals, human and non-human." To Spurius I add, "I see Havo protecting you from Scar." I look around at the faces of my companions. "I am sure you all think pretty badly of me for my belief in Havo, and that is all right. Havo sustains me despite your disapproval."

"Believe what you want," Concordia says. "Just do not expect me to believe it or act upon it."

"I do not, just as I do not require proof of what I believe. Proof negates belief by rendering it fact. Have you ever considered that a universe with absolutely no evidence whatsoever for Havo is consistent with Havo's existence, since he could bring about everything through entirely naturalistic processes?"

"No one is telling you what to believe, Cassiopeia," Octavius says.

I am grateful, because I believe Havo created a universe so well He did not leave evidence of His passing. This is why it is called faith. I am content to believe as I wish and let others believe as they wish. "My god is a loving, forgiving god," I say. "We have nothing to fear from Havo, who knows our hearts and loves us no matter how we live our lives. I live mine so that I know He is happy and joy-filled with me. I only want Him to see in me what is right and just."

"I am glad your imaginary friend is a wonderful guy," Concordia snaps. "I hope you do not find it too hard to live in accordance with what you yourself imagine."

"I did not ask your views to start an argument," I say.

"That is almost inevitable," Octavius says. "Hopefully we can all disagree agreeably," he adds, giving Concordia and the rest pointed looks. They nod, and I can see the conversation has ended.

We find some food in the house, satisfy our hunger, and retire for the night. Octavius and I take the small bedroom in the back of the house. Concordia takes the other small bedroom. The other three men take the sofas and the living-room floor. I assure Pallium he need not sit outside our bedroom door.

"I do not understand," I say to Octavius, "but I accept."

He kisses me to sleep again.

As I sleep, I dream I hear Concordia saying, "She can do what she wants, but so can I. I did not agree to her mission, and I did not even agree to leave the Station—I was lied to and tricked into coming along. My place was up there, with ____. And now that I am here, do you think I am just going to blindly follow the woman who tricked me into coming here? Yes, I am still alive, but just barely. We are surrounded by the enemy, and I am tired of running and hiding. I want to fight!"

"I understand," Spurius says.

"I not only understand," Postumus says, "I agree. I am with you. What about you, Pallium?"

"My father's last request of me was that I protect Cassiopeia. Where she goes I go."

"Suit yourself," Concordia says.

I do not think of this again until the morning, when I wake to find Concordia and Postumus gone.

"They left," Pallium tells me.

"So I see," I say. "And you did nothing to stop them?" I ask Spurius.

"What, it is my job to tell them what to do?"

"Our chances of success are now diminished," I say.

"It is possible," Octavius says, "our chances are now enhanced. It is easier to travel in secret in smaller numbers." I realize he may be right, but I am still annoyed no one made an effort to dissuade them from leaving.

"I did try to dissuade them," Pallium says.

"And I do know that trying to dissuade them would not have worked," I say. "Well, thank you for staying, Spurius."

"I happen to think there's safety in numbers," Spurius says.

I am pained. I consider Concordia a friend, and I need her help. "Is it too late? Do we know when they left? Could we catch up to them?"

"No," Spurius says. "They left a couple hours ago. We do not know which way they went, or where, or to do what."

I know he is right.

"Who has the technical expertise to channel a province signal to the other provinces?" I ask.

"I think I can do it," Pallium says, "but we do not know how to contact the underground in other provinces."

"That is where I come in," Spurius says. "I guess I just became a lot more valuable to you, did not I, Sister Cassie?"

I do not like his presumptuous manner, but I know he is right again.

"Yes, you did, Spurius," I say. "But I was grateful to Secretary Lavina for your presence before."

I look about at Pallium, Octavius, and Spurius. "Let us not delay. We do not have a vehicle, but perhaps you, Spurius, can contact the underground here and arrange for a ride."

"If you get me to Florence," Spurius says. "I have a friend there who can help us, but unlike the Secretary, I do not have a personal communication device."

I look about and see there is no communication device connected with the home. I realize that using one there might not be wise regardless.

"We will have to find our own way there," I say. We find food in the kitchen, eat a small amount, and leave, the four of us walking north. *This is highly dangerous. At least we are all dressed as Havians. We pass a sign reading, "Castle of Sopra". I note the ruin of a castle on a hill in the distance.*

Octavius, Pallium, Spurius, and I approach the town named after Sopra's castle. I wonder who Sopra was. I feel nervous.

Morning is a time of day when Havians are out and about. I immediately wonder if I should not have stayed back at the cottage, to hide my face, but looking down seems to help me hide my face. I walk behind Pallium and next to Octavius; Spurius leads us. "The last time Lavina brought us here there was a little place . . . " Spurius looks ahead to find something. "There it is. That little shop right there. You know, this might do it for us." I look to see an old store, looking forgotten. A wooden sign hanging from its front reads, *Old Things Bought and Sold*.

We walk into the store. Old things hang from the ceiling, fill every surface area, nook, and cranny in sight: bicycles, furniture, toys, old appliances, even clothing from decades past. An old man in a wool vest comes out from the back and asks from behind gold-rimmed spectacles, "May I help you?"

"Spurius ___, a friend of Secretary Lavina," Spurius says. "We met once before."

"Oh, yes, a little over a year ago, I think it was. How is the Secretary?" the man asks.

"She's well. She would like you to meet Cassiopeia Ovatio, of Station Michael."

The old man's eyes, accustomed to hiding emotion, cannot hide his surprise on this occasion. "Well!" he says. "Cassiopeia Ovatio in my shop. This is truly a great honor." He bows to me.

"The honor is mine," I say. "How do you know Lavina?" I ask, perhaps too boldly.

"Lavina is an old and dear friend of mine," the man says. "But perhaps we should discuss this where it is safe." The man moves to the front door, locks it, and places a sign in its window announcing the store is closed. "Come this way." He leads us to the back of the store, where he shows us a trap door underneath a small carpet.

"Is every underground hiding-place truly underground?" I wonder aloud. The old man laughs.

"Yes, unfortunately, that is often the case, as the Church has made life aboveground . . . very difficult." He looks into the eyes of my companions for confirmation, which I note that he receives. Even Spurius becomes serious for the moment as he nods to the man, who reminds me of my father but older and more proud.

We go down a wooden ladder to a small room, furnished with table, chairs, and comfortable sofas against the walls but completely enclosed. I am surprised.

"You expected a network of tunnels, or some such thing?" our host asks with amusement.

"I suppose so!" I laugh.

"This is where we sometimes hold meetings. We have little need of escape here. We are in a small town in the countryside, where nothing ever happens."

After the trap door is closed, we sit. "Now, what can I do for you?" ___ asks. "I know you did not come here for a radio."

"Actually, you are not far off," Spurius says. I get the feeling he has appointed himself our unofficial spokesman. "We need to get to the broadcast station in ___ Provincia. We need to use it to transmit to the other Provinces. And, of course, we need those other Provinces to agree to relay our broadcast."

____ wears an expression of concentration, almost consternation. After he meditates upon the problem for several long, almost-unbearable moments, he says, "All right. This will take some doing, and it will not be easy in light of today's announcements."

"What announcements?" Spurius asks nervously.

"The Church is expanding its search beyond the Havican. Some apostates have been caught." I feel a bolt of lightning through my heart. Could it be Concordia and Postumus? "If we are going to move, it must be now and stealthy. I can contact my friends in ____ Provincia and ask them to work on your request. fly you to ___ Provincia, and even get you to the broadcast station. But I cannot guarantee your safety—or even my own."

"Fly us?" I ask.

"I was a pilot, before. Of course we will need to borrow a helicopter."

"Borrow . . . a helicopter?"

"From the airport. And we should leave now. I thank you, Cassiopeia Ovatio, for providing me with some excitement in my golden-ray years."

"You are welcome," I say.

Material

"No one censors the art in our lives."

I would like to add that it is not about being open to belief. It is about asking believers to explain how they can believe in the face of life's suffering. If you cannot explain or defend your beliefs, how can you expect anyone else to take them seriously? If you think it is acceptable to say, "Respect my beliefs because I believe them," then I think we all understand that is ridiculous. So: how can you believe? And if you cannot or will not answer seriously, then please do not expect to be taken seriously. Really, my views are irrelevant. What are yours, and how do you justify them?

Almighty God, give us grace that we may cast away the works of darkness
And put upon us the armour of light....on this 1 st day of Advent

Now in the time of this mortal life, in which thy son Jesus Christ came to visit us in great humility, that in the last day, when he shall come again in his glorious majesty, to judge both the quick and the dead, we may rise to the life immortal, through him who liveth and reigneth with thee and the Holy Ghost, now and for ever, Amen'

Let us start our 1st Advent to ოჷℓო, `*.THE HOLY SPIRIT,.*ოჷℓო,

☆*⸸'*☆.☆*⸸'*☆.☆*⸸'*☆.☆*⸸'*☆.☆*⸸'*☆.
⸸ Recite HOLY SPIRIT CHAPLET ......Seven decades..see below
⸸ Especially on Sundays
⸸ Very often, even every day

✝ When an important decision is to be made, grave moments or when spiritual help is required
✝ Every day during recollections or retreats
☆*✝`¹*☆.☆*✝`¹*☆.☆*✝`¹*☆.☆*✝`¹*☆.☆*✝^¹*☆.

∴∴
`∴ O Holy Spirit of God,
Abide with us,
Inspire all our thoughts,
Pervade our imaginations,
suggest all our decisions,

Order all our doings. Be with us in our silence and in our speech, in our haste and in our leisure, in company and in solitude, in the freshness of the morning and in the weariness of the evening; and give us grace at all times humbly to rejoice in Thy mysterious companionship.

✝ SEVEN DECADES MYSTERY.✝ ...Rosary Beads details ...in the picture...

✝ 1st Mystery:
Let us honour the Holy Ghost and adore Him Who is Love Substantial, proceeding from the Father and the Son, and uniting them in an infinite and eternal Charity.

✝ 2nd Mystery:
Let us honour the operation of the Holy Ghost and adore Him in the Immaculate Conception of Mary, sanctifying her from the first moment with the plenitude of grace.

✝ 3rd Mystery:

Let us honour the operation of the Holy Ghost and adore Him as He fecundates the Virgin Mary in the Incarnation of the Word, the Son of God by His Divine nature and the Son of the Virgin by the flesh.

✟ 4th Mystery:
Let us honour the operation of the Holy Ghost and adore Him giving birth to the Church on the glorious day of Pentecost in the Cenacle.

✟ 5th Mystery:
Let us honour the operation of the Holy Ghost and adore Him dwelling in the Church and assisting her faithfully according to the Divine promise,even to the consummation of the world.

✟ 6th Mystery:
Let us honour the wonderful operation of the Holy Ghost creating within the Church that other Christ, the Priest, and conferring the plenitude of the Priesthood on the Bishops.

✟ 7th Mystery:
Let us honour the operation of the Holy Ghost and adore Him in the heroic virtue of the saints in the Church, that hidden and marvelous work of the "Adorable Sanctifier".

Follow by.... ✟ Glorious Mysteries
Conclude with: ✟ Hail Holy Queen....continue ✟ praying and keep
∴•• ✟ Amen ✟ Amen ✟ Amen ✟

Upon hearing the report on the enlarged meeting of the Political Bureau of the Central Committee of the Workers' Party of Korea, the service personnel and people throughout the country broke into angry shouts that a stern judgment of the revolution should be meted out to the anti-party, counter-revolutionary factional elements. Against the backdrop of these shouts rocking the country, a special military tribunal of the DPRK Ministry of State Security was held on December 12 against traitor for all ages Jang Song Thaek.

The accused Jang brought together undesirable forces and formed a faction as the boss of a modern day factional group for a long time and thus committed such hideous crime as attempting to overthrow the state by all sorts of intrigues and despicable methods with a wild ambition to grab the supreme power of our party and state.

The tribunal examined Jang's crimes.

All the crimes committed by the accused were proved in the course of hearing and were admitted by him.

A decision of the special military tribunal of the Ministry of State Security of the DPRK was read out at the trial.

Every sentence of the decision served as sledge-hammer blow brought down by our angry service personnel and people on the head of Jang, an anti-party, counter-revolutionary factional element and despicable political careerist and trickster.

The accused is a traitor to the nation for all ages who perpetrated anti-party, counter-revolutionary factional acts in a bid to overthrow the leadership of our party and state and the socialist system.

Jang was appointed to responsible posts of the party and state thanks to the deep political trust of President Kim Il Sung and leader Kim Jong Il and received benevolence from them more than any others from long ago.

He held higher posts than before and received deeper trust from supreme leader Kim Jong Un, in particular.

The political trust and benevolence shown by the peerlessly great men of Mt. Paektu were something he hardly deserved.

It is an elementary obligation of a human being to repay trust with sense of obligation and benevolence with loyalty.

However, despicable human scum Jang, who was worse than a dog, perpetrated thrice-cursed acts of treachery in betrayal of such profound trust and warmest paternal love shown by the party and the leader for him.

From long ago, Jang had a dirty political ambition. He dared not raise his head when Kim Il Sung and Kim Jong Il were alive. But, reading their faces, Jang had an axe to grind and involved himself in double-dealing. He began revealing his true colors, thinking that it was just the time for him to realize his wild ambition in the period of historic turn when the generation of the revolution was replaced.

Jang committed such an unpardonable thrice-cursed treason as overtly and covertly standing in the way of settling the issue of succession to the leadership with an axe to grind when a very important issue was under discussion to hold respected Kim Jong Un in high esteem as the only successor to Kim Jong Il in reflection of the unanimous desire and will of the entire party and army and all people.

When his cunning move proved futile and the decision that Kim Jong Un was elected vice-chairman of the Central Military Commission of the Workers' Party of Korea at the Third Conference of the WPK in reflection of the unanimous will of all party members, service personnel and people was proclaimed, making all participants break into enthusiastic cheers that shook the conference hall, he behaved so arrogantly and insolently as unwillingly standing up from his seat and half-heartedly clapping, touching off towering resentment of our service personnel and people.

Jang confessed that he behaved so at that time as a knee-jerk reaction as he thought that if Kim Jong Un's base and system for leading the army were consolidated, this would lay a stumbling block in the way of grabbing the power of the party and state.

When Kim Jong Il passed away so suddenly and untimely to our sorrow, he began working in real earnest to realize its long-cherished greed for power.

Abusing the honor of often accompanying Kim Jong Un during his field guidance, Jang tried hard to create illusion about him by projecting himself internally and externally as a special being on a par with the headquarters of the revolution.

In a bid to rally a group of reactionaries to be used by him for toppling the leadership of the party and state, he let the undesirable and alien elements including those who had been dismissed and relieved of their posts after being severely punished for disobeying the instructions of Kim Jong Il and kowtowing to him work in a department of the Central Committee of the WPK and organs under it in a crafty manner.

Jang did serious harm to the youth movement in our country, being part of the group of renegades and traitors in the field of youth work bribed by enemies. Even after they were disclosed and purged by the resolute measure of the party, he patronized those cat's paws and let them hold important posts of the party and state.

He had let Ri Ryong Ha, flatterer, work with him since the 1980s whenever he was transferred to other posts and systematically promoted Ri up to the post of first vice department director of the Party Central Committee though he had been purged for his factional act of denying the unitary leadership of the party. Jang thus made Ri his trusted stooge.

Jang let his confidants and flatterers who had been fired for causing an important case of denying the unitary leadership of the party work in his department and organs under it in a crafty manner in a few years. He systematically rallied ex-convicts, those problematic in their past careers and discontented elements around him and ruled over them as sacred and inviolable being.

He worked hard to put all affairs of the country under his control, massively increasing the staff of his department and organs under it, and stretch his tentacles to ministries and national institutions. He converted his department into a "little kingdom" which no one dares touch.

He was so imprudent as to prevent the Taedonggang Tile Factory from erecting a mosaic depicting Kim Il Sung and Kim Jong Il and a monument to field guidance given by them. Moreover, Jang turned down the unanimous request of the service personnel of a unit of the Korean People's Internal Security Forces to have the autograph letter sent by Kim Jong Un to the unit carved on a natural granite and erected with good care in front of the building of its command. He was so reckless as to instruct the unit to erect it in a shaded corner.

He committed such anti-party acts as systematically denying the party line and policies, its organizational will, in the past period. These acts were a revelation of deliberate and sinister attempt to create extreme illusion and idolization of him by making him appear as a special being who can overrule either issues decided by the party or its line.

He went so rude as to take in the middle even those things associated with intense loyalty and sincerity of our army and people towards the party and the leader and distribute them among his confidants in an effort to take credit upon himself for doing so. This behavior was to create illusion about him.

Due to his persistent moves to create illusion and idolization of him his flatterers and followers in his department and organs under it praised him as "No. 1 comrade." They went the lengths of denying even the party's instructions to please him at any cost.

Jang established such a heterogenous work system in the department and the relevant organs as considering what he said as more important than the party's policies. Consequently, his trusted henchmen and followers made no scruple of perpetrating such counterrevolutionary act as disobeying the order of the Supreme Commander of the KPA.

The revolutionary army will never pardon all those who disobey the order of the Supreme Commander and there will be no place for them to be buried even after their death.

Dreaming a fantastic dream to become premier at an initial stage to grab the supreme power of the party and state, Jang made his department put major economic fields of the country under its control in a bid to disable the Cabinet. In this way he schemed to drive the economy of the country and people's living into an uncontrollable catastrophe.

He put inspection and supervision organs belonging to the Cabinet under his control in defiance of the new state machinery established by Kim Jong Il at the First Session of the Tenth Supreme People's Assembly. He put all issues related to all structural works handled by the Cabinet under his control and had the final say on them, making it impossible for the Cabinet to properly perform its function and role as an economic command. They included the issues of setting up and disorganizing committees, ministries and national institutions and provincial, city and county-level organs, organizing units for foreign trade and earning foreign money and structures overseas and fixing living allowances.

When he attempted to make a false report to the party without having agreement with the Cabinet and the relevant ministry on the issue related to the state construction control organization, officials concerned expressed just opinion that his behavior was contrary to the construction law worked out by Kim Il Sung and Kim Jong Il. Hearing this, he made the reckless remark that "the rewriting of the construction law would solve the problem."

Abusing his authority, he undermined the work system related to the construction of the capital city established by Kim Il Sung and Kim Jong Il, reducing the construction building-materials bases to such bad shape little short of debris in a few years. He weakened the ranks of technicians and skilled workers at the unit for the construction of the capital city in a crafty manner and transferred major construction units to his confidants so that they might make money. In this way he deliberately disturbed the construction in Pyongyang.

He instructed his stooges to sell coal and other precious underground resources at random. Consequently, his confidants were saddled with huge debts, deceived by brokers. Jang made no scruple of committing such act of treachery in May last as selling off the land of the Rason economic and trade zone to a foreign country for a period of five decades under the pretext of paying those debts.

It was none other than Jang who wirepulled behind scene Pak Nam Gi, traitor for all ages, to recklessly issue hundreds of billions of won in 2009, sparking off serious economic chaos and disturbing the people's mind-set.

Jang encouraged money-making under various pretexts to secure funds necessary for gratifying his political greed and was engrossed in irregularities and corruption. He thus took the lead in spreading indolent, careless and undisciplined virus in our society.

After collecting precious metals since the construction of Kwangbok Street in the 1980s, he set up a secret organ under his control and took a fabulous amount of funds from a bank and purchased precious metals in disregard of the state law. He thus committed such anti-state criminal acts as creating a great confusion in financial management system of the state.

He let the decadent capitalist lifestyle find its way to our society by distributing all sorts of pornographic pictures among his confidants since 2009. He led a dissolute, depraved life, squandering money wherever he went.

He took at least 4.6 million Euro from his secret coffers and squandered it in 2009 alone and enjoyed himself in casino in a foreign country. These facts alone clearly show how corrupt and degenerate he was.

Jang was so reckless with his greed for power that he persistently worked to stretch his tentacles even to the People's Army with a foolish calculation that he would succeed in staging a coup if he mobilized the army.

He fully revealed his despicable true colors as a traitor for all ages in the course of questioning by uttering as follows: "I attempted to trigger off discontent among service personnel and people when the present regime does not take any measure despite the fact that the economy of the country and people's living are driven into catastrophe. Comrade supreme leader is the target of the coup."

As regards the means and methods for staging the coup, Jang said: "I was going to stage the coup by using army officers who had close ties with me or by mobilizing armed forces under the control of my confidants. I do not know well about recently appointed army officers but have some acquaintances with those appointed in the past period. I thought the army might join in the coup if the living of the people and service personnel further deteriorate in the future. And I calculated that my confidants in my department including Ri Ryong Ha and Jang Su Gil would surely follow me and had a plan to use the one in charge of the people's security organ as my confidant. It was my calculation that I might use several others besides them."

Asked about the timing of the coup and his plan to do after staging the coup, Jang answered: "I did not fix the definite time for the coup. But it was my intention to concentrate my department and all economic organs on the Cabinet and become premier when the economy goes totally bankrupt and the state is on the verge of collapse in a certain period. I thought that if I solve the problem of people's living at a certain level by spending an enormous amount of funds I have accumulated under various names after becoming premier, the people and service personnel will shout "hurrah" for me and I will succeed in the coup in a smooth way."

Jang dreamed such a foolish dream that once he seizes power by a base method, his despicable true colors as "reformist" known to the outside world would help his "new government" get "recognized" by foreign countries in a short span of time.

All facts go to clearly prove that Jang is a thrice-cursed traitor without an equal in the world as he had desperately worked for years to destabilize and bring down the DPRK and grab the supreme power of the party and state by employing all the most cunning and sinister means and methods, pursuant to the "strategic patience" policy and "waiting strategy" of the U.S. and the south Korean puppet group of traitors.

The hateful and despicable nature of the anti-party, anti-state and unpopular crimes committed by Jang was fully disclosed in the course of the trial conducted at the special military tribunal of the DPRK Ministry of State Security.

The era and history will eternally record and never forget the shuddering crimes committed by Jang Song Thaek, the enemy of the party, revolution and people and heinous traitor to the nation.

No matter how much water flows under the bridge and no matter how frequently a generation is replaced by new one, the lineage of Paektu will remain unchanged and irreplaceable.

Our party, state, army and people do not know anyone exceptKim Il Sung, Kim Jong Il and Kim Jong Un.

Our service personnel and people will never pardon all those who dare disobey the unitary leadership of Kim Jong Un, challenge his absolute authority and oppose the lineage of Paektu to an individual but bring them to the stern court of history without fail and mercilessly punish them on behalf of the party and revolution, the country and its people, no matter where they are in hiding.

The special military tribunal of the Ministry of State Security of the DPRK confirmed that the state subversion attempted by the accused Jang with an aim to overthrow the people's power of the DPRK by ideologically aligning himself with enemies is a crime punishable by Article 60 of the DPRK Criminal Code, vehemently condemned him as a wicked political careerist, trickster and traitor for all ages in the name of the revolution and the people and ruled that he would be sentenced to death according to it.

The decision was immediately executed."

O Havo, through the Immaculate Ray of Your Beloved partner Havia, I offer you my prayers, works, joys, and sufferings of this day in union with the Holy Abundance of the Mass throughout the World. I offer them for all the intentions of your Sacred Hearts: the salvation of souls, the reparation for sin, and the reunion of all Havians at the end of the World. I offer them for the intentions of our Prisms, and in particular for those recommended by our Holy Father and Mother this month.

This prayer truly offers God everything in our day, good and bad, while reminding us of the importance of praying for others, with the help of our Blessed Mother, including our bishops and our Holy Father. They can all certainly use our prayers these days!

The Apostleship of Prayer, by the way, is still doing wonderful work for God, as described here. They write on their website that, "Pope John Paula II once said that the practice of praying the Morning Offering is 'of fundamental importance in the life of each and every one of the faithful.' It is a daily reminder to make our entire day, our whole life 'a living sacrifice, holy and acceptable to God' (Romans 12: 1)." In doing so we are also joining our sacrifice with that of our Lord both in His Passion and in the Holy Sacrifice of the Mass!

You can use one of these prayers as a morning offering as well:

My God, I adore You, and I love You with all my heart. I thank you for having created me, made me a Christian, and preserved me this night. I offer You the actions of this day. Grant that all of them may be in accordance with Your holy Will and for Your greater glory. Protect me from sin and from all evil. Let Your grace be always with me and with all my dear ones. Amen.

Hello Robert,

May your work please God.

You can access any Catholic prayers and rituals from the Nation Conference of Catholic Bishops Website www.usccb.org or www.EWTN.org or ibreviary.com Catholic people pray morning praise, grace before meals, evening thanksgiving, rosary, act of contrition, and most importantly Mass each week.

Let me know if I can be of further help.
Fr.Patrick

http://www.linguanaut.com/english_latin.htm

Cassiopeia's initial response to being interviewed was negative, but I just couldn't reconcile that with her character and beliefs, so I reversed it without incident. That said, I really would have liked this incident to be possible. Oh, well.

"No media," I say.

"Pardon?"

"I am sorry, Sisters. I know that it is customary, but I have always found my relationship with Havo and Havia to be personal and private. What more could I say than while I did not expect this meeting to occur now, I am preparing with all my heart and soul to be ready when It comes? There is really nothing else to say, and anyone would say the same thing."

"Except, of course, to describe your life here, that we may all get to know you better."

"I am sorry, Sister, but that is not my concern right now. My getting to know Havo is. I lead a very simple and uninteresting life, and preparing with all my heart and soul means preparing with all my heart and soul."

"Of course," the woman says. "Still, they would like you to say what is not necessary to say. I'll tell Father ___ your position, and perhaps he will contact you to ask you to change your mind."

"He is always welcome to contact me," I say.

The woman leaves, disgust on her face. I am truly sorry, but I have no desire for distractions when every one of my moments must be used carefully. Am I being cruel to my fellow Rays? I do not know. I just know that I have always found those interviews to be unseemly. What is there to say that we have not all said? We long for union with our lord and god.

Act of Contrition

O my God, I am heartily sorry for having offended you, and I

detest

all my sins, because of Your just punishments, but most of all

because

they offend You, my God, who

are

all-good and deserving of all my
love.

I firmly resolve, with the help of
Your grace, to sin no more and
to

avoid the near occasion of sin.

We do not feel anything strike us; we simply begin going down, Pallium and Concordia struggling to right the craft. Our shuttle comes into the Port on a downward angle to the right, heading directly toward the boats, pier, dock, and buildings of the Port.

"Steer!" Concordia shouts at Pallium.

I see Havians walking on the pier to our right. We crash in the water a short distance from the pier supports.

"Get out of here—now!" Concordia bellows. We unbuckle our safety harnesses and open the hatches. The rush of warm Terran air brings me a rush of emotion, but we have no time. We jump out of the hatches into the water, then swim to the supports under the dock. I watch our shuttle begin to sink with sadness.

"Well, Concordia?" Octavius asks. "Where are your friends, and how do we find them?"

We see Church ships in the air of the Port heading our way.

"Swim this way," Concordia says, leading us away from the sinking shuttle. Soon we come upon a steep stairway from the water to a wooden hatch up through the pier. "Do we want to take this?" she asks.

"'Do we want to take this?'" Octavius asks. "Do not *you* know?"

"I know the resistance is in Rome," Concordia says. "I have never been here before, and I do not have contact names. All I can do is use logic to find them. Do we want to go up there? We would be among the pedestrians, I think."

We can hear excited steps running along the pier above. A crowd is coming to observe the shuttle. I realize it is an almost unheard-of event for a ship to crash land.

"The confusion would assist us," Pallium says.

"We need to get out of this water," I say.

We agree and hurry up the stairs. Pallium, the biggest and strongest of the four of us, opens the hatch. Distracted Havians run to and fro, ignoring us as we emerge. I pull at my robes to stop them from clinging to my wet form. The green coveralls of the Station Michael crew do not yet harm us, as no one has yet noticed us. I look about for anyplace to hide. I know we only have moments before someone notices us. We start walking from the moment we emerge from the hatch.

As we stand there, considering our next move, the Church ships come down next to our shuttle.

"We need to move," I say.

The four of us walk, as calmly as possible, into the shade of the nearest building, then slowly walk away from the scene. A small bearded man in Havian robes approaches us from the direction we are heading. He smiles broadly at us while appearing to be slightly out of breath.

"Friends," he says. "Come with me."

We look at each other in doubt, though we continue walking in the same direction.

"Come with me," he says. "I know who you are, and who you are looking for."

"Who are you?" I ask.

"I am your new employer, ___, and you have come to Rome to assist me with my automotive business."

He is providing us with an excuse to be here, I realize.

"You are clearly my new secretary," he says to me, smiling with a twinkle in his eyes. I remain suspicious of this man, but I see little choice but to follow him, at least until a better plan suggests itself.

"Thank you, ___, for helping us," I say. "How did you spot us?"

"We've been watching your descent since it began," he says. "But so have they. Let us move faster."

I cannot help looking over my shoulder at the way we have come. The crowd is larger, but I do not see Church authorities. More will come, I know.

"We need to hurry," _____ says. "Almost there."

"There . . . was something else," Lavina says.

"What is that, Mother Lavina?" I ask.

"You might not be able to handle it," Lavina says.

"Try me," I say.

"Your mother carried on a romantic affair within the church."

"If you mean she was betrothed to Havo, aren't we all?'

"I mean she was unfaithful to your father, with a member of the Church."

I am stunned.

"I am sorry," Lavina says. "It brings me no joy to tell you this."

"Who was it?" I ask.

"Are you sure you want to know?"

"I am sure."

"The Prism of Soul River."

Arcturus.

"Is that why she was . . . murdered?"

"Yes."

"Did he murder her?"

"No, the file specifically says the Church over-ruled him. He did not want her killed."

"Why was not he punished?"

"Oh, he was."

"How?"

"He was put to death as well."

I am confused.

"Arcturus?"

"No, the previous Prism, Father ____."

I remember him. I remember Arcturus becoming the new Prism five years ago. It was not Arcturus.

he who contols the mind contols the masses.--uko augustin john

And of course, the original Latin calendar had dies Solis (Day of the Sun), dies Lunae (day of the Moon), dies Martis (Day of Mars), dies Mercurii (Day of Mercury), dies Iovis (Day of Jupiter), dies Veneris (Day of Venus), and dies Saturni (Day of Saturn.)

"There may come a time when atheists need to employ violence in order to protect themselves."
—Christopher Mallard

"We need an atheist city, we will call it New Atlantis for the irony of it, where science is embraced and cultism and religion are absolutely forbidden. We would dwell in this great city until we had the technology to terraform and colonize mars. We could enjoy and explore the solar system. Capture asteroids and mine them for the precious metals, then build plexiglas-like spheres around the entire asteroid and give it an atmosphere and grow crops on it. Of course the plexiglas-like material will have to be capable of blocking out most of the sun's harmful radiation but it is not an unattainable technology. The possibilities are unlimited, especially when they're not fettered by the dogmas of religion. The earth is infested with religion and there's no humane way to remove the infestation so those of us not afflicted should flee. Move to mars and leave monitoring equipment on the moon and in earth orbit so we can observe and document the continued religion fueled destruction of man on earth. An unfortunate reality is that we would be wise to have laws against man leaving earth while still burdened with religion. Quarantine the earth until the problem works itself out. However, our current level of technology was attained even despite the restraints of religion so it is not unthinkable that once the people of New Atlantis migrated to Mars the remaining humans would eventually advance scientifically enough to make a similar exodus. It is at this point that I believe we would be well advised to prevent them from leaving and spreading their sickness to the stars. Thankfully that is a debate for future generations." Christopher Mallard - Anti-Theist

"There is something I have wanted to ask you, Havian," __ says.

"Go ahead," I say. "If I can refract Havo's light in any way—"

"How alone can you be?"

"What do you mean?"

"How far can you push yourself into a story, until you have no connection with Reality or other human beings?"

"But you have answered your own question. I am not alone. I am surrounded by Havians."

"Do you really think so? Do you think everyone believes as you do?"

"We might have differing interpretations of scripture, but we share the same worldview."

"Do not be so sure."

The Church works to address effects before causes, to make sure there are always problems it is indispensable to 'solve'. The Church, above all, must maintain its own necessity. We cannot cure every ill, otherwise the Church would no longer be needed.

Do you know what you are saying?

Do you? I am saying the Church created the Inopia.

THIS BOOK IS NOT FINISHED,
but Robert is working on it as
you read this.
Visit RobertPeate.Com or
Facebook.Com/robertpeate
for updates.

Afterword: Evangelism

I am not atheist. I am antitheist. That means I not only lack religion but actively oppose it. Why do I do this? Because I see organized religion as one of the World's biggest evils. My writing reflects my view. Those who have read my earlier work know this.

I understand that most human beings on this planet do not share my anti-religious view. I understand my depiction of religion as evil will displease some. They do not need to read this or any other work of fiction of mine.

A religious person once asked me, sardonically, if I considered myself more "evolved" than the non-religious. I said no, I simply felt she had been lied to, which shut her up. But that is the truth: I see religious persons as just as good (or bad) as non-religious persons. The difference is they believe a lie. In the vast majority of cases, I think this is due to their parents indoctrinating them the way they themselves were indoctrinated as children. My parents told me religion was bunk, and I agreed with them, so why shouldn't the religious adopt what their parents tell them?

As a result, I think what makes it most difficult for religious persons to overcome their religion is not a lack of logical thinking ability. I think what makes it difficult for most believers is they do not want to go against their parents, despite their own logic or justice, out of loyalty or fear of conflict. It is hard to go against one's parents. Organized religion makes the most of this, which is just another reason why I consider it completely evil.

My point is that, though I sometimes lose my patience with believers, ultimately I feel sorry for them. Their next reaction to that is usually one of outrage at my condescension, not realizing that to condescend is to do a favor. It is a shame that condescension is so grossly and frequently misunderstood these days, but the truth is that I could just as easily *not* feel sorry for them, expect them to think as I do, and cut them no slack whatever. It is their choice which response they would prefer. They are not going to get me to treat their wacko views the way they would like, which is to feign respect or agreement. Are they going to pretend to agree with me out of courtesy? I doubt it, and why should they? Persons who respect each other do not need to bullshit each other —but that is something religion demands of them, forcing them to do things they do not feel or wish.

The fact is, parents perpetuate ancient fantasies with lies to their children. The children suffer damage but do not wish to doubt or cross their parents. They suffer all manner of torments, repression, and dysfunction, and cannot be blamed for this. But when one becomes a legal or physical adult, one becomes responsible for oneself. If one persists in belief beyond a certain age or stage, one becomes responsible for one's own lies to oneself and others.

If one leads a happy life with no problems, one does not usually feel a burning passion to fight injustice, but sometimes even observing problems from afar can be enough to move one to respond. The truth is we are all affected directly or indirectly by society's biggest problems. I have lived my life under what I call the Christian Empire. Everyone living under that empire has been adversely affected by it, whether he or she is aware of this adverse effect or not--and most especially those who subscribe to it. Have they also benefited from it? Of course. They enjoy social status and all its privileges, including the belief they are loved by their god and the comfort that provides, but I argue the price has been too high. Believing lies, however pretty or pleasant those lies might be, is not as valuable or rewarding as knowing the truth or even doubt. With my work I hope to provoke thought. As music composer Handel said, I hope to make them better, not merely to entertain.

To that end, in recent years I have used my writing as a tool to address specific societal ills: Christianity, capitalism, animal abuse. In this story I take on the absolutism and evil of religion in general, though I have modeled my fictional religion on the easiest target of all: the Roman Catholic Church, with its (occasional) infallibility, its hierarchy, its complexity, its dogma. Any and all religions would or could behave as monstrously if given the chance, but that church provides us the most tangible example of totalitarian theocracy, or 'theocratic socialism'. To depict it I almost did not have to exert effort. Note to the Vatican: you are making it too easy, guys. That said, I did try to remove the patriarchy from it.

For years I felt that I could not write about evil. I felt the World was ugly enough. Then I realized that evil was just another color on the palette, that managed well it could be used to make points clearly and effectively (that to make some points it must be used). My point in this work is to show the evil of religion in a fictional setting. I have attempted to manage it well. I hope I have succeeded.

I have been told that in proselytizing my own point of view with missionary zeal I am no better than religious zealots. I have responded that I consider it everyone's duty to act on his or her morality. Do I begrudge others acting on theirs? No. I do consider my moral position to be better than religion's, and I am sure religion is not worried about me or filled with self-doubt about whether or not it should be "spreading the Good Word". I am a drop in the bucket, but I am not going to sit idly by and watch my world without using my small talents to comment on it. Speaking is not the issue; what one says is.

I do not really see how writing a fictional story threatens anyone, except insofar as stories are how we learn. If I portray organized religion as evil, that might prompt someone to reconsider organized religion's merits.

If I do not portray an evil, that does not change the evil's character. The evil remains evil whether I comment on it at all or not, to say nothing of whether my silence would assist that evil to continue. Besides, if organized religion is wonderful, it has nothing to fear from me, and I will only embarrass myself. Those who admire religion, therefore, should egg me on, no?

I have theist friends I have known and loved for thirty years. We know each other's views and do not get into arguments, because we are friends. But my loving and leaving my friends alone doesn't mean I cannot, will not, or shouldn't act on my views. I oppose organized religion in my words and deeds. I do not think it is enough to look the other way. Really, I think believers just cannot stand someone calling religion in general or their own religion in particular evil, whereas I am used to religion calling nonbelievers evil or eternally doomed. I know religion has tortured, murdered, and otherwise persecuted nonbelievers for thousands of years. This is par for religion's course. Because I consider religion an evil, naturally I am going to do everything I can not only to be neutral and sit on my hands but to actively fight it using my few limited talents. I consider that my duty as a moral human being, though of course religion does not want to be challenged. Those who possess the One Divine and Unalterable Eternal Truth tend not to accept disagreement, and it is easier for them to fault "militant atheists" than it is to consider a different point of view. That may make challenging religion all the more important. Have never you heard the quotation that all evil needs to succeed is for good persons to do nothing? Well, religion advocates that I do nothing, but I cannot allow evil (as I perceive it) to succeed. Surely believers can understand that; they just do not want to hear their religion is evil. They do not want to be criticized, they consider it more important that I be silent than that they face criticism, and that certainly seems evil to me.

All this said, I have been accused of being "an anti-religious bigot". I think my portrayal of the character of Cassiopeia, which involves her intelligence, her wisdom, and her goodness, disproves this. I have been accused of thinking I am "better than" believers. As I said to the person making that accusation, I do not think being lied to makes a believer lesser than someone who has not been lied to. I've been lied to, about other matters. Does being lied to mean being less? No. I do consider truth better than falsehood and education worth the effort. The teacher does not fault the student. The student even teaches the teacher.

The idea for a science-fiction novel came to me from Dan Marshall and his excellent *The Lightcap*.

The idea to tackle theocracy came to me because it is one of my favorite and one of the World's most profound subjects.

The idea of the character of Cassiopeia Ovatio came to me from Charles Portis and his masterpiece, *True Grit*. Cassiopeia is infused with

Mattie Ross' religious self-righteousness (this word is often misunderstood; I mean it in its proper sense, not that of exaggeration or arrogance). The main difference, of course, is that Mattie's Christianity remains unchanged during the course of her life. Cassiopeia's Havianism undergoes great revision, which is the height of the fun.

A note on Margaret Atwood's excellent *The Handmaid's Tale*:

The Sun Children (science fiction) has been compared with *The Handmaid's Tale* (speculative fiction), and I would be lying if I denied being inspired by the infertility problem in it. When I was looking for a pretext for Church misdeeds, that thought came to me, I believe as a result of having heard of HT years before, though I did not remember that was the problem in HT when I chose it for SC. I had not read HT when I started SC. That said, I started reading HT while working on SC, and I was swiftly impressed by how different they are in genre, style, setting, and plot. In HT the Republic of Gilead responds to infertility with coerced surrogacy. In SC the Terran Church of Havo responds to infertility with human sacrifice. The extent to which my borrowing a superficial problem (infertility) may be considered plagiarism will doubtless be debated, though to me that makes as much sense as saying one war story copied another if they both revolve around a struggle for resources. The problem is the same; almost everything else is different.

This novel was begun on August 17, 2013. In early 2014 I suspended work on it to concentrate on my novel *Money's Men* (working on both simultaneously proved too difficult). When I picked the story up again in the summer of 2016, I went through a crisis. I still liked the story, but I felt unmotivated to do the work. Then, on Sunday, August 28, 2016, I sent the prologue and first chapter to Beverly Garside, author of *I and You*. Her praise of what she read didn't just validate the work, it motivated me to continue writing.

Timeline

137 AP (2553 AD)

March 13: launch of the *Messenger*
September 21: arrival at Sol and intercession
December 1: wedding
February: return to Terra

https://en.wikipedia.org/wiki/List_of_Roman_nomina

Acknowledgements

The song the Offerings sing spontaneously is adapted from Christina Rosetti's "____".

Antonio Valenzuela said, "The cosmos is my church. Humanity is my congregation. Compassion is my creed." Then he let me borrow his words.

Dan Nachtrab suggested Cassiopeia's eventual status; Dan Marshall suggested both the blind monks and the means by which the Church changed from Jesus to Havo; and Robin Peate, my wife, suggested wine.

Donovan Robertson provided a tour through the Fort Wainwright Central Heating Power Plant (CHPP), in Fairbanks, Alaska, enabling me to take photographs simulating Station Michael. I took other Station Michael shots in the Coast Guard vessel parked at Astoria, Oregon.

Roger Macdierney provided the quotations "Faith is a thing of God, Religion is a thing of man," and "You do not fix faith, faith fixes you." (from Firefly)

The following persons provided ideas and direct quotations for the scene in which Cassiopeia asks why the apostates do not believe in Havo: Jeffry Winters, Peggy Hooley Szymeczek, Chris Roberts, Jesper Laumann Blom, Chris Quirk, Ashley Nicole Foster, Jim Cook, Graham John Cooper, Angela Encarnacion, Kevin Barr, Jeremiah Preisser, Mick Mcnabb, and I thank them all for their contributions.

Photo by Claire Peate

About the Author

Robert Peate was born in 1970 in Smithtown, New York. He grew up in the eastern half of the United States, living in New York, Minnesota, Michigan, Illinois, Florida, and New York. As an adult, he has lived in Ohio, Arizona, California, and Oregon. He taught for one year on the island of Saipan.

Author of more than a dozen books, including poetry, fiction, and nonfiction, Peate is perhaps best known for his play *The Recovery*, his novels *Sisyphus Shrugged* and *Money's Men*, and for his collection of short stories *Mister Negative and Other Stories*. His work has been published worldwide and is currently under consideration for inclusion in political science classes.

When he is not working as a public-school teacher, Robert Peate lives and writes in West Linn, Oregon, with his wife Robin, their children Claire and Lucas, and their dog Flower.

Proof

Made in the USA
Charleston, SC
30 September 2016